white lies

ALSO BY LUCY DAWSON

The Daughter
What My Best Friend Did
His Other Lover
You Sent Me A Letter
Everything You Told Me
The One That Got Away
Little Sister

white lies

LUCY DAWSON

bookouture

Published by Bookouture in 2018

An imprint of StoryFire Ltd.

Carmelite House
50 Victoria Embankment
London EC4Y 0DZ

www.bookouture.com

ISBN: 978-1-78681-451-7
eBook ISBN: 978-1-78681-450-0

For Sarah

PART ONE

The Accusations

(Statements supplied 18 September 2017)

CHAPTER 1

Dr Alexandra Inglis

Blinking awake, I tried to twist on the pillow away from the bright sunlight steaming between the flimsy curtains. It was only a tiny movement but a white-hot flash of pain stabbed into my skull from behind my eyes. I moaned slightly, lifted up one hand – trying to hold my head together – my sticky tongue unpeeling from the dry roof of my mouth. I needed water.

Propping myself up on an elbow, I squinted at the bedside table and shakily reached for the pathetically small hotel glass which wasn't even a third full. I drank it anyway, but some bits of surface dust clung to the inside of my mouth as I gulped it down, and nausea swirled in my gut as the liquid hit my stomach. I had to crash back onto the pillow quickly to stop myself from being sick. The room was uncomfortably stuffy, and I shoved a bare leg out from under the twisted sheet to try and cool down.

Someone sighed and moved next to me. I froze and very slowly turned to look over my left shoulder, to see the back of a head; tousled sandy-brown hair tapering softly down a tanned neck that swept out into a broad, naked male back.

My heart stopped, and I lurched back into the airless, packed club of eight hours earlier; a light sheen of sweat on my skin, clutching my slopping drink as I pushed through the crush of hot bodies. The bass thudding through my muscles from the inside out while I looked around the club drunkenly for the girls… my eyes alighting on a face looking back at mine through a break in the throng. His eyes and skin alternated electric blue and hot pink as relentless, beat-blinding strobes of white light bounced off our bodies, and a neon cage of flashing triangles descended over the heads and waving hands of the dancing crowd. He straightened up, and I realised he was tall. I drank in a tight T-shirt, gym-honed arms, beautiful eyes – and didn't stop staring. He looked confused at my brazenness, but then came a shy smile.

I saw how it was going to go immediately.

He looked down, rubbed his chin and neck awkwardly, as if trying to make a decision, then walked towards me…

I turned away from him, keeping my head on the pillow, and urgently scanned the hotel room. My shoes were next to a tangle of jeans and his T-shirt, my dress was crumpled by the chair – a large trainer lying on top of it – my bra over by the door to the bathroom.

I slid a hand under the cover. I wasn't wearing anything at all. *Shit, shit, shit.*

I held my breath and, moving in triple slow motion so as not to wake him, reached for my mobile phone, lying next to the empty glass, and picked it up. There were ten text messages, all from Rachel, starting with

Where are you? I can't find you?

through to the last,

YOU DON'T WANT TO DO THIS!! Trust me, stop NOW!!!!

With a jolt, I suddenly remembered the sound of hammering on the hotel door; staggering over to throw open the lock and putting my head round to find Rachel standing there. She must have got a taxi all the way back to check on me. She would have seen our clothes on the floor.

I closed my eyes in shame.

The ping of another message arriving made me jump, but it wasn't mine. The body alongside me shifted again, and I lay motionless while the bed groaned as he leant out, presumably to pick his phone off the floor.

I realised I was going to have to turn over. I couldn't just pretend he wasn't there.

Cautiously, making sure I exposed nothing, I twisted to see that he was lying on his back. Thank God, the sheet was covering him; he'd tucked it in under his arms. My eyes moved over the top of a hairless chest, before briefly catching the edge of blue-black tattoo, some sort of Celtic lettering skimming a well-defined tricep and deltoid, then up again to an embarrassed smile and light-brown eyes looking right back at me. My heart crashed with horror as I realised he was young. About twenty-five? I swallowed and croaked 'Hi', before clearing my throat.

'Hey,' he replied, and gave me an awkward little wave. His hair was sweetly all over the place, and it occurred to me that he was exactly the kind of boy I would have killed to wake up next to when I was at university – a couple of decades ago.

Before I had the chance to say anything else, there was a knock on the door and a firm shout. 'Ally? Are you in there?'

'Just a second!' I lifted my head up and it almost exploded. Looking around desperately and finding nothing in reach, I was forced to drop the sheet and dart naked into the en suite, grabbing a towel to wrap around my body.

He was sitting up in bed – having already put on his T-shirt – when I returned, and watched quietly as I hurriedly kicked the rest of our clothes and his shoes out of the line of sight from the door. I took a deep breath and threw open the lock, before carefully leaning my upper body round to peer into the corridor.

Mercifully, it was just Rachel, freshly showered and dressed – and alone. Unable to see the bed, as it was hidden behind the door and me, she looked down the length of sanitised room visible from the door. 'You got rid of him then?'

I closed my eyes briefly and shook my head, pointing over my shoulder.

She looked horrified and covered her mouth with her hand, before simply turning on the spot and walking hurriedly back to her room.

There was no way he wouldn't have heard what she said.

I closed the door and returned to him. He'd drawn his knees up and had let his head drop awkwardly. What I could see of his face was burning bright red with humiliation.

I felt dreadful. 'I'm so sorry. My friend, she…' I trailed off. There was nothing I could say to make it any better. I hadn't wanted to be unkind. He didn't need to hear that. Throwaway comments can hurt for such a long time.

He hesitated, did his best to smile and said manfully 'It's OK', before slipping from the bed. I averted my eyes, but thankfully he had boxers on. He reached under the valance and pulled out his belongings, dressing quickly, as I sat down on the chair by the window and focused studiously on the luridly patterned carpet. He pushed his feet into his trainers, slid his mobile into his back pocket and brushed past me on his way out. I opened my mouth to apologise again, but the door was already swinging open, then clicking shut quietly behind him. Before I could find the words, he was gone.

I exhaled and leant sideways so that I was resting my head on the side of the chair and could hug my knees up to my chest. I stayed like that for a moment, feeling numb and hollow, then reached to wipe away a few tears with the heel of my hand. With my thumb, I began to twist my wedding and engagement rings on my finger. I needed to dress and go downstairs to join the others for breakfast. Staying shut away would only make things look worse. I glanced at the crumpled, empty bed and shuddered at what I'd done there with him in the night – things that I let happen. That I *made* happen. I put my hands up to my thudding head, threaded my fingers into my hair and closed my eyes.

Things that I will now never be able to undo.

I stood up, walked into the bathroom and let the towel drop, but the movement of being on my feet again was too much, and I threw up violently, kneeling on the cold, hard tiles in front of the loo before I was able to climb in the shower. It turned on with a clunk, and I winced as the water pushed into my skin like an old-fashioned wire brush. The pressure turned me slightly pink as I moved under the head and washed clean every bit of me that he'd touched. Brushing my teeth afterwards made me retch, and even once I was dressed and had some make-up on, I was shocked by how pale and ill I looked in the mirror.

My previous benchmark for alcohol consumption was passing in and out of consciousness on a toilet floor having necked half a bottle of vodka at a student ball in the Birmingham Botanical Gardens – again, some twenty years ago. Strange faces had loomed over me, asking me if I was all right, and someone even pulled my dress down to preserve my dignity before my friend, Tim, eventually found me and took me back to the coach. But that was immature stupidity. I couldn't pretend that I didn't know what I was doing in Pacha – I admit I drank that much deliberately. I was desperate not to think any more. I wanted to blank everything out.

Once I'd grabbed my room key and phone, I let myself out and started to walk unsteadily down to breakfast. A little girl shrieked as she ran up the wide staircase towards me, her younger brother in hot pursuit, and I winced visibly at the pitch her voice hit – the jaunty parents apologised cheerily for the noise as they passed by, already on their way back to their rooms after breakfast, and I smiled weakly in return. They would have been up for hours and were probably envying me my late start and child-free status. I watched them happily walking away and was suddenly so desperate to be back at home that I had to grip the bannister and stand still for a moment.

That was how Rachel found me, as she appeared at the bottom of the stairs and looked up. She tried to rearrange her expression of shock at my appearance but failed. 'Have you been sick yet?' she asked once she was alongside me, holding out a steadying hand.

I swallowed. 'Yes.'

'Well, that's good. You should start to feel better soon, and it'll help if you have something to eat, come on.' She started to lead me gently, as if I was the patient for once. 'Everyone is down there,' she lowered her voice and leant in slightly. 'All they know is what they saw: you kissing him at the club. They don't know you came back here together. I told them I went with you in a taxi and put you to bed. They were all pretty wrecked themselves by then.'

'Thank you, Rach.' But my initial relief quickly gave way to shame. 'I'm sorry for ruining your evening. I'm so embarrassed that you had to come back here looking for me to make sure I was safe, and that you saw all of his clothes on the floor.'

'You don't need to apologise. I shouldn't have come crashing in so thoughtlessly this morning.'

'It wasn't your fault.'

'It was unnecessary.'

'The whole thing was unnecessary,' I replied blankly.

We fell silent for a moment, and she turned to me as we reached the bottom of the stairs. 'Ally, who you tell about this, if anyone, is your call, but no one will hear a word from me.' She gave my hand a final, supportive squeeze, and released me. 'Come on, let's do it.'

I took a deep breath and followed her into the busy restaurant. The smell of warming buffet food began to make me feel queasy again. We arrived at the table where our six other friends were already sitting in varying degrees of morning freshness. Clare was enthusiastically and noisily scraping the last of her yogurt and muesli into her mouth – Stef glaring at her, hunched over a mug of black coffee. Marie and Cass were staring down at their phones, while Carolyn had propped her head upright with one hand and was holding a piece of buttered toast in the other. Only whippet-thin Jo had gone down the full English route, and as I stared at her loaded plate, I felt a small amount of sick rise up into my mouth.

They all looked up and there was a brief pause before Rach said warmly: 'Here she is!' Everyone tried not to exchange awkward glances as I sat down.

Only Stef made no attempt to smile. 'You look like I feel,' she said. 'We need a Bloody Mary.'

'God, no.' I blanched. 'I'm never drinking again.'

There was another awkward pause, which Rachel covered by saying brightly: 'Checkout isn't until half eleven, I've discovered, so I might have a swim after breakfast if anyone's keen?'

Stef looked at her, briefly appalled, and then turned back to me. 'So you had a good night then?'

I cleared my throat. 'I don't know what I was thinking.'

'It's always the quiet ones you've got to watch,' Cass teased, reaching out to rub my back supportively. The motion made me want to vomit into her lap. 'It was just a snog, Al. None of us is going to breathe a word to *anyone.* Don't beat yourself up.'

They all nodded in agreement. Their kindness was harder to deal with than the disapproval I knew I deserved. I wished we'd just gone to a nice boutique hotel somewhere near home and stayed over for a night or two, like we normally did on our annual weekend away. A spa, wine and chat. When I suggested a last-minute Ibiza jaunt two months ago, it really *was* innocent. I'd never been, I'd always wanted to, and I thought it would be fun. There was no agenda.

I tried to smile but felt very near to tears all of a sudden. They all looked at me worriedly, and Rachel passed me a napkin. 'We're jealous as hell, if truth be known. I'd like something as pretty as him to keep in my pocket.'

They all laughed and the tone felt momentarily lighter, but it didn't ring true. *She doesn't think that at all, I know she doesn't. None of them do.*

'He looked like he was in a boy band,' whispered Carolyn.

'And I think we can confirm *you've* definitely still got it, baby,' said Marie. They all murmured agreement.

Cass even brightly said: 'Hell, yeah!' which sounded un-comfy in itself – as if she were issuing trotting instructions to a pony – but I couldn't join in with a sheepish, or even slightly smug, smile... Still got it? I didn't want it. I wasn't the woman from the night before, craving attention while feeling drunkenly dangerous, reckless and determined. I could sense their pity, and I knew exactly what they were thinking: *"Ally has had such a shocking time of it these last three weeks. It was just a kiss – and you know what? This might have actually done her confidence the world of good."*

I swallowed and remembered his body on top of mine. I could hear my own gasps. Acting a role. *No one has to know. I don't even know your name. And now you have to go.*

But this wasn't some glossy music video a million hungry kids were watching on YouTube as they memorised the 'empowering' lyrics. There was no glamour. It was just so sad. A tear crept down my face – and my friends didn't know where to look. Marie reached out and gently took my hand, which I had to pull away when my phone started to vibrate. Glancing at the screen, I saw it was Rob. I couldn't pick up. I just couldn't. If he'd put the girls on the phone I'd have broken down completely.

They all watched me dismiss the call, and then, even more embarrassed, I tried desperately to think of something to say. It was our last morning and I was ruining it for everyone, making it all about me and my selfish domestic drama. I made a huge effort to gain some control again. I took a deep breath and drew myself up with as much confidence as I could muster; the same blank authority and professional persona I tap into when a patient starts verbally laying into me.

Dr Alexandra Inglis will see you now.

'I've changed my mind, Stef. I think that Bloody Mary might be just what I need.' My voice was calm and steady.

Stef plonked down her coffee cup. 'Now you're talking,' she said. 'That way, I might just about be able to contemplate getting on a plane later today.'

'Hair of the dog,' I said automatically. Hair of the dog, life in the old dog yet, only mad dogs and Englishmen go out in the midday sun. I scratched the itching sunburn on my neck.

I am nothing but a cliché. Let sleeping dogs lie.

Except I knew I was going to tell Rob when I got home. I had to, because while my friends may have said they weren't going to breathe a word to anyone, I knew they would each gossip to their husbands about what I'd done pretty much the second they got back. I would have, too, if I were them. I wouldn't have been able to resist. And then a dozen people, at least, would know I had kissed another man. That was bad enough. I trust Rachel implicitly, but she'd learnt the truth, and when it all came out eventually – because these things always do – Rob would not be able to handle the humiliation of being the last to know and feeling like a fool.

Anyway, I wanted to tell him. He deserved no less.

*

Rob must have been watching for the car, because the outside light switched on and he opened the front door the second I pulled up in front of the cottage. He waited on the step for me, framed in the doorway, wearing a stripy shirt I bought him years ago, his old jeans and slippers. Behind him was a tantalising glimpse into our house as a nosy stranger looking in would see it: cosy and comfortable – a properly lived-in home. It was made all the more enticing by the unseasonable early September rain and high winds gusting in the dark as I staggered towards the door clutching my suitcase, my hair blowing all over my face, shivering in my too-thin coat and sandals.

'Here,' he reached out as I made it, 'let me take that. You didn't bring the weather back with you then? Must have been a bumpy flight?'

'A bit.' I passed the case over the threshold, stepped in and watched as he closed the door gently behind me and placed the case quietly down on the floor.

'The girls are both asleep then?' I asked foolishly – as we wouldn't be tiptoeing otherwise – and slipped my arms out of my coat.

He nodded and kissed me briefly. I tensed as we touched, but he didn't seem to notice.

'Cup of tea?'

'Yes, please.'

'Have you eaten?'

I thought about the numerous chocolate bars and plastic-tasting tuna sandwich at the airport. 'I might have a bowl of cereal in a minute, or something. Don't worry for now, but, thank you.'

'Why don't you go through to the sitting room and I'll bring your cuppa in? You look shattered.'

'I am.' I swallowed. 'We went to Pacha last night.'

He laughed. 'Bloody hell. No wonder you look like you're about to die. Go on – sit down. I'll be right there.'

I did as I was told and once I was in the living room, eased gingerly down onto the sofa. My head was absolutely thundering. For a moment I considered waiting another twenty-four hours before confessing, and just going to bed. I only wanted to close my eyes and sleep… although – I looked around me – the room was a tip. Toys everywhere. Rob had made no attempt whatsoever to tidy up once the girls had gone down. There was a half-full cup on the side and a squashed-in Coke can on the floor next to the sofa, alongside a dirty plate and the ketchup bottle. He'd had fish fingers and chips for tea. I got up again and placed the can on the plate, knowing that there would be enough sticky liquid in the bottom to be a complete pain in the arse when it got knocked over by one of the girls in the morning.

'Just leave it.' Rob appeared, holding my tea, and a plate with a couple of chocolate digestives on it. 'I'll do it in a minute.'

He placed them down on the side, crossed to the sofa – moving the remote and his laptop – and sat back down, opposite me. 'So, did you have a good time? What was the weather like?'

'Very hot.' I reached for my tea and sipped it slowly, holding it with both hands. 'I got burnt yesterday.'

He rolled his eyes. '*Quelle surprise*. What was the hotel like?'

'Nice. Bit too cool for school. It had a weird seventies feel to it. Lots of retro clocks and chairs. Bright rugs, that sort of thing.'

He wrinkled his nose.

'The food was good though.' I cleared my throat. I had sex with a bloke I met in Pacha last night. I momentarily widened my eyes at my silent confession. 'How are the girls?'

'Fine. Bored of me though, they kept asking when you were coming back, and Maisie made you this.' He reached over to the sideboard again and picked up a heavily glittered picture of a mummy, daddy, and two children, all smiling. A very happy picture.

To Mummy. I love you so, so, so much!

I read.

You are my best mummy and I have got you a treat! Love from Maisie xxx

'She saved you a Percy Pig,' Rob said. 'She kept saying, "what about Mummy?" Tilly just carried on scoffing them, but Maisie thought of you. She missed you. We all did.'

I nodded, and my eyes filled with tears.

Rob looked at me carefully and frowned. The atmosphere was suddenly heavy, all the promise and potential of my return cooling faster than the comforting tea in my hands. He opened his mouth to speak. 'You seem to be—' but I got there first.

'Rob, I slept with someone last night.'

He jerked his head back like I'd just thrown something dangerous near his eyes. He didn't say anything for a moment, but then unexpectedly moved forward on the sofa, widening his legs so he could rest his elbows on his knees, and put his hands over his mouth. I could only see his eyes, staring ahead. He blew out slowly through his fingers.

I watched him, frightened. Now the words were out there, I was uncertain of how it was going to go and what I'd just risked on behalf of our daughters, how badly I'd let them down. Now, nothing was ever going to be the same again. Everything we'd worked so hard for – gone, in an instant.

'You wanted to hurt me,' he said – not a question, a fact. 'Were you drunk?'

'Yes. I wouldn't have been able to go through with it otherwise.'

'Fucking hell, Alex!' He grabbed a section of the Sunday newspaper and scrunched it up so tightly I could see the veins in his hand standing out as he flung it to the floor. 'You didn't *have* to go through with it at all! Were you even in Ibiza?'

That confused me. 'What? Of course!'

'Who is he?'

'It doesn't matter.'

He flushed and clenched his jaw. 'OK. You've made your point. Yes, it does matter. Who is he?'

'No one you know. I met him in the club.'

He looked appalled. 'A complete stranger? You went back to someone's hotel?'

I faltered slightly. 'No, I took him back to my room.'

'Christ, Alex.' He was furious. 'He could have hurt you; he could have *killed* you.'

I thought of the boy. 'That's a bit melodramatic, Rob. I was safe.'

He ignored me. 'Please tell me you used something.'

This was not going how I had imagined it. I coloured. 'Of course.'

He nodded, as if that was something at least and stood up suddenly. 'I'm going to bed. I don't want to discuss this any more.'

'No!' I said desperately. 'We need to talk about this. We owe it to the girls.'

He half laughed. 'You're thinking about them *now*? Wouldn't it have been better to do that last night?'

'Like you did?' I asked him immediately. 'When you fucked Hannah after her leaving party?'

He looked up at the ceiling, eyes wide open, and breathed out again – as if preparing to do yet another exhausting lap of the track – and sat back down. 'All right. What is it you want me to say, Alex? That this hurts? Because yes, of course it does. Which was the point, surely? Do I have the right to get angry after what I did? No. Does that make what *you've* done OK? No.'

'So suppose you'd discovered I'd had a brief fling with someone at work – let's say David.' I deliberately picked the colleague of mine I knew he didn't like. 'Can you can look me in the eye and tell me you absolutely wouldn't have thought – at any point – "Fuck you, Alex", and looked for someone else to validate *you*?'

He looked at me in disbelief. 'That's why you did it? To feel *better* about yourself?'

'Of course that was part of it!' I exclaimed. 'When your husband has sex with someone else it doesn't make you feel great, funnily enough. You feel—' I hesitated, and the familiar tears began to prick again, 'even fatter, frumpier, older and more invisible than you already did.'

He looked at the floor. 'You're none of those things. No, I wouldn't have done it to feel better about myself. On the wrong day, I'd have been so angry with you, I'd have done it for revenge.'

'That was a part of it, but it was more complicated than that.'

'You got pissed and had sex with someone you met in a club,' he said bleakly. 'That's pretty simple, surely?'

When he put it like that, I barely understood what I'd done myself.

We sat there in palpable silence, neither of us knowing what to say about how on earth we had arrived at *this* Sunday evening, or how we were going to get out of it. Eventually he cleared his throat. 'Alex, you and I have had…' he paused and struggled to find the right words, 'an ongoing lack of intimacy for months now, way before what I did. I've tried to discuss it with you. I know you're tired; I know we have two young children. You have a job that wrings you out. You give all of the time, to everyone. I also accept that I'm not always easy to live with either, but we have no time for *us*. And perhaps it *is* different for men than women. We don't lose interest in sex the way women do. At least, I thought that's how it was. Given what you've just told me, maybe it's not that you don't like sex, you just don't like it with me.'

I was crying properly by this point, all of the events of the last three weeks having at last caught up with me; my lack of sleep and being unable to eat properly, the exhaustion of thinking of nothing but Hannah when I'm awake and imagining Rob kissing her, in bed with her – my Rob, *my* husband – while trying not to make a dangerous mistake at work that I'll lose my job over; all while staying under control in front of Maisie and Tilly, because I want all this to be something they never, ever know about.

'That's not true,' I said. 'Before all of this, I enjoyed sex with you, you know that. Although, yes, there are things I've tried to discuss with you too. I know I'm tired and stressed most of the time, but Rob, you never made an effort to just hold my hand, or kiss me, all you did was tell me things between us were shit and I'd better hurry up and do something about it – which didn't make me feel much like going to bed with you, to be honest. You can't just turn it on when there's no emotional closeness. At least, I can't.'

'Unless you're drunk and in Ibiza with a stranger?'

'I wanted you to know how it feels when someone does that to you,' I admitted. 'I think about Hannah all the time.'

'She's back in Australia,' Rob said. 'You know this. She's not coming back. I'd had too much to drink. It was a mistake.' He collapsed back on the sofa, exhausted. 'For the record, it does hurt, Alex,' he said quietly. 'It hurts a lot.'

'I didn't plan to do it before I went, just so you know,' I said miserably. 'The others were so excited when we arrived, and I wasn't. I didn't want to go. I felt so out of it, but then they started drinking, it was hot… everyone was dressing up, it was the kind of music in clubs that I used to dance to all the time. I was drunk, and it was flattering that someone could have found me that attractive, based on nothing more than looks.'

'I don't need to hear this,' Rob said.

'I'm trying to explain that it all went to my head. And my head wasn't in a great place to start with anyway.' I looked across at the father of my children, my husband of eight years. I'd shared the most significant moments of my life with him, and I had absolutely no idea what he was thinking. 'I'm sorry.'

'You *are* attractive.' He didn't look at me when he said it.

This time the silence was a sad, empty one.

'Do you still want to try and make this work?'

'Yes,' he said. 'Do you?'

'Yes.'

'I mean, it'll always be different now, but…'

'We could maybe try couples therapy? That might help us with the adjustments we need to make?' I sounded like I was making a professional recommendation to a patient.

'OK,' he said. 'Do you want to organise that then?'

I nodded, then, without meaning to, yawned.

'Although, wouldn't we be better off just going on a date once a week instead?' he ventured. 'Rather than going to counselling to talk about the effects of never getting any time together?'

I hesitated.

'I'd like to take you out to dinner.'

'OK. I'd like that too.'

It was all so horribly polite and formal.

He didn't smile. 'Good. Well, I'll sort something then. Go to bed, Al, you're going to be knackered tomorrow otherwise.'

I stood up. 'I think I will, actually, if that's OK?'

'Of course. Do you want me to sleep in the spare room?'

There was a pause, and I shook my head. I turned to go, but as I reached the door, he said 'Al?' and I turned back.

'Who else knows what you did last night?'

'Only Rachel. The others saw me with him in the club—'

Rob looked down at the floor.

'But they don't know any more than that, and Rachel won't say anything.'

'But everyone knows what *I* did?'

I nodded, confused. 'Do you want me to be open about what I've done too? In the interest of fairness?' It had become a surreal conversation I could never have dreamt we'd have.

'No. I think we just try and put all of this behind us now and move on. A clean slate.'

I hesitated. 'Are we doing this just for the sake of the girls, or for us too? Just so I know?' I caught my breath, because, in spite of everything, I love my husband. Very much.

He frowned and looked up at me. 'Of course, for us too.'

I exhaled with relief. ‘OK. I really am sorry, and I promise you it’s over, Rob. I didn’t even know his name.’

*

That is the truth.

I believed I had slept with a stranger.

When I graduated from medical school, I swore to ‘utterly reject harm and mischief’.

I did not knowingly break my vow that night, whatever that bastard has said to the contrary.

CHAPTER 2

Dr Alexandra Inglis

I went back to work the next morning and was grateful for patients to focus on. I wanted the needle to slip back into its regular groove – or vein – so everything else would melt away because I was too busy to think about it.

The packed morning surgery was the usual heady mix of elderly ailments, toddlers with various viral infections and finished up with a teenager's septic nose stud. By lunchtime, I'd managed to forget I'd had sex with someone who wasn't my husband – and that my husband had recently fucked his work colleague – for at least two hours.

'Well, at least everything is out in the open now,' Rachel said, when I grabbed a quick five seconds to call her back at lunchtime after she'd texted to make sure I was OK.

'True.' I sorted through some referral letters with my mobile clamped to my ear. 'Although two wrongs don't make a right, obviously, and I shouldn't have done it at all—'

'But you did,' Rachel interrupted. 'People make mistakes, and you've both been brave enough to admit that to each other. The critical thing now is whether you can properly move on from everything that's happened?'

'I really hope so. I'm not going to lie, Rach, you know that, before kids, my relationship red line was someone cheating on me, and I hate how differently all the Hannah stuff has made me feel about Rob. Yes, he's still fundamentally the same person. We're still looking after the kids, sorting packed lunches, brushing teeth, working, food shopping – but now he does one wrong thing and immediately I'm thinking: That's it – divorce. So, after what I told him yesterday, is he thinking that too? I don't know.' I hesitated and sat back in my chair, closing my eyes for a moment. 'But then thinking divorce because you're angry and hurt is one thing – actually doing it… who can even afford to split up these days? Two houses and all of that shit. That's before you think about what it would do to the girls… You couldn't find two little children who adore their father more than Tilly and Maisie. And I love him too. The very real thought of him leaving us, meeting someone else, marrying her and having another family, is unbearable.'

Rachel sighed. 'Life is never straightforward, is it?'

'No, it isn't. And I'm really not saying this is an excuse, for him or me, but it is bloody frightening how easy it is to make such a huge mistake that you genuinely regret. Is that worth chucking away ten years over? I think I might feel different if he'd had an actual affair, but it was one night. What *I* did was one night.' I shivered uncomfortably, not wanting to think about it in any detail. 'Obviously there are problems, otherwise neither of us would have done anything in the first place, but we both want to fix them.'

'Well, I'm really pleased,' Rachel said sincerely. 'No one's saying it's going to be easy, but surely you both wanting it to work is half the battle?'

*

There was no question we were both making a lot more effort to consider each other. Rob politely asked if he could go to the gym on Monday, unless I wanted to? I made it to a spin class on Tuesday evening, and on Wednesday, Rob volunteered to collect the girls so I could dash to an early parent's evening at their school, to be told what we could expect Maisie and Tilly to be learning during the autumn term in Year 2 and Nursery 2, respectively.

When I got back, he'd opened a bottle of wine – because, although it was our all new date night, I hadn't been able to find a babysitter – and made his pasta dish. I turned my phone off, so did he, and we watched *Passengers* together: a movie about a spaceship transporting thousands of hibernating people to colonise a new planet. One man wakes up ninety years too early and, after a year alone, deliberately wakes a female passenger he's been watching sleep to join him. I silently wondered if Rob would choose to wake me up if his pod malfunctioned, or if he'd select Hannah instead, but then pushed the thought firmly away.

We went to bed too late after it ended disappointingly, and I didn't really want to have sex – although I knew we probably ought to. Thankfully, Tilly woke up while I was brushing my teeth, and by the time I went back to bed, Rob was already dozing. We hugged until we fell asleep, however. It was a start. We were both trying.

On Thursday, 14 September, four days after I'd come back from Ibiza, the last on my list of lunchtime call-backs was a Christy Day. The name was unfamiliar to me, and Jen, the receptionist, had made the note

Would rather not say reason for call

which probably meant Ms Day had some sort of gynae issue. I scanned through her medical record – her last appointment had been with David, on 7 August, at which he'd prescribed Zopiclone for insomnia.

I dialled, and a slightly breathy, high voice said: 'Hello?'

'Can I speak to Christy Day, please?'

'Dr Inglis? Thank you for calling me back.'

'How can I help?' I glanced at the clock and tried to sound friendly. I was barely going to get five minutes to eat my sandwich at this rate.

'Well, this is rather embarrassing, but I've had severe diarrhoea and vomiting for the last three days. I can't seem to keep anything down at all.'

I unwrapped my sandwich and got it ready. 'Not even water?'

'Not really, no. I'm getting a bit frightened. I'd go to the hospital, but I don't want everyone there to get it. Do you think you could come and see me at home today, Dr Inglis? I'm sorry to ask.'

I cursed inwardly. I wanted to get home in time to see the girls before they went to bed. 'We don't do home visits unless they're absolutely necessary, Mrs Day.' I glanced at her notes again, how old was she? Forty-nine. 'You're sure you couldn't come into the surgery?'

'But what about the infection risk?'

'That's OK,' I assured her. 'We could let you in through our side entrance and take you straight through to a consulting room.'

'I honestly don't think I could make it through the journey, if you know what I mean, doctor. I wouldn't ask unless it was absolutely necessary.'

I tried not to grit my teeth crossly. After three days and now not keeping water down, she definitely needed to be seen, but… I forced a smile instead to make my voice sound cheery. 'OK, Mrs Day. I can't promise exactly what time it'll be, as I have a couple of other house calls first, but I will come tonight.'

'Thank you, doctor. I'm very grateful.'

So you should be, I thought gloomily, finally picking up my sandwich. The first appointment of the afternoon pinged onto my screen before I'd even had chance to take a bite.

*

My mood had not improved by the time I tiredly programmed my satnav with Christy Day's address at around half past six.

She lived on the leafy south side of Tunbridge Wells, up a private drive off one of the nicest roads. It had once been an area discretely scattered with detached arts and crafts houses and their huge gardens. Over time, they'd all been sold to developers who had built luxury closes and cul-de-sacs of still very desirable executive homes. Christy's was a large contemporary version of the original thing – a half-tiled hung double frontage with leaded windows and immaculate lawns. I whistled enviously as I drove down the drive. I wanted to move in immediately.

Crunching over the gravel past a sporty little Merc and a chunky black Range Rover, I rang the bell, and a dog started distantly barking somewhere. The enormous honeyed oak front door opened to reveal a classically attractive man in exceptionally good shape, not just for his late forties. He was unseasonably dressed in tennis whites, shorts and trainers – presumably to show off such a muscular, hard-earned physique – and was a little too tanned with an absolutely immaculate full head of suspiciously brown hair that looked almost sprayed into place. He flashed a bright white smile at me, and I extended a hand.

'Hello, I'm Dr Alex Inglis.'

He took it and we firmly shook. 'Pleased to meet you. I'm Gary Day, Christy's husband.'

I struggled to think who he reminded me of, only to realise it was Maisie's Ken doll, who'd been kicking around her plastic princess house dressed in nothing more than a bandana and moulded pants for months. The likeness was uncanny. I suppressed a smile, at which his eyebrows briefly flickered with interest. That was enough to refocus me instantly.

'Your wife is upstairs?' I said pointedly, taking back my hand.

'No, she's in the kitchen actually.'

Kitchen? With severe D&V? My mood darkened as I stepped into a vast oak-floored hall and he closed the door behind me. A tiny, fluffy, white dog began to bounce down the stairs yapping and wagging its tail enthusiastically. Gary bent to scoop it up as it got to the bottom step and let off another volley of yips.

'Shhh, Angel! I know, you want to say hello. You're such a girl's girl!' He strode across the hall, opened a door, and dropped the dog in, before shutting it again quickly. He turned back to me and grinned. 'All safe. Come this way.'

I followed him through yet another set of double doors, which, this time, opened into a cavernous cream kitchen/diner and TV area, complete with a dazzling ceramic floor that a thousand ceiling spotlights appeared to be bouncing off. I blinked and saw first my own reflection in the acre of wall-length bifold doors opposite – incongruous in my navy trench coat against the otherwise completely sterile palette – before my gaze moved left to where a woman was perched on a bar stool next to an island, on which sat three fizzing glasses of what appeared to be champagne.

She was wearing white, tight jeans – an odd choice for a woman with chronic D&V – and a soft, grey sweater that clung to an obviously still fabulous figure. She flicked back Farrah Fawcett hair, gave me a megawatt Charlie's Angel smile, and stood up, before putting an immaculately French-polished nail in her mouth and saying coyly: 'Hello, Dr Inglis, I'm Christy Day. Please don't hate me, but I've been a little bit naughty.' She picked up one of the flutes and offered it to me.

I stayed exactly where I was. 'Mrs Day, I'm confused. You told me you needed urgent medical attention.'

Gary came round and stood between us, before adding smoothly: 'We'll cut straight to the chase, Als. We want you to come and work for us.'

Als? I looked at them blankly. 'I'm sorry?'

'We moved to this house about eight months ago to finish developing and overseeing the opening of our fifth new spa and country club. It's about six miles away from here; you'll have seen the plans in the local press,' Christy said cosily. 'Gary's heading up the gym side – that's his area of expertise – and I'm doing the spa. I know you used to run a Botox clinic locally. A friend had some filler work done by you and it was fab.u.lous!' She twinkled at me. 'She also knows your friend Stef Knowles, actually, who said you might be keen to talk to us? The trouble is, we joined your practice when we moved to this catchment area, and I knew that if I called the surgery legitimately and was up front about what we wanted, because I'm your patient, you would probably have just thought "conflict of interest" and dismissed it; whereas I was sure if I could just get you over here to look at our plans and see how exciting what we have to offer is…'

My mouth fell open in disbelief. She wasn't ill at all.

'We need someone with proper experience and the credentials, you see,' Gary interrupted. 'We've done some digging around, and you've got both.' He closed one eye, pretended to take aim and fired at me with his thumb and finger. 'We know we've found our girl.'

I tried not to think about the very ill little four-year-old I'd seen just before them, and her frightened mum, who had apologised profusely for dragging me out, even though she'd been quite right to. Then I thought about Maisie and Tilly, patiently waiting for me to get home, and cleared my throat. OK, so it seemed we loosely had friends in common, but they couldn't possibly think getting me here under false pretences on NHS time was acceptable? That I should be *flattered*? 'As you don't actually require any medical attention, Mrs Day, I'm going to leave now.'

'Oh, you're not, not *really*?' Christy's smile slipped, and she pouted.

Who on earth did she think she was? And what made them think I'd want to work with them after this anyway, when they'd been prepared to adopt such underhand techniques?

'You're here now,' Gary wheedled, friendly wide smile at the ready again. 'Just a quick look at the plans, Als. Come on.'

His tone had become firm. It was almost an instruction. I turned and stared at him, as I considered the elderly patient I'd seen earlier in the day who had somehow managed to get himself to the surgery on the bus despite being in severe pain. He wouldn't have dreamt of asking me to come out to his house. I began to feel very angry indeed. 'It's Dr Inglis, thank you.'

He looked surprised, and Christy put her hands on her hips. 'All right, I don't think there's any need to be a snotty bitch about it.'

I sighed wearily. Great. She was one of *those* sorts of women.

'Chris,' Gary said warningly.

'No, I think perhaps we have actually made a mistake, Gary.' She stared challengingly at me and crossed her arms.

I ignored her insult. Experience had taught me not to go there. 'Mrs Day, if you had been honest with me and asked me to come and meet you here to discuss your business opportunity, I would have quickly run it past a colleague, but I probably would have said yes.' I addressed her politely and sincerely. 'As things stand now, I think I'll see myself out.'

I turned on my heels, clutching my bag tightly, smugly pleased that I'd kept both my temper and the moral high ground.

I'd almost made it to the kitchen door when voices and laughter carrying down the hall towards us grew suddenly much louder and an extremely pretty teenage girl burst into the room. She was clutching her phone in one hand and giggling flirtatiously, winding a piece of long blonde hair round her finger with the other. Her school shirt was untucked over a grey miniskirt that just about covered her arse, and a tall boy in school uniform behind her was yanking on a bag slung across her body, trying to pull her back towards him.

Everyone jumped as *my* bag, having slipped from my fingers, dropped onto the hard tiles with the dull crack of something smashing within. The girl pulled an 'awkward!' face – clearly thinking that they'd had the house to themselves – and added a slightly insincere 'sorry.'

But I was paralysed, my limbs hanging useless by my side as I stared at the young couple, or rather the boy.

It was *him*.

The twenty-five-year-old from Pacha I'd woken up next to four days ago.

Right in front of me.

In school uniform.

It was like feeling someone's outstretched fingers dragging across the bare skin on my shoulders, then clawing up the back of my scalp, before hands settled around my neck and started to squeeze. I was literally unable to breathe.

He stared back at me, those big brown eyes wide with confusion, his mouth slightly open. He knew exactly who I was too. I simply couldn't make any sense of how he was dressed. Without the ridiculous nub of a school tie at his neck – worn deliberately short to tick a box – he could have been mistaken for an office junior. He didn't have any of the gawkiness or angular thinness of a typical male teenager, rather the solid arms that I remembered holding me – and there was the bottom of his tattoo just visible under the edge of his rolled-up sleeve – but there was no mistaking that it *was* a school uniform he was wearing.

My mind began to panic and scramble. I had to do, or say, something; they were all looking at me. Why was he even here? He must be their daughter's boyfriend. I needed to leave. I *had* to get out. I bent wildly to grab my belongings, almost going over on my ankle in my haste. Gary put an arm out to steady me, only for us all to see – as I righted myself and snatched up the handles – a wide crack snaking through the centre of the glossy tile underneath. The medical equipment in the bag had been heavy enough to break it on impact.

'Oh, for fuck's sake!' exploded Christy, marching straight across, all pretence at sweetness and light now completely gone. 'Look what's she's done!'

'I'm so sorry,' I swallowed, stepping back, as Gary bent down and ran his finger over it and they all peered at the floor. Only the boy continued to stare at me. I couldn't help but give him another horrified glance. 'It was an accident. I'll go. I'm sorry.'

Desperate to escape, I pushed roughly past the daughter, who said 'Hey!' in irritable amazement, and rushed away down the hall. Struggling with the front door, terrified that one of them was going to follow after me and demand an explanation, I managed to get it open. Just about staying upright in my heels, I practically ran over to the car, scrabbled in my pocket for my keys and jumped in. Fumbling with the fob, I began to shake as Christy appeared in the doorway of the house, angrily calling something after me that I couldn't hear.

I somehow got the car started, as Gary appeared alongside his wife, just in time to see me lurch forward and spin round on the gravel, almost hitting a silver Golf with a personalised plate that had been dumped right in my way. Spitting up an arc of sharp stones over their other cars, I swung sharply round it as Gary shouted furiously, pushing past Christy. I whimpered aloud as I roared off up their drive, glancing back in my rear-view mirror to see him bent over, inspecting the front of his Range Rover.

I kept going until I was back on the main road, then turned right, and hurried down the hill that led to the bottom of town and the Sainsbury's roundabout. The traffic was still heavy, and although I kept checking behind me, I couldn't see either of their cars in pursuit. I turned left, and drove sharply out of the town, towards Eridge and home.

'Oh my god, oh my god,' I whispered aloud in the car, as I stared at the road in front of me. *School uniform.* Exactly how old was he? He couldn't be under sixteen. He just couldn't. He didn't physically look that young, but then, that didn't mean he definitely wasn't. I'd patched up plenty of rugby players over the years who'd looked years older than they actually were. I took one hand from the wheel and put it to my head in shock. I'd been surprised by how fresh-faced he was the morning afterwards, I remembered thinking that, but not that he looked like a *child.* I forced myself to think about him again, standing there in the Days' kitchen, and tried more accurately to mentally gauge his actual age, within the context of his uniform. Oh please, God, I hadn't had sex with a minor? I slowed down as I reached the top of the hill, turned right opposite Bunny Lane, and drove into Broadwater Forest.

If he was under sixteen I would face criminal charges. I'd lose everything; my job – without question, almost certainly Rob, possibly even my girls. A moan of fear escaped my lips. I didn't know. *I didn't know!*

I tried to think rationally. I needed to find out *exactly* how old he was. What about his tattoo? He would have to be eighteen to get that done. Although, I'd also seen enough botched jobs over my career to know scores of less reputable parlours would turn a blind eye to legalities. It wasn't a reliable reference point. My mind turned instead to the Days' daughter. I would be updating Christy's patient record in the morning; I could look on the cohabiting part of her record, which would give me her daughter's date of birth. Girls never went out with boys younger than them, did they? At least then I'd have a minimum cut-off point to work from. Except, what about Stef? She might know the daughter's age and that would be even quicker. Christy Day clearly said Stef recommended me, or told a friend to recommend me, someone who I'd done work on?

I pulled over immediately, chucked the hazard lights on and, ducking down, bent quickly to pull out my mobile. I thought Stef was going to let it go to voicemail, but, thank God, she picked up at the last minute.

'Hey, Al? You all right?' she asked curiously. I never normally called her around the girls' bedtime.

'Which of your friends have I done fillers for, locally?' I blurted, not even bothering with hello and barely noticing the dark forest either side of me. Normally I hate driving through it alone at this time of year. Rob insisted when we bought the house that I'd get used to it, but six years later, I still haven't.

'What? At your clinic, at The Stables, you mean? I don't know.' She paused. 'Melanie, Tessa; I think you did Nicola too, didn't you? I can't really remember, why?'

'OK, which of them know a couple called Gary and Christy Day?'

'Oh – that's Nic. The Days own all of those luxury spas. Nic said she'd get you in there! Why, has she come good?'

'Yes. I've just been to the Days' house. They're actually patients at the practice, but I didn't recognise them. They said a friend had passed them my name, via you.'

'Great!' Stef sounded delighted. 'Hang on though – you don't sound pleased? Is there a problem?'

'No,' I lied hastily. 'I shouldn't have told you that they're patients, but they've got a teenage daughter and I want to find out how old she is. That's all.'

'Sorry, Al. I've no idea.'

'Could you ask Nicola? Sorry to be odd and vague. It's just… doctor stuff. Honestly nothing to worry about though.'

'I can if you want me to – but that's going to be a weird question for me to ask her out of the blue? She's going to want to know why.'

'Of course, sorry.' I realised she was right. I wasn't thinking straight. 'Forget I asked.'

'Maybe try Google instead?' she suggested.

'I don't even know her name.'

'Well – it might be listed in a news item or something. Hope you get the info you need, Al.'

What I needed was to go back seven days and not get on that plane to Ibiza.

I hung up and googled

Gary Day spa country club

It took me straight to a very upmarket website. I discovered that the new club would indeed be the Days' fifth in a rapidly expanding chain and Gary was listed as the CEO, but that was it. No further information, and Christy didn't appear on the site at all. I checked Gary's LinkedIn profile and that was no better. I wanted to scan Facebook too, but realised suddenly that I was already creating a paper trail; links to my online searches that – if this boy did turn out to be, technically, a child – would almost certainly be examined. Could I explain everything on there so far? The Days had offered me a job out of the blue. It was only natural that I would have done a search on them after the event. But already, I felt too scared to continue, and almost dropped the phone in fright when it began to ring in my hands.

It was Rob, so I ignored it. I was practically home anyway and didn't trust myself to speak to him. Seconds later a text pinged through, checking where I was, as it was getting late. What time should he put supper on?

I looked up into my frightened eyes reflected back in the rear-view mirror and tried to calm myself down, forcing myself to breathe deeply. It was just beginning to work when, in front of me, illuminated by my stationary headlights, I saw a movement to my left, in among the shadowy trees. I froze, and screamed, as something burst from between them and a bloody great deer leapt into the road. It stopped and eerily stared right at me, head lifted on high alert as the lights shone into its shiny black eyes, ears cupped forward and body stiff. Just as abruptly, it broke right and wheeled off into the thicket on the other side of the road, vanishing ghost-like into the dark.

I pulled away immediately, utterly unnerved. I just wanted to get home… but then I imagined myself telling Rob what had just happened at the house call and automatically took my foot back off the accelerator.

I'd told him the man in Ibiza was a stranger. I'd not even hinted about his age. How could I tell Rob, a mere four days later, that, not only had I just seen him again, in our home town, I also wasn't one *hundred* per cent sure, but he might be sixteen, or under.

The car began to slow as I pictured Rob's face: disbelief and disgust at this very different kind of betrayal. I had to know exactly how old this boy was before I said anything to Rob. I needed to be dealing in certainties so I knew what we were facing.

Sitting up a little straighter, I swallowed. A possible minor. Cold stillness settled over me. I began to feel oddly composed. I knew this was not going to go away and I had no intention of trying to pretend it would.

I couldn't deny being at the Days'. Christy's call was logged on the practice system; Jen had documented it and put it through to me. I'd called back. The Days had witnessed me in the boy's presence, while he was wearing school uniform. I would not be able to argue, going forward, that I was unaware of his age.

I was already committed.

I thought back to the Ibiza hotel room as I drove steadily past the Forestry Commission clearing and round the last bend before our cottage. In truth, I remembered very little about the act itself, I'd been so drunk – but we had definitely had sex. Being in the club and kissing him was only marginally clearer in my mind. I could almost hear a barrister asking, in disbelief, *'and you're a family GP, Dr Inglis? A mother yourself?'*

I reached home, pulling straight into the drive because the gate was open, turned the lights off and sat for a moment in the safe, quiet car. I would wait and not say anything until I'd looked at Christy Day's record in the morning. Then I would decide what to do and what action I needed to take. There was a chance that he could possibly be as old as seventeen, or even eighteen. Still horrendous, but legal.

The front door opened, and Rob appeared, frowning curiously as he waited. I tried to smile, reaching for my bag and phone, before taking a deep breath and getting out.

'Too tired to stand up?' Rob said sympathetically as I reached him. 'You look shattered. I've made you some food and it's almost ready. Come in.'

He bustled off into the kitchen, and I kicked my shoes into the understairs cupboard before removing my coat and slinging it over the bannisters. True to his word, Rob had laid the table and was carefully dishing up a stir-fry when I appeared in the room.

'Long day, then?' he asked conversationally.

I hesitated and, in that split second, despite all of my reasoning, I almost told him the truth, but was distracted by something on the table that caught my eye; I paused, reached over and picked up another picture.

'I know,' Rob sighed. 'More Maisie "happy family" drawings.'

I looked at the smiling Mummy, Daddy and daughters – all holding hands.

'Do you think she's picked up on some of the tension over the last three weeks and is trying to communicate her anxiety about it the only way she knows how?' Rob looked at me worriedly.

Oh Maisie. My eyes flooded with tears. What had I done? I heard myself on the phone to Rachel saying so blithely that Rob and I were going to put all of this behind us and move on. 'Probably, yes.'

'To be fair to us, I don't think it's only that,' Rob said. 'She asked me if she could look at my wedding ring while we were having tea and said: "you and Mummy always wear your married rings". Like she was checking, or something. We had a chat and it turns out Polly's parents in her class are getting divorced. We talked about what that meant, and she asked me if I'll always keep loving you, and you'll always keep loving me. I said of course. I promised her we won't get divorced. Because we won't, Al.' He looked across at me. 'Don't cry. It's true.'

I nodded and tried to wipe away my tears. Would he still be saying that, if he knew?

We ate tea; we watched some TV. We went to bed and, for the first time since Rob had told me about Hannah, we had quiet, under-the-duvet sex.

'I love you,' Rob gasped, afterwards.

'I love you too,' I said, and I meant it. It was one of those moments where actually saying the words wasn't enough to explain the depth of what I felt for him.

*

I admit that I initiated sex that evening, which does not prove I was 'excited' at having seen the boy again. I wanted to be close to my husband. I wanted to pretend everything was going to be all right, but mostly I wanted to pretend that none of it had happened in the first place.

CHAPTER 3

Dr Alexandra Inglis

Unsurprisingly, I didn't really sleep and was up well before Maisie and Tilly, anxious to get out of the house so I could go straight to work and look at Christy Day's record. By half past seven, we were strapping the kids in the car; breakfast done, packed lunch for Tilly made, teeth brushed, shoes on.

'You're sure you've got everything?' Rob asked doubtfully, bending over to kiss Tilly. 'Have a lovely day, sweetheart.' He straightened up and closed the door, calling across the car roof to me, 'you picked up Maisie's reading bag?'

'We're good to go.' I smiled back at him tightly. Come on, come on…

He walked round to kiss Maisie. 'You have a good day too, darling. We'll do something fun tomorrow all of us, shall we?'

'Minor Mania?' they both said instantly, and Rob rolled his eyes. 'Soft play? Oh good. Well, we'll see.'

He closed Maisie's door, and I began to climb into the front seat.

'Hey, hang on.' He put a hand out to stop me, leant over and kissed my mouth, briefly.

'Sorry. I'm only rushing because I'm duty doctor today and I want to get in early to get sorted before the chaos,' I said quickly.

Somehow trying to explain why I hadn't thought to say goodbye properly only made it appear even more significant.

'It's OK. Long week, I know. Nearly there, Al. Almost the weekend.' He gave me an encouraging smile.

We were being so achingly polite it hurt.

I quickly got in the car and barely waved as Rob watched us pull off up the drive.

'Right, off to breakfast club we go!'

'Where's Daddy working today?' Maisie asked.

'At home,' I said, looking both ways and turning left.

'Who's getting us from school?'

'Me, sweetheart. I'll come and get you from after-school care.'

Maisie slumped. 'Again? I don't want to go. Mummy, you won't ever take off your married rings, will you?'

My heart skipped a beat but, without a moment's pause, I replied brightly: 'No, darling, of course I won't. I promise.'

Well, what else could I say?

We hurried into breakfast club in the nursery attached to the main school, to find several other stressed parents herding their children into the cloakrooms too.

'Morning Tilly! Hi Maisie!' said Melissa, one of the other mums I saw regularly at drop off. She was stood behind her son Zack, who was slowly fumbling with his zip. She shook her head at me. 'So *slow*' she mouthed, looking pained, and glanced at her watch. Zack glanced up at her, and she smiled brightly: 'Keep going, darling, you're doing really well!' As my girls wriggled out of their coats, let them slip to the floor and galloped off to the main room before I could stop them, Zack finally succeeded and passed the pesky jacket to Mel before running off to join the others.

'I hate rushing him all the time, but to get out of here, back to the car park and then get over to the office…' She stepped back as I bent over to grab the girls' coats from the floor, then we both hung the stuff up together. 'When did life get so busy, Ally?'

'I know. It sucks.'

'Morning! Morning!' Another mum, Catrin, burst in, grappling with slipping lunch boxes, a PE kit and two coats. 'Thank God it's Friday. I had Harry dressed in a Mike the Knight costume until ten minutes ago when I realised I'd got the date wrong and their castle trip is *next* week. That is right, isn't it, Al? I lost the "advance notice of dates for the rest of term" letter the first week back.'

I smiled. 'The castle trip is definitely next Friday. I'll Whatsapp you the letter when I get home tonight.'

'You're a star, thank you. Right, I'm out of here.' She shoved everything on pegs then looked down at herself, confused, starting as she realised she'd hung up her own bag too. 'For fuck's sake,' she breathed, looking at Mel and I. 'It's going to be one of those days, isn't it?'

Despite being accosted by one of the teachers on the way out, to sign a consent form I thought I'd already dealt with, I still managed to arrive at work before everyone else, bar Cleo, the practice manager. I said hello to her, disappeared off to my office, started up the computer and logged on. Pulling up Christy Day's record, I went straight to the cohabitants section, so I could see everyone living at the address and their dates of birth:

Gary Andrew Day, 23.11.65

Ruby Claire Day, 11.01.97

Jonathan Christian Day, 23.09.99

I stared at the names, until it dawned on me that I'd got everything completely wrong. Yes, the Days had a daughter, but she was twenty. Too old to be in school. She wasn't the girl I'd seen.

They did, however, have a seventeen-year-old boy; Jonathan.

He was the Days' *son*?

I thudded back in my chair in horror. OK, so he wasn't underage, which was the main thing – but he was still my patient, and his parents were too.

Jonathan Day.

I had no recollection whatsoever of seeing him full stop at the surgery, let alone one-on-one in this room. I could, of course, check immediately – his notes were a click away. But I was well aware of the guidelines. I needed a legitimate reason to view his patient record, and the second I opened it, the access would be logged, a trail started and questions asked.

I had to close my eyes for a moment to try and take it all in. I was in no doubt about the General Medical Council guidelines for all GPs, which are very clear; relationships between current patients and doctors are unethical. We are expected to maintain professional boundaries at all times and never to exploit the 'inherently unequal' balance of power between a patient and doctor. The more vulnerable a patient is considered to be, the more serious the abuse of power, and the greater the threat to my position as a doctor.

Jonathan Day was only seventeen and would be considered a young adult – certainly vulnerable – but as I'd been totally unaware of his identity in Ibiza, sleeping with him couldn't possibly be a punishable offence. It did, however, present significant problems that I was now going to have to deal with.

I leant forward and put my elbows on my desk, head in my hands, rubbed my temples and across my brow with my fingertips and tried to think.

Fuck, fuck, *fuck*.

'Bit early for that sort of language, isn't it?'

I jumped guiltily and swung round to see my practice partner, David, standing in the open doorway, smiling, which quickly turned to a frown. 'You all right? You look like someone just died.'

'I didn't have time to put enough make-up on this morning, that's all.'

Embarrassed, he smoothed down his tie. 'Sorry. Have you got five minutes before kick-off?'

I hesitated. 'Sure. I'll be through in just a second.'

He looked at me curiously for a moment longer… but I stayed silent, made myself smile brightly and waited for him to go, until he shrugged and disappeared.

First things first. I turned back to Christy's record. Christine Jane Day.

I took a deep breath and began to type up my notes.

Written retrospectively, home visit, seen 14.09.17 at 18.37. Patient had requested home visit as unable to come into surgery because of severe D&V. Unable to keep water down, day three of symptoms. On arrival, Mrs Day was dressed, mobile and on visual assessment appeared in good health. She offered me one of three glasses of poured champagne in her kitchen. She admitted she had 'been a bit naughty' and had called me out to discuss her Botox business. Her husband Gary Day was present and they verbally offered me paid employment. Mrs Day confirmed she felt that had she approached me 'legitimately' I would have refused to meet her, because it might represent a conflict of interest. I declined their offer and Mrs Day became verbally abusive, referring to me as a 'snotty bitch'. I informed Mrs Day that as she did not require medical attention I would be leaving. I accidentally dropped my bag on vacating the property and damaged their floor, for which I apologised. I did not offer to examine Mrs Day, due to her aggressive demeanour.

It was a fair and accurate account, except, was 'verbally abusive' too strong? But then, she *had* sworn at me, and I needed to make it clear why I hadn't examined her, other than giving her a visual assessment. I made no reference whatsoever to her son's presence

– because it wasn't relevant to anything that had happened, nor at the time did I know his identity.

I exhaled heavily and went through to David's room, pausing to knock on the open door.

'Hello,' he said absently, eyes on his screen and shirt sleeves already rolled-up. 'Have you had login issues? I'm getting a system error message. I can't access anything. Bollocks, bollocks.' He reached under his desk and his screen went black as he turned it off at the wall. 'When in doubt, switch it off and on. Techies get paid a lot of money to come out and do what I just did. Cross your fingers.' He flipped it on again and peered anxiously at it. 'Are you sure you're all right? You seem stressed to beyond and back. It's coming off you in waves.'

Deeply dismayed to hear that, I sat down. 'I do actually need to run something past you that happened last night, just so you're in the loop.'

'Thought so,' he said. 'Go on then, hit me with it. Oh, this *bastard* system. Cleo!' He yelled like a major general. 'Are we completely down – or is it just me?'

'Hang on,' came a shout back from her office down the corridor. 'I think it's everyone. Bear with me.'

David looked at his watch. 'Eight minutes until the phone lines open. God. So, what are you about to tell me that's going to make this morning even worse?'

I cleared my throat. 'I did a home visit last night, a woman with D&V. I'd tried to persuade her to come in, but she wouldn't. I got there, and she was sat in her kitchen with a glass of Champs on the side for me, at which point she tells me she's made-up the D&V and wants to offer me a job in her new spa, doing Botox and fillers.'

'Bloody cheek,' David snorted. 'Her, not you. Why do I never get house visits where people offer me booze and lucrative private work?' He pressed the enter button on his keyboard repeatedly. 'Oh come on!'

'So, I tell her I might have thought about it if she'd been upfront, but now, not so much, whereupon she tells me I'm a "snotty bitch" and that she thinks she might have made a mistake after all.'

'Lovely,' said David. 'CLEO?'

'I DON'T KNOW YET, DAVID!' came back the equally cross bellow.

I continued manfully. 'Her husband is there, trying to talk me round, but I go to leave and then—'

Cleo stuck her head round the door. 'It's the whole system, and we've got no Internet connection either.'

'Fuck, shit and arse,' said David. 'Have we been hacked? Is it just us or bigger?'

'No idea, but can we all just come through so everyone knows how we're going to handle this and it's not complete carnage this morning?'

David jumped up, my situation already forgotten, and followed Cleo out to the main reception. Within a couple of minutes, all seven of the GPs, the two practice nurses and reception staff were congregated.

'We've no active records, obviously,' Cleo explained, 'so you'll be pen and paper, and retrospectively updating as soon as we're back up and running. Reception will tell you who you have for your next appointment when you ring through to say you're clear from the last. Alex, you're duty doctor today, aren't you?'

I nodded.

'OK, reception, can you draw up ONE list of the emergency slots, keep it at the front desk and block them out as the calls come in? *Please* make sure you work from the same master sheet so we don't get any double bookings.'

'We're going to need longer appointment times for everyone though, surely?' pointed out one of the salaried GPs, Megan. 'If we've got no notes and we're going to be prescribing from the BNF?'

I saw one of our newest receptionists, Jen, mouth 'what's that?' anxiously to one of the other women sharing the front desk with her – Tina – who hadn't been with us that long herself.

'It's the reference book we use for getting the correct dosage or side effects of drugs, that sort of thing. If you don't have patient records to hand you have to manually look up whatever you're going to prescribe them,' I said. 'That's all. You don't need to worry about it.' They looked relieved and smiled at me gratefully.

'You'll just have to do your best to stick to the ten-minute slots, I think, in answer to your question, Megan – and we'll explain at the front desk when everything starts inevitably running late.' Cleo was already looking strained. 'I'll be around if anyone gets really arsey.'

'I suppose we've got no idea when we'll be back up?' asked David, hands on his head. 'It's probably another accidental NHS internal send-to-all test email and a million users hitting reply all again, isn't it?' He sighed crossly.

'Well, it could be a massive user error again, yes, or a hack or just a glitch.' Cleo gestured widely. 'Who knows? But for now, we need to open the phone lines, and it's ten minutes until morning surgery, so good luck everyone. I'll keep you posted.'

The computers stayed resolutely dead, however, and I had an increasingly hellish morning, as already grumpy patients became more and more fed up as we began to run later and later. It got to eleven o'clock and, having got rid of a particularly vile mother who had given me an earful about her daughter with tonsillitis being kept waiting for 'a disgusting length of time', I rang through for my next patient.

'OK, this one is a Shahid Khan.' Poor Jen sounded really harassed. 'Fresher at the university, not registered yet. I told him you'd got a slot if he wanted to wait, which he has, and he doesn't want to say why he needs to be seen. I've given him a GMS3/99,' she spelled it out carefully, tripping up with unfamiliarity, 'temporary services form to fill out and give you, because obviously I can't enter him on the system.'

'OK thanks,' I sighed. 'Send him through.'

'Bev's going to shout him for me now – I'm desperate for a wee. Sorry!'

I drew a dividing line on my pad under the tonsillitis child's notes and reached across my desk for a tissue to blow my nose. I needed a glass of water too; I felt mildly dehydrated, having not had enough time to drink anywhere near enough all morning.

On cue, there was the next knock of the door.

'Come in,' I said, trying to sound cheery.

I heard the door open, turned round with a ready smile, clutching my tissue, and froze.

Standing in front of me was Jonathan Day.

He was slightly stooped, as if conscious of his height. He raised his eyebrows expectantly as he slowly lifted his head, ruffling a hand through his hair while his face split into an embarrassed smile. For the first time, I got the distinct impression he knew exactly how heartbreakingly attractive he was and was imagining what he was looking like to me; almost posed as if in front of a camera on a modelling shoot. He was in uniform again, but he'd removed his tie and undone his top button, so he looked like any other young professional. Too smart for a fresher, that's for sure.

'What are you doing here?' I could hear the fear in my voice.

He turned and looked briefly over his shoulder, before coming right into the room and closing the door behind him. 'You know why. To see you.' His voice was urgent, excited.

My stomach had already shrunk into a small, hard, rubber-like ball. 'Jonathan, you shouldn't have come. If anyone sees you…' My mind had gone three steps ahead to how it might appear that he'd been in my room with me like this, alone.

He flushed slightly with surprise, and then pleasure, at the sound of me saying his name for the first time. 'I'm not stupid, no one knows who I am. Don't worry. There's no trail. I'm Shahid Khan, remember?' He thrust a blue and white piece of paper at me, his temporary services form. 'I look like just another patient. Here is the safest place for us.'

Us? An alarm bell began to ring quietly in the back of my mind.

'But that's exactly the problem, Jonathan,' I said urgently. 'You ARE a patient here. I could get into very serious trouble for seeing you like this in view of... the relationship we've had.'

He shook his head. 'But *I* haven't seen you, have I? I already said, no one knows I've been here. I gave a false address and everything.' He pointed at the form; then, when I still didn't take it, leant over and slid it across my desk. 'Relax. I had to do something, anyway, because you can't exactly come to school and you definitely can't pull that crazy shit again and come to my house like you did last night, Alex.' He laughed, his voice confident and well spoken, but all I noticed was that he knew my name.

'Don't get me wrong, it was amazing to see you,' he smiled at me suddenly, 'but they all started asking loads of questions after you drove off. Especially my girlfriend. Even my dad knew something was up the way we looked at each other. I couldn't believe you took such a big risk.'

What? 'Wait, Jonathan—' I held up a defensive hand. 'I had absolutely no idea you lived there. Your mother requested a home visit for medical attention.'

'It's OK, you don't have to be embarrassed. I was pleased.' He looked around him and pulled up a chair, so uncomfortably close to mine that his knee was almost touching the outer part of my thigh. I could smell the same aftershave that had been all over my dress the morning afterwards, to the point I'd actually thrown it away in the en-suite bin instead of packing it to take home.

I twisted back in under my desk more tightly so that the plastic arm of my seat blocked our legs from any further direct contact.

'Mum told me how you got one of your friends to put you forward for a job they've got going,' he continued. 'That was clever. I've been thinking about you too.' His smile faded. 'I haven't been able to get you out of my mind, and I'm really pleased you've changed yours. I thought you might, but…' He shrugged, shyly.

Changed my mind about what? I could feel my panic starting to build. 'Jonathan, I want to make it absolutely clear that my friend recommended me to your parents without my knowledge. I didn't come to see you yesterday. I'm your doctor at the practice you're registered at. There are very strict rules about that sort of thing.'

He looked at me suggestively, then drawled: 'Yeah, right. Like that bothered you on Saturday night in the club?'

'But I didn't know then. We were just two strangers.'

'What?' He laughed. 'No, we weren't!'

A much louder bell began to sound in my head. 'You knew who I was when you approached me?'

'Of course!' He threw his hands up incredulously. 'Are we having two separate conversations here?'

I caught my breath. 'Jonathan, have I seen you before? Here, I mean, as a patient?'

He looked at me, his mouth slightly open. 'Seriously? You don't remember?' He frowned, completely confused, and put his hands up to his hair again, to reveal a very expensive, chunky watch on his wrist. His eyes were wide, but then his features suddenly relaxed again. 'Shit, Alex, don't do that to me! I believed you for a minute there.' He let his arms fall back down heavily – then gave an odd, slight shake of his head as if he were jolting back into reality. 'Can you stop messing around now?' he asked. 'We need to talk.'

'Jonathan, when we met at the club, did you think I knew who you were? Because I didn't. You do understand that, don't you? I *didn't* know who you were.'

He exclaimed again and rolled his eyes. 'OK, OK. You "didn't know".' He mimed inverted commas. 'I get it, but we still need to talk.'

I started to slide sideways in my chair, as far away from him as I could get, very slowly. So if I'd seen him in a medical capacity… for what? Something general, or more serious? Did he have mental health issues? Was I potentially in danger right now? I squished myself in the corner, turned slightly so I could face him, and said as calmly as I could manage: 'OK, what do you want to talk about?'

He hesitated at my deliberately measured tone, noting it immediately. 'Don't do that doctor voice. I see you in a club in Ibiza, of all places, so I smile. You don't say anything, but you don't have to, it's written all over your face. I walk up, we start kissing. We go back to your hotel. You make it clear what you want, we do it and then the next morning you basically tell me "thanks very much, now fuck off". I've never had a girl do that to me. Girls *don't* do that to me. I leave, and I still don't get it. But, whatever. Shit happens. Except then you're suddenly standing in my *house*, because you knew that if you showed up, I'd come and find you afterwards. And I have. I'm here.' He sat back and threw open his arms. 'What is it you want from me, Alex?'

I looked at him, frightened. 'Nothing! I don't want anything from you!'

He glanced sideways and snorted. 'Is this some sort of game to you? Bored, married woman seeks attention? I'm not that kind of bloke, sorry. I had a massive row with my girlfriend last night just for looking at you yesterday, so can we cut the crap? Yes, I want to see you again. Very much. Yes, I like you, a lot. Tell me where, and I'll be there. I won't say anything, no one needs to know and we'll just… see how it goes.'

I was astonished; for a moment, completely lost for words. 'To reiterate, when I saw you in the club on Saturday I didn't recognise you, at all.'

'I know that's not true.'

I was taken aback by his bluntness. 'OK, well, I'm sorry to hear we disagree, but regardless of what you think, I was completely unaware you were known to me. Having relationships with patients is not allowed when you're a doctor, Jonathan. Especially a patient who is', I swallowed, 'only seventeen.'

He looked at the floor. 'So like I said, that's a problem now, but not so much when I was fucking you?'

I jerked back in my chair in shock. 'Can you please not talk to me like that?'

He shrugged and smiled lazily – all while looking straight at me. I could see exactly why, drunk, I'd not thought for one moment that he was too young, too innocent.

I blinked, completely disorientated by everything that was happening in this, my work room. It was as if I were watching a hideous slow-motion car accident unfold in front of me, while somehow also being trapped in the driver's seat – the car spinning round in circles, seconds before impact. 'You know, I think it would be best if you left now, actually,' I managed eventually. I was shell-shocked. I didn't know *what* to say.

'You want me to leave?'

'Yes, I do.'

He leant forward and put his hand on my leg. 'I don't believe you.'

I pushed it off, horrified at his touch.

He flushed violently at my instinctive reaction, sat up even taller and rapidly drummed his fingers on his legs, before abruptly getting to his feet. 'OK.' He reached out and grabbed back his temporary treatment form, scrunching it up and shoving it in his pocket.

Even though he was towering over me, he looked humiliated, and I foolishly tried to make it better. 'I really am very sorry, Jonathan, that you thought my coming to your house was some sort of signal, but please don't feel embarrassed. I can see it was an honest mistake.'

That only made it worse. He swallowed, almost painfully, and his Adam's apple bobbed in his throat as he reached into his pocket and pulled his school tie out again, before turning, holding it loosely in his hand so it trailed behind him as he quietly left the room.

Somehow that was the worst bit of the whole encounter, because, for all his height and masculine body, the bravado, expensive watches and tattoos, that one action revealed the youth he evidentially still was.

I turned back to my desk and covered my mouth with my hands, elbows resting on the cheap faux mahogany as I stared at the blank computer screen in front of me. I remained paralysed for a few moments, before jumping up and rushing out, walking smartly down the corridor back to the waiting room. I scanned the sea of faces looking hopefully back at me, in case I was about to call *their* name, but he wasn't there, he'd gone.

Any relief was short-lived, however. I drew back and pushed through the door into the reception office. Jen, Tina and Bev looked up at me wearily, and Jen blurted: 'Oh no! Did you ring through and I haven't sent the next one in?'

Before I could answer, another phone began to ring.

'Hang on!' She snatched it up as, simultaneously, a terse voice called 'Excuse me?' from the front desk and Tina swore under her breath. 'I'm JUST coming, Mrs Peters!' she called out. 'One minute.' She pushed past me as Bev looked desperately at the clock. 'I'm so sorry, Dr Inglis,' she said to me. 'Can you wait for whatever it is for five seconds? I HAVE to go to the loo.'

'Of course.' I stood back to let her pass.

Tina had her back to me; Jen was scrabbling round looking for something. Thinking she wanted the duty appointments list, I reached over to Bev's desk and picked it up, offering it to Jen. She shook her head and pointed at Bev's pen instead.

I passed it across as Jen mouthed 'thank you' and started writing quickly. I looked down at the list in my hands of the appointments

I still had to come and had already done. There he was, *Shahid Khan*. What a bizarre name to have chosen. I stared at the only evidence of him having come into the practice – then placed it down and headed back to my desk.

Jen rang through to me seconds later. 'I'm so sorry. You're ready for your next person, I know, but we can't find the list anywhere.'

'I put it back on Bev's desk.'

'Oh, I'm not saying *you've* lost it,' she said quickly. 'Sorry. It's mayhem out here. Anyway, give me a second and I'll send them through when we find it, or them.'

*

The system came back on about ten minutes after morning surgery finished. By the time I'd done my house visits, come back, dealt with the prescription requests and processed some blood test results, David stuck his head round my door to find me about to start on the sea of paperwork swimming on my desk. 'You all right, Al? Worst morning for a while, eh?'

I glanced up at him. 'Yes, it was. David, can you come in for a minute? I need to talk to you.'

'Ah, yes. You didn't get to finish your house call story, did you? I'm sorry.' He came in and collapsed tiredly onto the chair Jonathan had pulled right up to my knee an hour earlier. David was tall too, and the stark reminder of Jonathan sat there, staring, made me shiver.

'Alex? Do you want to carry on?'

Blinking, I realised David was waiting patiently.

'Sorry. Things have moved on a bit, actually.' I took a deep breath. 'Let's suppose, hypothetically, one of your colleagues had a one-night stand with a much younger man—'

David started, and sat up a little straighter.

'And it turns out he's a patient of hers,' I continued, looking down so I couldn't see the expression on David's face, 'which obviously she didn't know at the time – a patient she has apparently also treated in a professional capacity, although she has no memory of that. Let's also suppose he's the son of some patients who don't like her very much and that he turned up at surgery this morning, to see her, because she inadvertently went to his parents' house last night on call, and he thinks it was some secret signal for them to start something up again.'

There was a moment of silence, and I looked up eventually to see David sat back, his expression grave, hands clasped round the back of his head.

'So what would you advise her to do, hypothetically?' I said and gave a nervous, miserable laugh.

'When you say one-night stand, you mean?—'

'Sex, yes.'

'And exactly how old, is "much younger"?'

'Seventeen.'

'Oh, Alex.' He closed his eyes and put his head in his hands instead.

'I know, I know.' I found myself near to tears and tried to choke them back.

'I assume, hypothetically, she made it very clear to him that it was a one-off, something she wouldn't have let happen in a million years had she known who he was, and how old he was, and that under no circumstances would it be happening again?'

'Of course.'

'And he got the message?'

I nodded. 'He left, embarrassed and a bit angry, but he was under no illusions.'

'Does this hypothetical colleague of mine think he'll leave it there?'

I paled. 'God, yes, I hope so. I can't see why he wouldn't. He said that he'd had a row with his girlfriend and his parents had asked questions. He went to the trouble of creating a fake identity to get an appointment with me, so he obviously doesn't want it out in the open either.'

'Does anyone else know about this?'

I shook my head. 'Just you. He screwed up his temporary treatment form, and took it away with him, and the paper list of duty appointments documenting his fake name has gone missing. Nothing was logged, obviously, because the system was down.'

David sat back. 'He didn't ask for medical advice. He didn't give his real name, so one can reasonably assume he would be unhappy about his real notes being accessed. There's no paper trail, so it's as good as if he wasn't here. He's got the message that it was a one-off. You didn't know when you slept with him that he was your patient…' He exhaled. 'Nothing punishable, as far as I can see. Although now, of course, you must remove him from your list pronto – his parents too. But that's fine, because you can use their duplicity from last night as the reason for that.'

I lowered my voice to a whisper. 'I genuinely have no recollection of treating him professionally. I don't remember seeing him here at all.'

'Well, you sure as hell can't open his notes to look, Al. You're absolutely certain he got the message then? It's just… you can really do without any love-struck kids hanging around giving people the wrong idea, given your history.'

I could feel my face turning red as I coloured, guiltily. 'You mean Rob?'

'Yes, of course. Who else could I have meant?'

'Rob was a consenting adult, and we're married now! We've been married for eight years!'

'I'm not disputing it turned out to be the real deal. He was, however, already married to someone else when you both met, here, and you were his doctor,' David gently, but correctly, pointed out. 'You saw Rob over a course of appointments – it wasn't a one-off – and while you were bloody lucky to get away with just a warning after his ex made that "anonymous" complaint against you; it's still sitting there on the list of Registered Medical Practitioners. So, get this boy off your list *now* because, frankly, if he shows up to see you again, it's going to make you look like this is how you pick up men, Al.'

'Knock, knock.'

We both jumped, David twisting round in his chair, to see Rob himself standing in the doorway, his hand raised and against the doorframe. My mouth fell open. How much had he heard?

Rob reached into his pocket with his other hand and pulled out my mobile, holding it aloft. 'You left this at home in the rush this morning. I just found it and thought you might need it in case the school called or something, so I brought it down. Bev let me in.' He looked between David and I. 'Everything all right?' His tone was light, but I could hear a very slight edge to it.

David jumped up, smiled warmly and offered Rob his hand. 'Rob! Good to see you again, mate!'

I winced inwardly. David wasn't the kind of bloke who could pull off 'mate' with any conviction at all.

Rob shook his hand and looked at me silently.

'We've had the morning from hell,' David said chattily. 'Systems all down, Internet up the spout, patients kicking off. Still, we got there in the end, thank God.' He laughed. 'Anyway, I'll let you both get on, but as I was just saying, Alex, if you can *pick up* that man's *record* we've got to *report* on, that would be great.'

He looked at me pointedly, obviously thinking that Rob might have heard the last thing he said, too.

'Will do,' I said quietly, suddenly exhausted.

'Cheers, Rob, see you soon, pal!' He patted Rob's shoulder heartily and, head down, scurried off to his office, like the White Rabbit.

Rob came in, sat down and slid my mobile across to me.

'Thanks,' I said. 'That was kind of you.'

'That was a lot of "pal" and "mate" from David. He's very chipper today considering the morning it sounds like you've had.'

'Just relief that it's over, I expect. It makes you go a bit giddy and weird when you're working under high stress like that and trying not to mess up by giving someone something they ought not to have.' I couldn't meet his eye.

'You look shattered.' Rob reached out and beckoned with his fingers. 'Give me your car keys and I'll swap with you. I'll take the Qashqai back and collect the girls from school – that way we don't have to switch the car seats over. You take the BMW and come home when you're done here.'

'Are you sure?' I glanced at him gratefully. 'I don't want to mess up your work.'

'You're not.'

'Well, thank you.' There was another pause and I said quickly: 'I'm sorry that I can't stop and say let's go to lunch or something, but I'm not even going to get time for a sandwich today; I've got all this morning to catch up on as well as a load of other stuff.' I smiled apologetically and gestured at the paper mountain.

'There's nothing going on that I should know about, is there, Al?'

I stopped short. He waited, and I shook my head.

He appeared to consider that. 'OK.' He got to his feet and leant over to kiss me goodbye. His mouth lingered on mine for a moment longer than I was expecting. I'd started to pull back before I realised my mistake. I managed to salvage it, though, and even felt myself starting to respond to his touch.

He broke away. 'I think we'd better stop there, don't you? I'll see you back at home.'

*

I didn't tell him then and there about Jonathan because I was at work. It wasn't the time or the place. That's all. And it's lunacy to suggest I could – or would – have compromised an entire medical centre to prevent there being any computerised record of subsequent patient appointments that morning, even made-up ones. I was not anticipating Jonathan would come into the surgery, nor did I ask him to. We didn't have any contact whatsoever after I left his parents' property. I was only in early to look at and update Christy Day's record because I was frightened the boy I'd seen at her house was below the age of consent.

Neither did I apprehend and destroy the handwritten appointment list, and I take issue that it's even being considered an official document. It was barely more than a piece of scrap paper. In any case, I put it back on Bev's desk. I wasn't nervous and panicking. I was simply looking at the list to see if he was telling me the truth and been documented as Shahid Khan.

I'm just not that devious. It's as simple as that.

CHAPTER 4

Dr Alexandra Inglis

By the time I'd finally finished at half past five, I was exhausted. My limbs felt heavy with fatigue and I couldn't stop yawning, partly through dehydration. For the first time since the previous weekend, I was thinking longingly of a large G&T.

I said goodbye to Cleo and David, the last ones left to lock up, and stepped out into the overcast early evening. Looking for our BMW in the car park, I saw that Rob had typically left it right in the farthest corner, carefully reversed into a space over by the wooded bank that backed onto the gardens of the terraced houses behind. My husband never parks conveniently close to anywhere he wants to be if he can pointlessly park miles away. My shoulders sagged slightly, and I began to walk across the tarmac, thinking about Jonathan sitting in my room talking about fucking, and David's advice.

It hadn't even occurred to me that what I'd done might appear to be an emerging pattern of my using appointments to 'pick up men'. I could see, however, when the two events were placed alongside each other – even with an eight-year time lag between them – it might make my insistence that I'd not known Jonathan was my patient appear unreliable, at best.

David was right, I needed to remove Jonathan from my list quickly. I'd drafted the letter to Gary and Christy Day explaining that, after my house visit, I'd decided it was in everybody's interest for them to move as a family from my list to my colleague Peter's, but after the fallout from the morning's computer fiasco, I hadn't managed to catch Peter or Cleo in time to confirm that was OK with them before the post went.

I also couldn't believe Jonathan seemed to think I'd known exactly who he was; it was ridiculous. Knowingly have sex with a seventeen-year-old patient? I'd be struck off immediately – and who in their right mind would risk that happening? Never mind the financial impact, which would be hugely significant for our family: why would I waste all of my years of hard work and gamble away a career I enjoyed? All for one night? It could never be worth it. And that's before even considering the effect it would have on Rob and the girls.

I imagined our innocent children back at our safe, cosy house, eating tea. By the time my mother was my age, she had a twenty-year-old daughter – older than Jonathan. Christ… I pictured him trailing his school tie behind him as he'd left my office, then recalled the blur of our naked bodies in the dark hotel room and shivered with disgust. I'd had sex flashbacks about various exes many times over the years that had made me feel slightly grossed out, but this was in a different league altogether. It was repulsive. Seventeen.

I reached into my pocket for the keys my husband had given me earlier. I blipped the car unlocked as I approached, walked around to put my bag in the boot, and almost screamed to discover Jonathan, hidden from view by the car, sitting down on a spread-out coat on the grass hillock, next to a rucksack, waiting for me.

'What the hell are you doing?' I gasped. 'You scared the life out of me! You can't jump out at people like that – Jesus Christ!' I stepped back, shaking.

'I didn't jump out.' He got up stiffly. He'd obviously been there a while. 'I just want to talk to you, that's all.' Then he opened the passenger side and climbed in.

Aghast, I opened the driver's side. 'Get out of my car, *now*!' I ordered.

He sighed, as if I was being completely unreasonable, and did as he was told, walking round the bonnet to stand in front of me.

'Did you not hear what I said to you earlier?' I demanded. 'Even if I wanted to, doctors aren't allowed to have relationships with their patients. I would lose my job.'

'Jesus, stop being so dramatic. No one's here. No one's looking. I just want to talk, not do you in the back of your car.'

I shrank away. Where was the vulnerable boy sitting on his coat of just *two seconds ago*? He was suddenly talking like some slightly bored and irritated much older man. His shape-shifting was impossible to keep up with. I didn't know how to place him, how to *deal* with him.

'I want you to leave.'

He sighed again. 'Fine, if we can't talk privately in the car, I'll say it here then. I know what's in this for you, Alex. You wanted attention; I gave it to you. I made you feel better about yourself… but I also liked it. You're different.'

'Stop.' I held my hands up. 'You don't understand what it was about at all. I'm not different, I'm a mother. I've got two little girls and a husband. I'm old enough to be *your* mother.'

'Age is just a number.'

I half laughed in disbelief. 'You don't get to say that yet. You're too young. Just go home, Jonathan.'

He stepped forward suddenly, only inches away from my face, and grabbed my wrist. I could feel his body trembling. 'We can be careful. No one needs to know.' He was holding me tightly enough to hurt.

'Let go of me, now.'

'I'm sorry. I didn't mean to frighten you.' His voice was calm, and I had no idea if he was being sincere. After a moment's pause, he released me. 'Just sleep with me again,' he said suddenly. 'One night, sober, and I'll leave you alone after that if you still want me to.'

I stepped back, rubbing my reddening skin. 'You've not heard a single word I've said, have you?' I struggled to keep my voice level. 'Or do you just not care that I could lose my job?'

'OK, then sleep with me again or I'll tell everyone what we did.'

I gasped and, as I looked at him, rage swept up inside me. He reminded me, suddenly, of Hannah. I'd gone round to her flat to ask her what the fuck she thought she was doing, coming on to my husband at her party, asking HIM to be the one to save her from the letchy hands of the more senior managers. Her *protector*. She'd had the same untroubled expression as Jonathan was now wearing when I'd screamed 'he's MARRIED' in her face, before she slammed the door in mine.

'Tell everyone then,' I said. 'I didn't know who you were, and my husband already knows I've been unfaithful, so the only sordid detail left is you trying to blackmail me into having sex with you. You're really trying to do that, by the way?' I was revolted.

Quick as a flash, he stepped over to me, ducked his head, and kissed me on the mouth. He gasped as his lips briefly touched mine, before I stumbled back and looked around us, only to see David, overcoat on, keys in his hand, right by his car, silently watching.

Our eyes met, and David looked away first before getting into his Land Rover and pulling sharply out of his space.

I watched him drive off, my mouth slightly open in shock, realising instantly how that must have appeared. I turned slowly back to Jonathan. 'That was my colleague who just saw us then. I'd already told him about you coming to the surgery today, but I also said you'd got the message and you'd be leaving me alone.'

'Alex, I—' Jonathan began.

'Be quiet,' I said. 'You've just made it look like we're having some sort of affair. He'll now be duty-bound to report this; so, yes, everyone *is* going to know what we did. Well done. But you know what? I'm going to make sure they understand exactly what you just said to me, that you tried to blackmail me into having sex with you. What a deeply disgusting thing to do.' Glaring at him, I wiped my mouth with the back of my hand, turned away and threw my bag on the back seat of the car.

'Alex, just stop—' he began,

'Get out of my way,' I said, climbing in and slamming the door.

I started the car and he moved reluctantly to the side, seconds before I roared across the car park to the exit, only pausing to look furiously in the mirror before I pulled out onto the main road. He was still standing there, watching me, his face now expressionless.

I swung right, violently, and started to drive, gripping the steering wheel tightly, before screaming out loud and slapping the wheel with both hands, my anger and fear exploding without warning, causing me to swerve dangerously close to the parked cars lining the road on either side. The bastard. The nasty, stupid, little bastard. I hurtled up to the traffic lights at the end of the road, on red, and stopped with a jolt, breathing too fast, before shoving the gearstick into first again and swinging out onto the main carriageway. My jaw was clenched so tightly – as I drove too close behind the painfully slow-moving traffic – that my muscles started to ache. 'Just fucking MOVE!' I yelled, as a bus, one vehicle up, pulled over to pick up passengers, forcing me to stop completely. I had no choice but to sit there helplessly as traffic streamed past on the other side of the road, the swirling rage beginning to solidify within my stomach into a huge, leaden lump as a suffocating tightness began to spread from my chest outwards and up my throat. David no longer believed me, I could tell. Unless I could convince him what he'd seen in the car park was not how it appeared, he really would report me. I hadn't lied to Jonathan – he had a duty to.

I swallowed, acutely aware of the seriousness of this new situation, and glanced left to see a mother marching up the street crossly pulling the hand of a little girl who was crying and trying to keep up – almost having to run. She was about the same age as Maisie. My eyes welled up; I could feel her unhappiness so acutely it physically hurt. She was only small. Too tiny to be made so sad by her mummy.

What had I done? What the fuck had I done?

I had to look away and wiped my wet face with my hand as the tears started to spill over. I tried to think about when I should tell Rob what had happened. Should I do it straight away or wait and see if I could drive the girls to his mother's first, in the morning? Tilly was such a light sleeper, she'd definitely wake if he started crashing around upstairs packing a bag, then Maisie would be disturbed too. It would be unbearably traumatic for them to see him leave in the night; because wouldn't I do exactly that if I were him and was told the 'stranger' his wife slept with turned out to be a seventeen-year-old she had a connection to after all, and had been seen kissing only hours earlier?

The traffic began to move again. My anger had drained completely, leaving dry fear in its place as I tried to think clinically about practicalities. It probably *would* be better if the girls weren't there. Nothing was going to formally happen until Monday morning now, so, although another fourteen hours wouldn't make much difference to Rob, it could potentially be a great deal to our daughters.

When I finally pulled onto the drive, through the window I could see Rob playing monsters with Maisie and Tilly, chasing them round the sofas, arms outstretched as they tried to run away from him. I couldn't hear the growling and the delighted screams but knew exactly how they would sound. I sat in the front seat and watched them for a moment, before climbing out and walking up to the front door, smiling as the girls saw me and pointed. I was just about able to hear the shouts of 'Mummy!' from behind the glass as they turned and ran to come and find me.

My key turned stiffly in the lock, and I pushed the door gently open in case either of them was already right behind it, but they were still rounding the corner. The house was warm and smelt comfortingly of cooking. Maisie jumped happily into my arms, and Tilly clasped at my leg. 'Mummy's home, Daddy!' Maisie called, and Rob appeared in the sitting room doorway, puffing slightly, hair all over the place. He smiled happily at me. 'Busy game of monsters on the go,' he said as I kissed Maisie and then Tilly.

'So I see! What fun!' I laughed. The actions were all there, but I was completely numb inside. I could only picture myself reaching out and in slow motion sweeping the family photos off the sideboard, throwing the vase of roses on the floor, the glass smashing everywhere, the girls screaming for real, Rob rushing forward to stop me… because I had as good as broken it all. I put my bag down and caught my reflection in the hall mirror. I had to quickly turn away. I couldn't look myself in the eye.

We put the girls through a bath and they busily told me all about their day; who they'd played with, what they'd had for lunch, their best and worst bits. I read Tilly stories as she lay on her tummy on her bed, and I sat on the carpet next to her. She listened carefully to *The Highway Rat*, twisting my hair absently round her finger. After her songs, I tucked her in, told her I loved her and added 'Best littlest girl!' to which she beamed and replied: 'best mummy!'

'That's a lovely thing to say, darling, thank you! Night, night.' I bit my lip to stop my tears, and quickly bent to kiss her before she noticed anything was wrong.

I took a moment outside Maisie's room to compose myself before snuggling her down too and singing *her* songs, as I sat on the floor stroking her hair. She listened contentedly and when I got to my knees to lean over and kiss her good night, whispering 'best biggest girl', she wrapped her arms round my neck before gently, ever so softly, kissing my cheek. It was so uncomplicated and pure, it felt almost like a blessing, and I wished with all my heart it could absolve everything. I so badly wanted to be the best version of myself that she believed I was. I thought about how safe my mother had always made me feel, even though there must have been times when she was falling apart inside during the divorce from my dad and, as I left the room, I resolved then and there to do my best – whatever the aftermath – to make everything as bearable as possible for my daughters, and Rob. I wanted, very much, to blame Jonathan's public kiss for what was going to come but, deep down, I knew my failings were all my own.

*

I changed out of my work skirt, top and tights and threw some pyjamas on over my underwear, before going downstairs into the sitting room to find my husband. He was on the sofa, computer on his lap. I sat on the sofa adjacent to him and curled my legs up and under me.

'All right?' he said.

'I need to talk to you, Rob.' So much for making sure the girls were out. I didn't know I was going to say it, but the words were there before I realised they would be.

In any event, I was immediately proven to have made the right decision, because Rob replied: 'Yeah, I know you do.'

He moved the laptop onto a cushion next to him and clasped his hands. 'There's a text on your phone from David that says: "I thought you'd told him it was over? Didn't look like it to me, today. I can't pretend this isn't happening".' Rob glanced up at me briefly. 'I went through the messages while you were upstairs because when I came into your room at work today and you weren't expecting me, there was very obviously something going on between the two of you.' His voice was flat and quiet. 'You weren't with the girls last weekend, were you? You were with David. When you told me you'd slept with someone else, it was actually him, wasn't it, and now he wants you to leave me?'

For a moment or two, I was dumbstruck. What had we done to each other?

'He's always had a thing for you.'

'He lives with his mother, and I'm almost certain he's gay.'

'No, he's not,' scoffed Rob.

'In all the years I've known him, not once has he ever talked about a woman. But that's irrelevant. I really was with the girls in Ibiza. David's talking about something else.' I took a deep breath. 'The man I slept with last Saturday turns out to be a current patient of mine, and he's seventeen.'

Rob's mouth fell open. 'What?'

'I didn't know he was my patient or how old he was – obviously, I hope – until today,' I continued quickly. 'He came to the surgery this morning using a fake name to get in to see me. Apparently, I've treated him before, but I have absolutely no memory of that. Once I realised who he was, I made him aware that I could no longer be his doctor and that he wasn't to come near me again. That's what I was discussing with David when you arrived at lunchtime. After I'd finished work, though, he was waiting for me alongside our car. He kissed me, which David witnessed. *That's* what David's text is referring to; he's going to have no choice but to do something official about it now, after what he saw. This "boy" also told me that unless I had sex with him again, he would tell everyone what we did; so either way, it's all going to come out.'

Rob closed his eyes, before saying hesitantly: 'You've had sex with a patient who David saw you kissing this afternoon?'

'No, he was kissing me,' I corrected instantly. 'But, yes, he was the one from Ibiza. He says he recognised me in the club but, as far as I was concerned, he was a complete stranger. I was very drunk, but, even so, he didn't look seventeen in the slightest.'

Rob's eyes snapped open. 'That's supposed to make this better?'

'No,' I said quietly. 'I'm just trying to explain because I can hear how this sounds to you.'

'Can you?' His eyebrows lifted. 'Can you, really? So how do you think I feel right now?' There was no mistaking the rising anger in his voice.

I took a deep breath. 'Disgusted, revolted, angry, unable to believe it. All the things I felt when I discovered his actual age.'

'How could you?' Rob interrupted. 'And before you say ANYTHING, Hannah was twenty-six. That's different to this.'

Thrown by this unexpected comparison, I nonetheless managed to choose my words carefully. 'I'm not about to do the "men get to sleep with young women, so why shouldn't women get to sleep with young men" bit,' I said clearly. 'Personally, I don't think it's OK for anyone of our age to have sex with someone who is emotionally vulnerable, or at the very least impressionable, which I think most young adults are, up until their late twenties.'

'Oh come, on!' Rob exclaimed. 'They're not even vaguely on the same page!'

'I'm not actually trying to defend anything. Had I known what I was doing, it would have been a complete abuse of power. But—' I raised my voice slightly, holding a hand up because Rob was starting to exclaim angrily again, 'I had no idea. Yes, what *I've* done – albeit unwittingly – makes me feel sick to my stomach. Yes, it's horrendous that he's only seventeen but, come on, Rob, you must know I would never, *ever* have had sex with him if I'd known how old he was? I didn't actually do anything wrong other than have a one-night stand with a stranger, or so I thought.'

'He kissed you this afternoon?' Rob ignored me. 'I don't even know how to process this.' He got up suddenly and started to pace around the room. 'So…' I watched him start to do the maths. 'He's still at school?' He looked at me horrified, and I nodded.

'Jesus fucking Christ, Alex!' He glanced at me again, as if I might somehow be an imposter sitting in the room who just looked and sounded exactly like his wife of eight years. 'I can't believe that you wouldn't have known; you've got eyes, haven't you? And you must have recognised him.'

'There are thousands of patients on the surgery books: I see someone every ten minutes at work; plus, I was drunk and, like I said, he looks much older. He's very tall, he—'

'No!' Rob said. 'I don't want to hear it. I don't want detail.' He shook his head. 'I don't want to talk about this any more full stop. I need some space.'

'We have to talk about it. We need to decide what—'

'No, we really don't.' He started walking towards the door.

'Rob – wait!' I jumped up and put my hands out to stop him, but he pushed me to one side and kept going. 'Please, stop!' I whispered desperately, tears rushing to my eyes but not wanting to wake the girls with shouting. 'Please stay and talk to me about this.' I grabbed onto his arms with both hands, and he started to shake me off.

'Don't touch me! You're a *mother*, Alex! You've got two children yourself.'

'But when you say you're going, what do you mean? Going where? Please just stay and hear me out!' I begged.

'What more is there to say?'

'I didn't know who he was!' I implored, trying to take his hand. 'This is *me*, Rob. I'm your wife!'

'I said, don't touch me!' He stepped back, defensively pulling his hands up high, out of my reach, before putting them on his head, looking at me with wide eyes. 'I cannot believe this. I just want you to leave me alone.'

'No!' I insisted, standing in his way. 'This isn't fair. I didn't do this to you when you told me about Hannah.'

'She's an adult, I'm not her doctor and I wasn't caught in a compromising position with her this afternoon!' he exclaimed. 'Excuse me, please.' He tried to pass again, and once more I blocked his way. 'I said, get out of my way!' He raised his voice.

'Please, shhhh! I don't want to wake the girls.' I pleadingly held a finger up to my lips. 'How many more times can I say it – I didn't *know*, but if you leave me now, it'll make it look like I did. Everyone will believe I'm the person you're saying I am now. And I'm not! I'm *not*.'

I lost all control at that point and was so deeply distressed that I started crying in that completely abandoned way that feels scarily child-like because of its lack of boundaries, and for the person watching borders on them wondering if you've become dangerously unhinged. I sank to my knees on the carpet, at his feet, and sobbed.

'Stop it,' he said, after a moment. 'I don't want the kids to hear you like this.'

I wasn't able to. Everything that had happened in the three weeks since he'd nervously confessed to having sex with Hannah – over breakfast the Saturday morning after the night before, when the girls had just left the table and scampered off into the sitting room to watch TV in their pyjamas, and I'd asked if he wanted another coffee – had crashed over me like a wave and dragged me out to sea. I couldn't catch my breath.

He looked down at me silently, then stepped past me and left the room, closing the door behind him.

Winded with pain, I collapsed into the foetal position, hugging my knees to my chest as I cried. I saw Hannah's hard little eyes staring at me in the doorway of her flat and heard Jonathan catching his breath when his lips had touched mine. I was bereft that Rob and I had allowed them into our marriage, and terrified at what now lay ahead.

*

I'm not sure how long I lay there, long enough for the tears to simply run out, but eventually I heard the door open again, and a large wodge of loo roll appeared in front of my face. Rob was crouched behind me.

'Here,' he said. 'Take this.'

I reached out and, lifting my head, obediently wiped my eyes, and my nose.

'Sit up,' he said, and taking my shoulders, he rocked me upright, then sat down on the carpet, leaning back on the sofa adjacent to me, his hands resting on his knees. We sat in silence for a moment before he asked: 'Do you swear that you didn't know who he was in the club?'

'Of course,' I said, exhausted.

'And he kissed you earlier? Not the other way around?'

'Yes.'

He started twisting his wedding ring. 'You can't just tell someone over breakfast, "Oh sorry, I fucked someone else last night", and not expect it not to have some kind of impact on their behaviour. I shouldn't have tried to dump my guilt on you about Hannah. I know I've hurt you. I made you very angry too, and that's part of why you did what you did in Ibiza. Mostly I just think this is all such a mess, and I don't want Maisie and Tilly to suffer because of mistakes we've made. It's not like he was underage and what you did was illegal.'

'Thank you.'

He exhaled. 'You don't have to thank me. We're married. We're supposed to support each other. What will happen now?'

I cleared my throat and tried to focus. 'For me at work, you mean?'

He nodded.

'Well, unless I can convince David he didn't see what he thinks he saw, he'll report me, I expect. I'll ring him tomorrow, but I'll have to sit down with him and Cleo on Monday morning and go through it all with them formally, just to cover my back in case this boy comes good on his threat and tells everyone we've had sex.'

'What if David doesn't believe you?'

'The process would be the same as when Bella made her complaint about you and me.' I watched Rob tense at the mention of his ex-wife. 'It'd go to the Primary Care Trust and the General Medical Council. Unlike last time, because of him being much younger and a current patient, it will be investigated immediately, I imagine. I'd need to contact the MDU for some legal advice. I might be suspended in the interim while the investigation is ongoing and they gather statements from everyone; but I haven't done anything punishable, so ultimately I don't see how I could be struck off. It would be massively stressful though.'

'Fuck,' he exhaled and let his head drop.

'I think I just need to talk to David in the first instance.'

'What's this boy's name?' Rob said.

'I don't think I can tell you yet. I'm sorry.'

'But he threatened to shop you unless you slept with him again?'

'Yes.'

'David wouldn't have heard him?'

'I don't see how. He was on the other side of the car park.'

'Is the warning you got after Bella made the complaint about *us* still on your record?'

'Yes.'

We sat there in silence for a moment more as he digested the implications of that.

'OK. Well, we'll just have to deal with it as we get there, I guess.' He held out his hand. I could just about reach it, and we entwined the tips of our fingers. 'I love you.'

My relief as he said that was immense. 'I love you too.'

Neither of us moved. I wanted to stay like that forever, safe with him, our babies upstairs asleep in their beds – as if none of it had happened.

'We need to be a lot better at protecting us,' he said. 'You, me, Maisie and Tilly. But we'll get through this, together. I promise you.'

*

I've no doubt he meant every word, but sometimes love isn't enough, no matter how hard you want to believe it will be.

I felt glad to have told him everything, though, and went to bed relieved that there were at least no more surprises to come.

How very naïve I was.

CHAPTER 5

Dr Alexandra Inglis

The morning of Monday, 18 September was one of those clear, bright blue sky days that gives everyone hope winter is still way off after all, and the supermarkets are just being ridiculous in already stocking gingerbread biscuits iced with pumpkins and ghosts, plastic spiders, light-up eyeballs and trick-or-treat buckets. I'd dressed carefully in a navy trouser suit with a bright red top to help me feel stronger than I felt and had got up early to wash my hair and dry it properly. I wanted at the very least to look professional when I spoke to David and Cleo about Jonathan's Friday surgery visit and the unwanted kiss.

Stood with my back to the kitchen table while I stared out of the window into the garden and tried to gather my thoughts, I sipped my coffee apprehensively. Rob was attempting to get Maisie and Tilly started on their raisin wheat, although both girls were crossly registering their complaints about missing the rest of the episode of *Paw Patrol* he'd not allowed them to pause. I stared silently at our holly tree. Contrasted against the sky, the glossy green leaves and already shiny scarlet berries reminded me – not for the first time – of a painting that had hung for years in my grandfather's house: a Naïf Vermont winter landscape of children bringing home a Christmas tree on a sled and ice skaters twirling on a frozen lake. I used to want to live in that picture and run through the unblemished snow past the little weather-boarded church to the cosy hay barn and play inside.

'We should all go to New England next autumn for a holiday,' I said suddenly. 'I've always wanted to see the woodland colours in the fall.'

Rob straightened up and looked at me, worriedly. 'OK. Why not? Sounds fun.' He cleared his throat. 'You all right?'

I nodded. 'All good.' I put my cup down on the draining board and turned to face my girls. 'Right, sweethearts, I'm going to go to work now. Daddy's going to take you to school and I'll come and collect you later. Have a lovely day, won't you?' I bent to kiss the top of Maisie's golden-haired head and breathed in the scent of the Johnson's shampoo I still used on both of them. I had a sudden urge to stay at home with them, for all four of us to go and do something completely different with such a rare, beautiful day; one we'd remember for all of the right reasons.

I crossed round the table to Tilly, who leant her head back blissfully and closed her eyes to receive my kiss on her soft forehead, before twisting round while still clutching a dripping, milky spoon, arms open wide. 'Hug me, Mummy!' she offered generously.

I couldn't possibly refuse but eyed her spoon warily. 'Thank you, darling, what a lovely goodbye.' After a snuggle for her, and one for Maisie too – who wasn't about to miss out on anything Tilly was getting – I inspected myself anxiously, all of my thoughts and fears temporarily replaced by the simple challenge of getting out of the front door without needing to change again. I glanced up at Rob. 'Do I look OK?'

'Perfect.' He pulled me into a hug, creasing my jacket, but I managed not to say anything, and instead, gratefully took the support in the spirit it was given. 'Call me at lunchtime, hey?' He looked at me pointedly, and I nodded. We both knew I'd have something to report by then.

I'd had a long telephone conversation over the weekend with David, who had at first been briskly, almost icily matter of fact. I'd implored him to give me the chance to talk to him as a friend rather than a colleague – and as we spoke, he began to thaw, until to my huge relief, he'd started to sound like his normal self again. He hadn't heard Jonathan blackmail me but was appalled when I told him exactly what Jonathan had wanted in return for his silence.

'What the fuck is wrong with kids these days? It's all about sex now, isn't it? Sexting, watching porn on their phones, child on child sex offences on the rise. Jesus Christ! What have we all let happen to this generation?' He paused, genuinely bewildered, before adding quickly: 'Not that I'm saying you saw him as a child. Sorry, that wasn't helpful.'

'It's fine. I'm just relieved you understand that there is NOTHING going on between us, and what you saw was him forcing himself on me.'

'I think that's actually the point there, Alex,' David said suddenly. 'I made a massive assumption based on what I thought I saw, but he came to your place of work, and after you'd told him to leave he still hid behind your car and waited for you, threatened you unless you slept with him again, grabbed your wrist to restrain you and foisted unwanted sexual contact on you. Just because a woman chooses to have sex with someone once does not give said person the right to assume any kind of relationship or contact after that. And yes, he's seventeen, but he's also physically able to overpower you and old enough to know the difference between right and wrong. He knew it was wrong to try and blackmail you like that. Let's formally document everything with Cleo on Monday morning, so that if he comes back and starts harassing you again, we've got a record of everything. Hopefully we won't ever need it as evidence, but I don't want to take the chance. I'm so sorry that I leapt to the conclusion I did and I didn't immediately support and protect you, as I should have.'

'It's OK. I'd already told you I'd slept with him, plus you probably were thinking about the warning already on my record because of Rob. It's easy under those circumstances to let your mind arrive at a conclusion despite the absence of proof.'

'I'm still sorry I didn't at least give you the benefit of the doubt. I should have known better.'

*

I took a deep breath as I pulled into my designated 'doctor on duty' space outside the surgery, and looked in the mirror, wiping a smudge of mascara from under my eye. At least I didn't feel as if I was now walking into a room where I had to convince Cleo and David of my innocence, and David was right, if Jonathan was stupid enough to come back, I needed to have taken steps to defend myself.

I closed my eyes for a moment, and took a few deep, calming breathes, before climbing out and closing the car door. I shivered as I walked around the side of the building. I had made an error of judgement with my choice of clothes: it was actually much colder than it looked and my jacket was too thin, so I hastened briskly to the security keypad and punched my code in, before opening the staff door and stepping into the corridor. I gave an involuntary shudder as the warmth began to spread through my body: the surgery was always hot to the point of roasting. I walked down to my office, put my bag down on the floor, took my jacket off and hung it over the back of my chair, before smoothing my trousers and going in search of David and Cleo.

They were in David's room and, as soon as I walked in, I knew that David had already brought Cleo up to speed. They both had a cup of tea on the go; she was clutching a notebook and pen – which already contained some notes – and inclined her head to one side, smiling sympathetically.

'Morning, Alex.'

'Morning.' It was hard to know if it was appropriate to smile back. 'Good weekend, both?'

'Not bad, thank you,' she said.

'It was pedestrian, thanks,' David replied, pushing his chair back and stretching his legs out. 'Do you want a tea or coffee before we get started, Alex? I'll make it.'

I shook my head. 'No, thanks. I'll have one in a bit. I'd rather just get on with it if that's OK?'

'Sure.' Cleo nodded understandingly. 'So, it might be best if you just tell me in your own words what happened on Friday when Jonathan Day came to see you for an emergency appointment while you were duty doctor?'

I cleared my throat. 'OK, so at about eleven o'clock Jen buzzed me and said my next patient was a Shahid Kahn. She told me he was a temporary resident and—' I stopped, interrupted by the sound of persistent dull thudding drifting up the hall. I paused and we all listened carefully, but there was nothing. 'That he was a fresher,' I continued, 'who didn't want to say why he needed—What *is* that?' I broke off as the noise resumed again.

David frowned, got up and opened his door wider, leaning out into the corridor. 'Jen? Bev?' he called. 'Are you there? Everything OK?'

'It's just some bloke knocking at the main door,' Jen called back. 'I think he's gone over the road to Lloyds. Probably a prescription mess up, or something, I expect.'

'OK, well, shout if you need us.' David turned around, came back over to his desk but, in the process of sitting down while simultaneously picking up his mug, he didn't manage to get a proper grip on the handle and promptly dropped the cup of hot tea in his lap.

'Ow! Fuck!' he exclaimed, leaping to his feet. The cup fell to the floor and bounced on the laminate, jerking the remains of the liquid in the air. Cleo jumped up out of the way, and I swung my legs to one side as the cup clattered to a stop, and David started to scrub, vigorously and pointlessly, at the front of the wet patch on his trousers with the sheet of tissue he'd already snatched off the patient bed behind him. 'That's really bloody hot!'

'Are you all right?' I said, concerned. 'You haven't scalded yourself, have you?'

'I'm fine, thank you. Anyway, I'm not taking off my trousers so you can have a look, even with a third party present.' He nodded at Cleo, who was bending to pick up the cup. 'They'll have you pegged as a medical Mata Hari at this rate.'

'I hope not. She ended up in front of a firing squad, didn't she?' I replied. 'Which would seem a little harsh, even for the GMC.'

David snorted. 'Let me just sort myself out and we'll reconvene in a minute, OK?'

We didn't get the chance, however, because the man Jen had seen at the front door came back. It was Mr Daniels, one of our regulars who, Jen, having only been our receptionist for two weeks, had not yet had the pleasure of meeting. He had significant mental health issues alongside physical problems with his blood pressure and was convinced that the medication we'd prescribed was in fact poison because we couldn't be bothered to work out what was really wrong with him. He'd been verbally abusive to Megan on several occasions and was now registered to Steven, a gentle but firm bear of doctor who, like Mr Daniels, was not far off retirement age. This had seemed to placate Mr Daniels initially, having 'a man of experience' looking after him, but, as ever, it was only a temporary fix and he was back with a vengeance. We ended up letting him in but then had to call the police when he refused to leave and started shouting obscenities at Bev while our curious patients gathered outside the front door waiting for the morning surgery to start.

'Well, that ought to give them all enough drama to keep them busy while they wait,' said David drily from behind the reception desk as the now full waiting room watched a bitterly protesting Mr Daniels being manhandled into the back of a police car. 'Poor old sod, what a shitty start to a week.' He sighed and, for a moment, I wasn't sure if he was talking about himself or Mr Daniels. 'Anyway, as we were. Alex, Cleo, can we conclude at lunchtime instead?' I nodded, and Cleo gave him a thumbs up.

'Everyone else,' Cleo addressed the rest of the assembled staff squashed into the back room to see what all of the fuss was about, 'can we have a brief meeting at one p.m. for five minutes, because we—' she stopped as more shouting broke out beyond the desk. 'For goodness' sake! What now?'

'That can't be Daniels back again, surely?' David said worriedly.

We quickly opened the side door to the office and pushed through the double doors at the top of the corridor back into the waiting room. My first thought was that perhaps Mr Daniels had finally tipped over the edge and become actually dangerous. I was worried for our full waiting room of potentially vulnerable patients, including children.

We both quickly scanned the room – and my heart stopped to see the couple in front of the reception desk who had been raising their voices. Gary and Christy Day were stood slightly in front of their son, who was dressed neatly in his school uniform. Gary, fully suited and booted, turned and saw me.

'There she is!' he exclaimed angrily, pointing right at me. 'That's the doctor who's been sexually abusing our son.'

The whole room was instantly silent, as if someone had hit the mute button on a television. I was only aware of my heart starting to thump violently in my chest as every single pair of eyes in the room swivelled to look at me. I saw frowns, mouths falling open and, on some faces, immediate disgust.

Christy Day pushed round her husband and positioned herself right in front of me, facing me full on. She was heavily made-up, dressed in skinny black jeans, spikey sock ankle boots and a tight black top under a real fox fur gilet. Her long sharp nails gripped the handle of her designer bag furiously. She'd evidentially come dressed for a fight.

'Shame on you!' She practically spat the words at me. 'And you came to my house? You have the brass neck to get one of your slapper friends to put you forward so you can *come into my house to get at my child*?'

She took a step closer, and I tensed as David leapt between us and put up his hands. 'We need to calm this down. This is a very serious allegation you're making here, and this isn't an appropriate—'

'*Appropriate?*' Christy turned on him. 'Don't you dare talk to me about what's appropriate! You're supposed to be able to trust your doctor with your children. She's been preying on him for months!'

'What? No, I haven't! That's a lie!' I exclaimed, horrified.

'So you haven't had sex with my son then?' Christy demanded.

I hesitated and looked at Jonathan. His face was absolutely blank, and he stared straight ahead.

'You see!' Christy exclaimed triumphantly to the room. 'She's not denying it! She can't, because it's true. Well we're not going to let you get away with this. I'm going to make sure you never get your dirty hands on anyone else's son.' She leant round David and pushed her finger into my face, jabbing me on the forehead between my eyes hard enough to make me jerk my head back in shock. It was horrible, like she was miming a bullet hitting me.

'That's enough,' David said. 'I've just had the police here and I'll call them again if you attempt another assault on my colleague. Please, just come through into somewhere we can—'

My wife isn't the one doing the assaulting.' It was Gary's turn to step forward and interrupt. 'You *best* get us a room where we can make our complaint properly.' He looked David up and down, distastefully, taking in the visible stain on the front of his trousers. 'I assume it's you who runs this place as you're acting the big billy bollocks.'

'Dad.' It was the first word Jonathan had said.

'Don't worry, son, I'm dealing with it.' Gary didn't look at Jonathan, just held up a hand to silence him. 'She's not going to be allowed to hurt you again.'

'Yes, he's the one who runs it,' Christy said, nodding at David. 'He's the doctor I saw last month.'

'This is outrageous!' I exclaimed. I was starting to shake. 'You're making public allegations that are completely false, and which you can't have any evidence of because they're not true. That's slander, and I'll sue you if say another word.'

'You're threatening me?' Gary laughed incredulously. 'Did you hear that everyone? The kiddy-fiddler doctor says *she's* going to sue *me*!'

'I mean it, I'll call the police if you continue this.' David turned to face Gary. 'We either discuss this privately or not at all.'

'Jonathan – you know this isn't true.' I addressed him over his parents, directly and loudly. 'Why are you making this up? Is it because I said I'd tell everyone you tried to blackmail me into sleeping with you?'

'Don't talk to him,' Christy pointed at me furiously. 'Don't so much as look at him, love, all right?'

'Please, Alex, don't say anything more.' David swung round to face me. 'Just go into my office and wait there, OK?'

'Jonathan?' I looked at him desperately as he raised his head, met my eyes… and stayed silent. I was almost certain I saw the ghost of a smile play about his mouth, but when I blinked in disbelief, his expression was implacable once again.

I had no choice but to turn around and leave the room, everyone watching me. As I opened the door I heard one of the older patients tut and repeat Christy's verdict with a muttered: 'For shame!'

I did as I was told and went into David's office, sat down in my chair of earlier and noticed there was still tea on the floor. Automatically, I got back up, pulled some more tissue sheets from the large roll in the dispenser, folded them and placed them on the floor, stepping on them to absorb the liquid, as I did at home when one of the girls knocked over a drink. When I saw it had soaked as much as it was going to, I carefully put the tissue in the bin and sat back down. I didn't have my phone in the room with me, so I couldn't call or text Rob. I never rang him from the work phones and I realised I didn't even know his mobile number in any case, so I just sat very still, in shock, and waited. Jonathan had done this because he thought it was all going to come out about him trying to blackmail me. He'd made sure he got in there with his accusation first.

David returned at nine a.m., looking ashen. He sat down opposite me. 'The Days have alleged that you've been involved in an inappropriate sexual relationship with their son, Jonathan, for three months now, which, they say, began after his first appointment with you. I've checked the records and you did see him on Thursday, 15 June, at three p.m. The phrase Jonathan's mother keeps using is 'sexual abuse', although Jonathan himself, while agreeing you've been having a relationship, has stated it has always been consensual.'

I exhaled with a sort of violent gasp. I hadn't been aware I'd been holding my breath.

'Although Jonathan now says he feels "uncomfortable" with what's happened. So, while the good news is there's no basis for a criminal charge here, professionally – for us as doctors – meaningful consent is pretty much an impossibility in this situation. He's without doubt going to be viewed as a vulnerable patient and trust is the cornerstone of the doctor-patient relationship. I don't have any choice under the circumstances but to ask you to accept suspension with immediate effect pending an investigation, as the Days are making their complaint to the GMC as we speak. I'm so very sorry, Alex.'

I nodded, silently.

'You should get some legal advice, I think.'

'They're going to strike me off, aren't they? It'll be my word against his, and they'll look at the warning I received over Rob and think they know exactly what happened.'

'I think your registration is at risk, yes.'

'You know he's lying, don't you, David?' I looked him straight in the eye.

'Oh Alex, if it was only all down to me… but this is out of my hands now.' He said it kindly, but we both knew he was being a good doctor, carefully offering as much comfort as his professional parameters allowed. 'Do you want us to call Rob to come and get you? Will you be safe to drive?'

I swallowed, feeling near to tears. 'I'll be fine, but, thank you.' I reached out my hand and put it on his knee, to show that I understood what he was having to do, even though we were friends – but he visibly flinched and, horrified by how my action could have been misinterpreted, I snatched it back. 'God, I'm so sorry. I didn't mean—'

'It's fine – don't worry.' He quickly reached across his desk for a tissue for me. 'Go home and please phone the MDU, Al. You're a female doctor – which is rare in this kind of situation in any case – and the Days yelled their allegation in the most public way they could. This is already out there, and I think we have to expect a high level of media interest.'

*

I drove home slowly through the bright sunshine to tell my husband I'd just been accused of sexually assaulting a teenager and was now suspended pending further investigation. I was exactly the same woman who had left for work several hours earlier preparing to document the beginnings of harassment by a male patient. But now, everyone was only going to see my reflection in the seventeen-year-old mirror Jonathan was holding. It was horrific.

I was devastated.

David was right – both Christy and Gary Day knew exactly what they were doing when they walked into the surgery. They wanted maximum exposure, and I don't believe they considered either the effect it would have on their son, or my daughters, for one second. They just intended to punish me for what they believed I had done wrong… but Jonathan? He wanted to be back in control after I'd taken it away from him on Friday.

I've thought about this a lot; Jonathan Day has no autonomy in his relationship with his parents, so he seeks out situations where he gets one up on someone in a parental position instead – I was just a vehicle for his need to lose and then regain control. Sometimes he uses sex to get his own way, sometimes power. He's happy to play the poor little boy or the powerful man, as long as he has the upper hand. If I hadn't become his victim, I would have found it fascinating that he could suppress or invoke feelings for the purpose of control, rather than the authenticity of the feelings themselves.

In other words, what had actually happened between us was irrelevant to him. Like all good liars he adapted his story to suit his immediate circumstance.

Did that make me angry?

Of course it did.

CHAPTER 6

Jonathan Day

When I stood up the skin had basically been grated off my shin, knee and the bottom of my thigh. They all pulled pained 'Ooooh' faces, some laughed, and Dad came jogging over to have a look. 'You soft sod, what were you thinking?' He gave me the car keys to go and have a sit down but told me to put my coat over the seat so I didn't get blood everywhere – nice. I was only there because he'd paid me. They wouldn't have had enough players otherwise, after one of the usual blokes dropped out at the last minute. I got carried away and forgot we were on AstroTurf, went in for the sliding tackle and that was it.

Mum went into one when we got home, going on about it permanently scarring and the infection risk. She got me a dressing and cleaned it up, but the next morning it still felt like it was on fire, and when I tried to sit down at breakfast my trousers were already sticking to bits of the open skin the dressing wasn't big enough to cover. Mum took another look and insisted that she make a doctor's appointment.

It wasn't that bad – definitely not enough for her to drive me to school, come back later to take me to the surgery and sit in on the appointment herself, which is what she wanted to do. Instead we compromised on me driving myself over that afternoon if she could get me seen, because I'd realised it would get me out of having to hand in a piss-poor Economics essay; Mr Loftus being about the only teacher who still demands handwritten essays to be given to him in class, in person – twat. I got Mum's text at lunchtime, immediately got signed out and drove myself over to the surgery nice and early for the three p.m. appointment. I sat parked in the car for ages, dicking around on my phone, and watching people coming and going from the chemist opposite.

She arrived at about ten to three, pulling straight into one of the doctors' spaces. I looked up from my screen because the speed of the movement caught my eye; I thought the BMW was going to smack into the wall before it jerked to a stop – and then she climbed out.

I saw her slim, tanned leg emerge first, then the rest of her. She was wearing brown leather, strappy, heeled sandals and as I followed it up, I arrived at a sand-coloured skirt that she'd tucked a sort of silky cream shirt into. It triggered a memory instantly – the female archaeologist in Indiana Jones; she even had the same blonde hair. Elsa Schneider. I repeated the name to myself. I'd seen the movie about a hundred times. Mostly every Christmas with the family. *Doctor* Elsa Schneider.

She slammed the door shut and, even from just side on, it was easy to tell she was a) fit and b) pissed about something as she marched alongside the building and disappeared off round the back.

I YouTubed Elsa Schneider and watched Harrison Ford climbing off some boat in Venice before turning round at the sound of a female voice calling him. And there she was. Whoa.

I leant back, loosened my school tie and undid both front windows a bit more, to get more air going through. It was hot in the direct June sunlight.

I got to the bit in the ransacked hotel room where Indy grabs her, pretty much tells her to shut it because he's in charge, then kisses her. She gets all 'how dare you', but sucks his face off in return, bites his ear and tells him she hates arrogant men, before pulling him down onto some off-screen bed.

The clip finished there and, bored, I looked at the clock, climbed out carefully – my leg still pulling where the gammy hairs, sticky with blood, had glued themselves to the inside of my trousers – and walked slowly over to the main doors.

Mum had pulled a blinder and got me the first appointment of the afternoon, so, in theory, it was impossible for the doctor to be running late, but it was still nearly ten minutes past three when it finally flashed up on a screen above my head:

Jonathan Day, Dr A Inglis, Room 10

in bright red, digital old-school letters.

Feeling annoyed that I was pretty much on my own time now, not school's, and wanting to get it over and done with so I could go and meet Cherry, I shuffled down the hall and knocked on the partially open door to Room 10, to hear a brisk, not exactly warm: 'Come in.'

I did as I was told, and there, sat at a desk, was Elsa Schneider. I forgot about my irritation immediately. Up close I could see she was older than my first glance across the car park had her down for, but I was still intimidated enough by how she looked to lose the power of speech as I walked in. If I was a tosser, I might use the word cougar, but I'm not. I just thought she was beautiful.

She barely looked up from her computer screen, just said: 'please sit down,' so I did, stretching my bad leg out, and finally she turned to look at me, her face registering slight surprise to see it reaching all the way past her, behind her chair.

'Sorry, my limbs are always somewhere they're not supposed to be,' I said apologetically.

'They really are.' She laughed suddenly, and I felt pleased to have cheered her up. 'Anyway, how can I help?'

'I was playing five-a-side last night on AstroTurf, I slid and I've hurt my leg.'

'OK, let's take a look.'

I hesitated, not sure if it was best to try and roll my trouser leg up, or what. I leant forward and started to ease the material from the wound, clenching my teeth as it detached away from the raw flesh underneath.

She saw my expression and said quickly: 'that looks like it's really painful, does this burn go right up your leg?'

I nodded. 'To just above my knee.'

'OK, let's stop then. It might be better if you just undo your trousers and we try and go from above.' She frowned critically at the visible part of the hurt bit and stood up. 'Come over to the bed and just lean on that. I don't want you to fall over. When you've got them off, just sit yourself down.'

I stood up slowly, walked over to the stretcher on wheels and began to unbuckle my belt. She kindly turned away to busy herself with washing her hands, but I'd still started to panic. She was hot. I was wearing pretty tight boxers; I didn't want blood even slightly pumping, because a semi would be just as noticeable as a raging hard on. But also, the air conditioning was on full blast and I didn't want to look pathetic either. I took a deep breath, tried instead to think about Mr Loftus and his droning voice asking me where my essay was, unzipped my fly and pulled my trousers down – with one last quick check on the front of my underwear for obvious or disgusting stains. When I got to the top of the burn, I started to try and peel the fabric back, but it had stuck hard to the edges where it was beginning to dry out on my thigh.

She came back over and raised her eyebrows. 'Ouch. That's a really nasty gash.'

I looked down at the floor and bit my lip, trying not to smirk or think about gashes.

She coloured instantly and said: 'Cut, I mean. You can pull them back up again. I've got a better idea.'

I didn't need to be told twice.

She reached for a pair of scissors. 'I think I'm going to have to cut the leg off if that's OK?'

I cleared my throat. 'Will you at least use an anaesthetic?'

She half smiled. 'Cut the leg off your *trousers*.'

'I know. Sorry.' I felt a bit of a dick and wished I'd not said anything. 'Yeah, that's fine.'

I sat down on the edge of the bed as she came over and pinched up some of the slack material between her fingers, snipped delicately, then slid the bottom blade through the hole. I tensed as the metal point briefly touched my skin underneath, and she looked up worriedly.

'I'm not hurting you?'

I shook my head. 'You're not near the burnt bit.' Relieved, she started again.

The concentration on her face was fierce. She didn't take her eyes from the line once; the only sound in the room was the shearing of the blades through the material as they came together again and again. I could smell whatever almond body lotion or shower gel she'd used that morning, and as she moved round to the other side of my leg, leaning over to start again so that the two incisions would join together, I saw down the slight gap of shirt, where her breasts had fallen forward in her white bra. I glanced away to one side and focused instead on a diagram of the cross-sectioned human body stuck on the opposite wall.

She straightened up for a moment. 'OK, now I'm just going to cut the main bit of the trouser away so we can see what we're really dealing with.' She wiped her brow with the back of her hand and started to snip downwards. 'What are you, six foot?'

'Six two.'

'When did you start shooting up?'

I laughed that time, I couldn't help it.

'Oh, come on! You know what I mean.' She straightened up again and whisked away the redundant material. There was just the section stuck to my skin remaining. 'When did you grow so tall?'

'When I was about thirteen.' I answered her question but she barely seemed to hear me.

'Now we're getting somewhere.' She washed her hands again and pulled on some latex gloves. 'This is almost a third-degree burn. I don't know what pitch you play on, but it looks like there was no give on it whatsoever. I wouldn't be in a rush to go back if I were you.' She paused for a moment as she cleaned it up. 'You made the right call in coming in. I see from your notes that you're a type 1 diabetic, so you'll already know you have an increased risk of infection and it's harder for your wounds to heal, so well done for being sensible. I'll clean it up properly though, and you'll be fine. How is everything with the diabetes? Any hypos recently?'

I shook my head. 'I'm really good at my management.' I was hardly going to say that I was a bit shit, actually.

'Good for you.' She looked impressed.

'Thanks, I knew it was important to come and get checked out today, so…' I shrugged nonchalantly and obviously kept quiet about it having been Mum who pushed me. 'Will I have permanent scarring?'

'No, you should be fine. It won't affect any modelling or anything.'

I looked up quickly. 'Oh, I don't model,' I lied. 'Well, I've done the odd bit but nothing major.' I shrugged, making out like I was embarrassed to have to say anything about it at all.

We lapsed into silence again as I watched her quietly, only wincing a couple of times as she worked methodically but gently, cleaning it up.

'You're doing really well,' she said at one point and smiled encouragingly at me. 'Nearly there.'

Once she'd dressed it, she straightened up and peeled the gloves off, dropping them in a large metal bin that she opened with a foot pedal. 'All done. Now, you're going to need to get that dressing checked in forty-eight hours. Ah – except that's Saturday. You better come back tomorrow instead then. I'll make you an appointment with the practice nurse.'

'Can't it be you?' I said, and I couldn't see her face as she replied lightly: 'I'm not in tomorrow, I'm afraid.'

But I heard it. Her tone was almost teasing. *She was flirting with me?*

She sat down at her desk and started tapping on the keyboard. 'Do you have a mobile we can text the appointment time through to? Is ten-to-four tomorrow OK?'

'Before lunch would be better if that's all right?' I said, thinking of the psychology coursework I still hadn't completed but had promised without fail for the following morning's session.

'Half past ten?'

I nodded. 'And my number is 07976—' I gave it to her, then felt my phone vibrate in my pocket with a text. 'I've got it – thanks.'

'No problem – and here's your prescription.' She swung round to the printer and grabbed the green piece of paper, signed it and held it out to me. 'Sorry about your trousers.'

I looked down at my one bare leg. I looked like I was wearing grey shorts on one side. I shrugged. 'That's OK. It's a look.'

'It certainly is. Um – Jonathan.' She glanced at my notes on screen. 'I'm sorry if I said a couple of things that I could have phrased better, or differently. I wasn't… well anyway.' She looked flustered. 'Sorry.'

'You didn't say anything out of order at all,' I insisted, and held her gaze confidently before smiling.

'Just make sure you keep an eye out for the skin around the wound becoming red, or hot and hard—' She was killing me, but I held it together. 'Any inflammation basically, which would be a sign of infection.' She continued valiantly, despite having gone scarlet. 'Or any puss, and a strong unpleasant smell.'

That wasn't the note I'd hoped to end on but I stood up and smiled politely. 'Thanks for your time, Dr Inglis.'

'You're very welcome.'

I could feel her watching me as I walked out of the room feeling a lot better, despite my one leg out. Elsa Schneider. Sweet.

I probably would have just left it there. I should have just left it there, but I went over the road to get my prescription and while I waited for them to make it up, I stared at Dr Inglis's car.

'Could I borrow a pen and a bit of paper – if that's possible?' I asked the woman behind the desk. I gave her a small, slightly sad smile. I learnt a long time ago that it makes a certain type of woman want to mother me, or in this case, grandmother me.

She bustled about looking for a biro that worked. I hesitated, then scribbled

> Thanks for being nice to me today. Ever tried Snapchat?
> Don't forget to ghost mode tho.
> J Day

Then I added my username. I knew full well Dr Inglis wouldn't have a clue. She'd be Facebook at most. I folded the paper over, handed back the pen, got my meds and, once I was out in the sunshine again, walked casually over to her car and tucked it under the windscreen wiper.

I got back into my car and drove straight over to Cherry's. She went nuts over my bandaged leg and laughed hysterically at the cut-off trousers, which just annoyed me – it wasn't that funny – wanting to upload several pics of both of us in our school uniform, mine all messed up. 'You look so cute! My poor baby!'

Her parents were still at work, so we did it despite my bad leg. She made a big thing of avoiding my wound and going on top, but I kept looking past her at the dressing, where Dr Inglis had touched my skin an hour earlier. I closed my eyes and imagined her instead, trying to block out Cherry's loud gasping as *she* busily imagined how hot she looked right now.

Would she do it? Would she message me? The thought that Dr Inglis really might, made me come instantly.

*

At home over dinner, Mum tore a strip off Dad for not taking me straight to A&E the night before.

'My poor little bubba.' She dolloped some more mash onto my plate as I stared at my phone. 'And you just told him not to bleed on the car, Gary? How could you?'

'There's nothing wrong with him.' Dad picked up his lamb chop bones in his fingers to get the rest of the meat off. 'He'll have done his big eyes bit and the doctor will have gone overboard, that's all.'

'Hashtag old and bitter,' Ruby remarked, getting up to put her plate on the side before sitting back down at the table.

'Never mind me,' Dad retorted instantly. 'Will you *please* take them shoes off!' He nodded at my sister's feet. 'That's the second time I've asked you tonight. I don't want this floor scratched.'

Ruby rolled her eyes.

'When you live in your own place, you can carve your own initials in it for all I care, but no sharp heels past the front door, thank you very much.'

'He'll get his felting kit out if you're not careful, Rubes.' Mum sat down with her lamb chops and mixed roasted vegetables. 'And stick those little round circles on each of the stiletto bits. Do listen to your dad though, please, and take them off. The clack-clack does my head in, apart from anything else. It's like nails on a blackboard.'

'Oh my god! All right!' Ruby kicked them free. 'They're off, OK? I only kept them on because I'm out in five minutes. You'll have to make your own cup of tea tonight, Mum.'

'Hang on, I need someone to empty the dishwasher.'

'It's his turn.' Ruby flicked my arm.

'I can't stand up for long periods of time.' I didn't look up from my phone. 'The doctor said I had to keep my leg elevated as much as possible.'

'You're such a little shit. Fine. Whatever, I'll do it.' Ruby stood up. 'But *then* I'm going.'

'You don't want any sweet, Rube?' Mum said through a mouthful. 'There's a lardy cake in the cupboard. I bought one for Nan today, and one for us. Just as a treat.' She looked at me pointedly.

'No, thanks. I might as well just glue it straight on my hips.'

'I'll have some,' I said, messaging Cherry to tell her I wouldn't be able to pick her up on the way into school in the morning, because I'd forgotten I had the nurse appointment. She sent me the crying pile of poo and lips emojis straight back. Still nothing from Dr Inglis. 'If that's OK?'

'Of course it is.' Mum jumped up straight away, leaving her dinner. 'I'll get you a plate, sweets.'

'Mum, he's got a turf burn, he's not actually lost a leg,' Ruby said, and I flicked her the Vs as the lardy cake appeared in front of me, along with a knife and a side plate.

'Do I get any?' Dad said, 'or is it just for Brains?' He nodded at me.

Mum sighed. 'I didn't think you'd want any. You don't eat sugar during the week.'

I made the mistake of snorting, and Dad rounded on me, hand resting protectively on his flat stomach.

'Oh, so you are actually part of this conversation then? There was me thinking you were just busy messaging "ickle Chewwy. Wuv you!"' He nastily mimed a couple of kisses and rolled his eyes. 'Like every bloody night when we barely get a word out of him. You don't want to ask me or your mum how the new gym site is coming on?' he asked me. 'Or your sister how her day at work was?'

'Sorry. Do you want some cake then, Dad?' I looked across at him stonily.

He stared back at me. 'Yes, please. I do.'

I reached for the knife and cut him a larger than average slice and thudded it onto his plate, before passing it over. Then I cut myself a piece and bit into it.

He clenched his jaw, but picked it up and took a mouthful, trying to be all relaxed as he said: 'Very nice thanks,' to Mum, who glanced between us worriedly.

Ruby had wisely put the kettle on after all, keeping out of the firing range. I finished my slice. Watching Dad struggle with knowing exactly how many calories he was consuming left a very nice taste in my mouth.

'Thanks, Mum, that was great. Is it OK if I go and get on with some homework now?' I got up with a pained effort and a sharp intake of breath, before kissing Mum on the top of the head as Dad stared guiltily at the crumbs left on his plate. Tosser.

I went upstairs, collapsed on my bed and watched a few vlogs. One in particular made me furious; all he was doing was eating a fucking egg in the garden; it had been up for less than a week and he'd already got 400K views – and no doubt how many thousand click-throughs to his new book. I was so annoyed, I decided to watch a movie in bed, and didn't even feel much better when I walked past Mum and Dad's bedroom on my way to the bathroom and saw Dad frantically doing push-ups in their en suite, before jumping up and jogging on the spot to burn off his lardy cake.

I got bored of the film quickly and decided to call it a night but couldn't get to sleep. My leg genuinely was hurting, and I went back on my phone at about half ten, only to sit bolt upright when I realised a badscissors17 had added me. I accepted and waited, breath held.

I didn't have to wait long:

I don't think I like this...

I smiled. It was her.

Don't worry. You'll get used to it.

And she did, very quickly as it turned out.

But yes, it was her that messaged me first. I gave her the opportunity and she grabbed it with both hands, if you know what I mean.

CHAPTER 7

Jonathan Day

Those were the only messages we sent that first night, though. I didn't want to seem too desperate. Our chat had vanished the following morning anyway, and I wondered if she might regret it when she woke up, delete her account and pretend none of it had happened. But twenty-four hours later, stood in Spoons with everyone and having a *shit* Friday night because they were all drinking and I'd already had my allocated two, she started chatting again.

How's the leg?

Hurting. Mostly because people keep banging into me in pub.

Keep an eye on yourself!

Yes ma'am. Not drinking. Obv.

I worried I'd overdone it with that, but she sent me a thumbs up emoji.

Get you. Emoji! I replied. Impressed!

Immediately, the crying with laughter emoji came through. Followed by a unicorn.

Oops. Sorry. Fat fingers. Don't have a thing for unicorns.

Interested, I stepped away from the group. Was she a bit pissed?

Nothing wrong with unicorns. Very pretty.

I imagined her sat on a sofa somewhere, a second G&T on the go, maybe a third, her husband on an opposite sofa on *his* phone – I'm not stupid, I'd noticed the rings – an unwatched movie playing on Sky in the background. In other words, exactly what my parents would be currently doing. I waited, but nothing came back and suddenly Cherry appeared under my nose, arms crossed.

'So, I'm just checking out this situation. Who are you messaging?'

'My mum. She's making sure my leg is all right. Why?' I slid my phone quickly into my back pocket.

She brightened. 'Oh. OK. So in other news – I need another drink.'

Sighing, I reached into my wallet for a tenner and held it out between my index and middle fingers.

She smiled and whipped it away from me. 'Thank *you*.' She blew me a kiss, spun round on the spot and walked back to the bar, earning herself admiring glances from several huddles of blokes as she did, all of whom she completely ignored.

I got my phone back out – another notification. I opened it and caught my breath. I had to blink a couple of times.

I was wondering if you needed a house call? Monday lunchtime?

My mouth fell open. WTAF?

That would be great if it's not too much trouble? My address is—

*

I spent the whole weekend unable to think about anything else. I had no message to look back at, so I wasn't sure if it had even happened, or I'd dreamt it. Even if she HAD sent it, she was bound to have sobered up on Saturday morning and thought twice. Maybe she actually meant she was genuinely going to come and check on my leg? But then, I'd have had to have gone through the doctors officially, wouldn't I? I checked my chats religiously, but nothing more came through from her at all. I wasn't going to take any chances though, so on Monday morning I appeared at breakfast in my T-shirt and trackie bums.

'Mum, I don't feel well. Do you mind if I don't go in today?'

'Oh baby!' Mum was sat at the breakfast bar fully made-up, hair done and dressed for work, but held out her arms to me. I walked over and leant my head down so she could rest her lips on my forehead – which I'd just held a hot flannel to, up in the bathroom. The same trick, since I was ten years old.

'You do feel warm.' She pulled a sympathetic face. 'Your leg isn't playing up?' She glared at Dad, who sighed crossly, got up and put his bowl in the dishwasher, adjusting his suit trousers and glancing at his Rolex. 'Come on, Chris, we've got the planners meeting. I don't want to be late.'

'My leg is fine,' I told Mum truthfully.

'Are your sugars OK?'

I nodded. 'I just feel a bit dizzy, that's all.'

'You're going to have something to eat now though?'

'Yes. Of course.'

'I'm not back until four, sweetheart.' She looked worried. 'You'll be all right looking after yourself until then?'

I nodded. 'I'll at least open some soup later. I promise.'

'You're practically Bear Grylls,' said Ruby, getting up, snapping her phone shut and shoving it in her handbag.

I gave her a fake smile to which she stuck her tongue out. 'I'm off. I'll see you all later.' She kissed Dad's cheek as she passed him.

'Have a good one, bub,' he said, pleased. 'You look very nice today. Very professional.'

'Thank you!' She struck a pose, briefly. 'Media agency expert Ruby Day, at your service.' She laughed, happily. 'Hope you feel "better" later.' She looked at me pointedly and ignored my narrowed eyes as she spun round and tick tacked out of the room.

'Shoes, Ruby! Walk on tiptoe and not the heel!' Dad threw his arms open, exasperated, then looked at his watch again. 'Christine, *please*! Can we GO!'

'Don't call me that!' Mum said sharply but got up. 'Bye, love. I'll have my phone on all day.' She kissed me and looked at Dad, pointing a warning finger at him. 'If you're going to be like this, I'm not coming. Have a word with yourself, all right?'

'Fine, fine.' Dad held his hands up. 'I'm sorry. Now can we please just go? Bye, Jonny. Stay out of trouble, please.'

'Thanks, Dad,' I said absently, checking my phone again. Still nothing. I was starting to feel like a bit of a knob. Had I just skived off for no reason whatsoever? I made some good use of my time though, updating my Instagram with pictures of me lying in bed, shirt off. After five minutes of posting I hadn't had any likes at all though, not even Cherry, so I deleted them in a mood, got up and got ready, showering and choosing a white T-shirt and jeans. Then I put clean sheets on the bed.

At quarter to one, just as I'd given up hope, Angel began to bark and, my heart stopping, I jumped up off the bed, went over to the window and looked down. It was her car. She had actually come. *Fuck.*

She climbed out of the car dressed in a navy skirt and jacket and was holding a black bag. She half smiled as I opened the front door and walked slowly across the gravel to the front door.

'Hi.'

'You're here,' I said foolishly, and she smiled a little wider.

'I am. Can I come in then?'

She walked past me into the hallway and looked down at the floor. 'Do you want me to take my shoes off?'

I thought about Dad. 'No, you don't have to. It's fine. Everyone is at work, by the way. It's just me.'

She chewed her lip and looked around her, almost as if she was confused. 'I have no idea what I'm doing here,' she said softly.

I hesitated and, feeling so nervous I wanted to puke, I walked over to her, bent my head and kissed her. She stood very still, at first, but then she started to kiss me back.

We had sex in my bed. I've slept with plenty of girls, but I'm not going to lie, I was nervous. It was a bit vanilla, which is not a criticism – just straightforward and quick, but I think she came. I definitely did, as she lay under me. We didn't talk as she dressed and sorted her hair out, but she smiled at me, and I honestly thought I was going to wake up at any moment.

'Is that it now?' I blurted.

She'd looked amused. 'Do you want it to be?'

I shook my head. 'No. I'd like to see you again.'

She stood up, hesitated and said: 'How about Friday night? Ten p.m? I could meet you for a bit. At the bottom of the hill by Calverly Park?'

'OK,' I agreed eagerly.

I walked her out to her car, and then didn't know if I should kiss her or not, and ended up standing there awkwardly instead, like a twat.

She smiled. 'See you Friday then.'

I watched her drive off and went back into the house, closing the door behind me in amazement. That had actually just happened?

I'd just gone upstairs again, when the doorbell rang, making me jump. Had she forgotten something? I went back as fast as I could, smiling widely, and flung the door open, but bloody *Cherry* was on the doorstep.

'Hey, you're up and about! I bought you lunch!' She held up a Pret bag and bounced in past me. 'Look at you all pleased to see me. *You're* the cutest. C'mon. Let's eat!'

At the time I felt relieved; now I wish she'd been just five minutes earlier, because she would have seen Alex leaving the house. It would have proved she *was* there. To be honest, I spent the next four days wondering if it had happened at all. It was the unrealness that I couldn't handle, the feeling I'd made the whole thing up in my head.

I couldn't concentrate in class at all and got bollocked more than usual for not paying attention, although I honestly couldn't see what the problem was; under the new system, nothing counts at all until our exams at the end of Year 13 – a whole year away. I had plenty of time. They'd started banging on about making a head start on my uni choices *before* the summer holidays, saying I had to devise a long list of courses, going along to some open days and thinking about a personal statement. None of it mattered. I couldn't think about anything but Alex, naked and under me.

*

By ten to ten in the pub on Friday, I was slightly more than my usual two drinks up, purely from nerves. I told the others I was going to get some more cash out and staggered down the hill that ran parallel and behind the high street's glossy shop fronts, walking past all of the fire escapes and waste bins. It wasn't lit by street lights and I nearly fell once or twice, bouncing off one of the bumper-to-bumper parked cars. Part of me was convinced she wouldn't be there and it had all been a fantasy; but, sure enough, there was the BMW sitting on a double yellow in the black, lights and engine off.

I got in but she didn't even smile, just looked around her to make sure no one was looking. 'How long have you got?'

'Until people miss me? About three minutes?' My phone began to light up. Cherry was calling.

Alex glanced at the screen, then out of her window. 'Can you say you've gone home, not feeling well? I've got half an hour.'

'OK.' I let the call go to voicemail and shifted position to pull the seatbelt round me, accidentally kicking a plastic bag I hadn't realised was at my feet, which clinked. I reached down to check nothing had broken and saw a full bottle of gin lying on its side.

'My excuse for leaving the house,' Alex said. 'It's not for us.'

I shrugged. That was fine by me. My mother drank gin. I couldn't think of anything I'd want to crack open less.

She started the car and we quickly drove out of town – as I texted Cherry to say I'd got a taxi home, my leg was suddenly hurting again but otherwise I was fine, just tired – up onto the main road that led to a cut through the forest called Bunny Lane. It had turned properly dark and a bit creepy. Alex was driving fast and swerved slightly as an actual rabbit popped out of the hedge.

'Not Bunny Lane for nothing then,' I said for no reason, and she didn't reply. 'Are you all right?' I said a moment later as we went too fast round another corner and my hand instinctively reached to grip the door handle.

'I'm fine,' she said shortly, and after a few more minutes, took a sharp left into a dark car park of a farm shop, all closed up, the barn doors bolted across.

I'd been there with Mum and Dad a while back when Mum had wanted to stop and buy some bacon because someone had told it her was home reared or something. I remember Dad saying it wasn't just the pig that had been reared: 'Five quid for a pot of olives? They proper *can* get stuffed.' He obviously hadn't been the only one to feel that way, because I realised it wasn't just closed but had shut down. We bounced over the uneven surface of the dry muddied car park, full of potholes, and I felt a bit sick.

She drove right to the back, then up a small dirt track and stopped in front of a padlocked, five-bar gate that led into the dark woodland beyond.

'I'm not going in there,' I said, looking at the arms of the trees moving in the wind and wishing I'd not watched the trailer for the re-release of *It* the day before.

'Obviously,' she said cuttingly, and I started to regret getting in the car at all, but she undid her seatbelt quickly, turned to me, leant across and kissed me, hard, while undoing my jeans and sliding her hand down the front. I gasped – I couldn't help myself.

It's not easy to fuck in a car when you're my height. It felt awkward and all angles – not just because of fumbling for condoms in wallets. Not my best work. She didn't seem any calmer afterwards either.

We drove back into town in silence and I was worried that I'd messed up, and this was going to be it. She drove me back to the main road near my house and pulled over near our drive.

'Are you all right to walk the last bit?'

I nodded, glancing at the car clock. It was only quarter to eleven.

'Next time, can you not wear so much aftershave, please?'

I felt myself blush in the dark. 'Sorry.' I hesitated. 'I got you something, but I don't know if you want it now.'

She raised an eyebrow and said uncertainly: 'OK?'

I reached into the pockets of my coat and pulled out a small mobile and charger. 'Snapchatting like we did at first is too risky. If you want to reach me, use this instead. It's just a pay as you go. I've got one too. I'll message you later so you've got my number. Once the credit has gone you can top it up or just chuck it, but don't actually burn it… they're called burners,' I explained as she looked blank. 'You've seen *The Wire*, right?'

'No. They did this on *House of Cards* though.' She reached out and took one from me.

'On what?'

'Never mind.'

'People think Snapchat is safe because the messages vanish, and after thirty-one days, even Snapchat themselves can't recover the content, they can only see if users exchanged communication, but people don't realise the actual messages can save to your handset.'

She paled. 'Really?'

'Yeah. Don't worry. We barely used it, but this will be a lot safer from now on.' I pointed at the mobile she was still holding.

She smiled suddenly. 'You've put a lot of thought into this.'

I blushed again.

'That's sweet. I have to go now though, so, good night.'

This time, I just got out – didn't wait for her to kiss me or anything. After I'd closed the door carefully, I watched her pull away, feeling very happy for a moment. There was definitely going to be a next time. I should have been thinking, so what that I was wearing aftershave? but I wasn't. All I was thinking about was when I'd see her again.

Once I got home, I texted her from *my* burner:

Thio io mo

And was a bit disappointed when I didn't get a response – although I hadn't really expected anything.

I wish I'd stopped it then. I wasn't in love with her. I've never told a girl I love her and I'm not going to say it until I mean it but, from then onwards, I was thinking about Alex a lot. All of the time.

CHAPTER 8

Dr David Harper

I thought I'd immediately caught out Jonathan Day with his ridiculous 'lunchtime house call sex tryst' in the first half of his statement. Pretty much every single GP has the same sort of 'lunch' up and down the country. Yes, there are house visits, but then it's back to the surgery for paperwork, prescription requests, processing blood results, reading letters from consultants, filling in forms for patients. You're lucky if you have time to go to the loo. The idea that a GP would swan off in the middle of the day for some languid sex with a patient is beyond the realms of even the most deluded of imaginations. It's utterly ludicrous, in fact.

I'd realised Jonathan was, at the very least, prone to exaggeration from his initial account of the leg injury. Had it been *that* bad, Alex wouldn't have dressed it herself, he'd have been sent off to the burns unit; but, once we reached the part where Alex arrived at the Days' house, complete with medical bag, to seduce Jonathan, I started to listen for the enjoyment of watching him spin his web – and that I *did* find interesting.

It had seemed clear to me, from the moment that his father started yelling at all and sundry in my surgery waiting room, that Gary Day was in charge. Day junior only spoke to admonish his father once – and to all intents and purposes, he let his parents handle everything. The father was the sort of oiky, unpredictably angry chap who could smile at you one minute while selling you something out of the back of his paid-for-in-cash Range Rover, then knock you out the next. I had Day junior immediately pegged as a squashed-down teen who did as he was told, had probably formed an unhealthy attachment to Alex which had got out of hand and was also enjoying this unfamiliar feeling of parental protection and safety – hiding behind his father all too willingly.

Except the more he spoke – as we all sat there in my office – the more I began to wonder if I hadn't actually got him totally wrong. He was exceptionally articulate and controlled for a seventeen-year-old. It was hard to believe he was the offspring of the great ape sitting alongside him. I established quite quickly that he attended a nearby private school, which possibly explains it, but yes, it threw me. He was clearly very bright indeed and I watched him carefully as he talked. He was also astonishingly good-looking; there was no debate to be had there. He was on the cusp of that final shift from beautiful boyish vulnerability to masculine dominance; fatally attractive to a certain kind of person, in my experience.

But 'the Devil hath the power to assume a pleasing shape', and Jonathan Day was far more than a pretty smile and big brown eyes. I found myself engaged as he made some pithy observations and, to my mounting dismay, I began to see how Alex might well have had her head turned by such a boy. I was certainly concerned enough to check the days she'd worked in June and, on Monday, the 19th she *was* off – she does a four-day week because of her young children. My first assumption was that Day junior had struck lucky with this detail – I wasn't worried that it confirmed anything bar that it was logistically possible that she might have gone to his house that day, and yes, it was.

Would Alex be so foolish as to have responded to a note left by a young, male – attractive – patient on her car however? Surely not.

No health care professional would do that. They'd just completely ignore it… but while one would like to think she's learnt her lesson on that front, one also knows Alex can be far too easily led for her own good.

As I listened to Day junior, I started to think about the recent lunchtime when I found Alex crying at her desk. It would have been in August, I think. I didn't really know how to comfort her; like most British men of my age I'm fairly useless when it comes to being confronted with a crying woman in a social context, but when I worriedly asked her what was wrong, she confided that she was experiencing some marital difficulties.

I was very sad to discover that her husband seemed to be repeating his behaviour pattern of old, this time substituting Alex for some young colleague of his. As my mother would say, there's no fool like an old fool. She was obviously upset, but at the time I had no reason to think her mental capacity had been affected by what her husband had rashly done. I think I would have staunchly pointed out to anyone who suggested such a thing what an insult to the intelligence of an exceptionally capable woman that was. But as I listened to Day junior hold court, I began to wonder if perhaps a boy like this appearing in her office, flirting with her when she was already feeling rejected by her husband, had proven just too deliciously tempting?

There are lots of things that fascinate people about doctors, but one of the things I'm asked most at dinner parties is, do you ever fancy your patients? Is it tricky when you're having to intimately examine a very attractive person?

My answer is always the same. Most people – unless they are attention-seeking nut jobs – come to the doctors because they have something wrong with them: lumps, bumps, boils, bleeding bowels, rectal protuberances, pubic lice, ulcers, puss-filled hair follicles, heavy periods, testicular torsion, excessive bloating or wind… aroused yet? Exactly. It doesn't matter how attractive a person might be, I just see symptoms – and almost *everybody* looks better with clothes on, trust me.

Of course, sometimes a person will walk into your room who is exceptional. And yes, we're only human. But that's when the experienced doctor then simply detaches from that emotional response and focuses on the job. The patient is there to be treated, not flirted with. The professional within us must remain empathetic, naturally, but we do not allow ourselves to become compromised. How on earth would we cope with the extremely distressing cases – of which there are plenty – unless we are able to compartmentalise successfully? We would be basket cases, no use to anyone. It was one of the first lessons I taught Alex after the Rob debacle: *detach and compartmentalise. Protect yourself.* Surely she hadn't let Day undo all of her good work?

I admit I was unsettled and concerned enough to give the rest of Day's statement my undivided attention.

CHAPTER 9

Jonathan Day

Cherry was the first person to notice my mind was elsewhere. We've been going out for over seven months now: she was never going to miss it. The first time she confronted me was in her bedroom after school on the Monday after I'd left everyone in the pub and gone home.

We were watching Nigahiga. 'I literally don't get this,' I said, staring at the screen. 'Five million views for picking rubbish out of his bin and he's not funny. He's not actually funny.'

'I like him.' Cherry shrugged. 'He's authentic – which is the golden ticket. He doesn't pretend to be someone he isn't.'

'I know what authentic means,' I snapped, and she raised her eyebrows.

'You're very touchy recently,' she remarked. 'Talking of truth and lies, why aren't we doing it any more?'

'What?' I pretended to look puzzled. 'We are.'

'No, we're not.' She changed position and lay on her front on the bed, crossing her feet over at the ankle. Everything had become a selfie pose with her; she'd almost completely stopped moving like a normal person. 'Not since you got your leg fixed. Have you gone off me?'

'No.'

'Am I fat?' She twisted over on her back and stuck her long legs up in the air.

'Shut up.'

'Seriously. Am I getting fat? You can tell me.'

I sighed. 'Of course you're not.'

'No, Jonny, that's right. I'm not fat. I got 1K likes when I posted in just a suit jacket last week. Someone said I AM Lolita clickbait.' She sat up suddenly and crossed her arms. 'So it's not me. That's for sure. I'm still doing good business. You though? Not so much.'

'Can you please not talk like you're American? It really pisses me off. You were born in Bromley, not Brooklyn.' I reached over and turned the iPad off grumpily.

'OK. Stick this in your mockney pipe and smoke it, then.' She shrugged. 'Your numbers are shit. You're not getting any more followers because you're not putting in the effort. You need to be posting every day at this stage. There is no way we're even vaguely ready to be YouTubers yet. Joe and Zoe, on the other hand, are out there right now, living our lives with their millions of followers, houses, endorsements, and cute little dogs. How do you feel about not being part of that narrative?'

'Don't channel Taylor Swift like that. It makes you sound like an immense bell-end.'

'Whatever. I can tell you I do NOT feel good. I refuse to be part of generation mute. I love you, but I want to be out there loud and proud. If you've gone off the idea of YouTubing together, then fine, but at least have the courtesy to tell me, so I can get your replacement sorted.'

I scoffed. 'As in replacement boyfriend?'

She narrowed her eyes. 'I mean, someone more committed to creating their online presence. Of course I still want you as my boyfriend.' She sat up on her knees and pulled her tie loose, unbuttoned her shirt, unhooked her bra and just looked at me, half-naked. She was right, she looked amazing – and I felt absolutely nothing.

'There are so many people who would kill to see me like this in real life, and you're the only person who gets to, but you don't want it,' she said. 'So, who have you met? Where did you go last Friday night when you just disappeared?'

'I went home, Cherry. That's all. I was tired.'

'Do you think Joe Sugg gets tired, or do you think he's out there right now writing his next book? Your last Instagram was over five days ago. It's not good enough, Jonathan.'

I was suddenly bored. Bored of it all. 'I am NOT a mockney. That's just bloody rude.' I got up, grabbed my phone and banged out of the house.

She didn't come after me, and I didn't care. I got into my car and roared off down the drive, only stopping once I was back out on the lane, to text Alex from the burner.

Can I see you?

So much for my playing it cool. I sat and waited for ten minutes, but she didn't answer. I gave up and went home. Cherry messaged me later that night with an apology of sorts.

It's good that we argue! People are going to love this shit! Will they won't they, do they don't they? Trust me. We are going to rule!

I told her it was fine and I'd already forgotten about it, which I sort of had anyway – it was Alex I was concentrating on. I didn't understand what I had done wrong that meant she was now just ignoring me. I did think she might just be doing what *I* do with girls – blank them until they are grateful for whatever attention I show them.

If she was, it worked, because by Wednesday I'd reached the point where I needed to see if she was deliberately cutting me off or was on holiday or something and there was a rational reason for her silence. I'd just pulled into the surgery car park after school to look for her car – I'd decided if it was there, that was it, we were over, I was just going to get on with my life – when a text came through from her. I jumped with shock.

Are you at home?

I'd looked around me worriedly and spied the BMW. She was here somewhere. Could she see me from an office room? Was this a trick question? I decided to just be honest.

No, I'm in your car park at work.

I waited for a moment, but nothing happened. I climbed out of the car and walked up to the surgery hesitantly, then turned right and ventured around the side of the building where I'd seen her disappear off to that first day. There was a door there, but no one around. No Alex waiting for me. I hung about for a moment or two more, but nobody appeared, so I walked back to the car park. I even popped into the chemist, just in case – but she wasn't there either. Just a couple of old people waiting for prescriptions.

I went back to the car, and as I climbed back in, the crappy mobile finally went off in my hand, making me almost drop it in the scramble to look at the screen.

Go home.

I was confused. Was I being dismissed, or summoned?

Just in case, I started the car and drove as fast as I could back to the house, but she wasn't there waiting, and I also discovered, when I got up to my room, that my iPhone was missing from my bag. I'd had it when I left school, so some wanker must have nicked it from the passenger seat while I was pratting around outside looking for Alex. I was seriously pissed off by this point, as well as angry with myself. I could do without the hassle of getting a new phone, but far more importantly – I'd blown it with Alex and overstepped the mark. What I'd done must have looked stalker-ish to her, but it really wasn't. I was actually trying to resolve everything, but then her text had thrown me. I didn't know what it meant, or what I was supposed to do. I was completely confused, which was probably the point.

On Wednesday, 12 July – a whole two weeks after she'd effectively told me to do one – a message came through with an address and

This Sat – be there at 10 p.m.

That was it – but her precise schedule was a problem. It was Olly's party, which had been planned for ages to coincide with his parents going to Tenerife. I couldn't arrive before ten, then go and come back again, *or* show up as late as eleven either, at my mate's party. But I wanted to see her, I *really* wanted to see her.

*

So on Saturday morning, I went into Ruby's bedroom. She was still dozing and Angel was lying on her bed, looking up and wagging her tail when I came in.

'You know when she wags her tail like that she's effectively wiping her arse on your bedclothes, don't you?' I said as I sat down.

Ruby rubbed her eyes and turned over. 'What do you want?'

'Nothing,' I lied. 'I came to see if you wanted a tea or coffee.'

Ruby pulled a face. 'Shut up and just tell me; it'll be a lot quicker.'

I sighed. 'Are you in tonight?'

'Yes, why?' She looked at me warily.

'I need some cover for why I'm going to get to Olly's party about two hours late. Can I say that you had a crisis and I had to be here with you?'

She burst out laughing. 'Yes, because if that were true, you'd be the first person I'd call.'

'You might,' I said and pretended to look hurt.

'Don't try your baby deer thing; it's only Mum that works on. Why are you getting to Olly's two hours late?'

I hesitated. 'I can't tell you. I just need an excuse that they'll all buy, especially Cherry.'

She frowned. 'Is what you're doing illegal?'

'No, promise,' I said sincerely.

She propped herself up on her pillow. 'Are you cheating on Cherry? Because that's a bit shit if you are. I don't especially like her and she's got a balloon instead of a head, but she's obviously very into you and you shouldn't knowingly hurt people.'

'Believe me, Cherry can more than take care of herself. You don't have to worry about her. Please, Rubes. This is important.'

She looked at me again. 'So if anyone asks, you're going to say you've been at home consoling me, and as far as Mum and Dad go, you're going straight to Olly's?'

I nodded.

'Are you going to be somewhere safe?' she said, all of a sudden. 'You'll text me when you really do arrive at Olly's? I'm not doing it otherwise. And you've got your pen?'

'I swear.' I reached into my pocket and pulled out my insulin pen to prove it. 'Thanks, Ruby. I owe you one.'

*

I started to get ready way too early and was done by seven o'clock. I hesitated and texted Alex.

Can I come at nine, not ten? Would make a big difference to me?

No, it's not dark enough then. Someone might see you arrive.

She knew how to make me feel special, that's for sure. But the thought that I'd actually be with her in two hours overrode everything else. I refused Mum's offer of an Indian because I didn't want to smell, having a salad instead – to much piss-taking – and sat on the sofa watching *Bridget Jones's Baby* with the three of them, jittering my leg nervously until Dad turned to me.

'What's rattled your cage?'

I stopped instantly, shrugged and looked blank. 'Nothing? I'm going out in a minute, that's all.'

Dad looked at his watch pointedly. 'The night's as good as over!'

'It's not even quarter to ten yet.' I looked at my phone then out of the window. It was dark enough now, surely?

'Leave him alone, Gary.' Mum popped a chocolate in her mouth. 'Just watch the film. You said you were enjoying it a moment ago.'

'I said it's better than the first two,' Dad retorted. 'That's not the same thing. McDreamy's getting on my nerves now and it's not realistic. She's stopped smoking just like that, has she? I don't buy it. Where are you going anyway?' He swung back round to me, and I jumped guiltily.

'Olly's.'

I glanced at Ruby, but she didn't look up from filing her nails.

'Make sure you text me, please, if you're going to be later than one,' Mum said. 'And remember that you've got school on Monday. It's not the holidays yet. You got a snack with you?'

'Yes, of course.' I stood up – Dad was still looking at me.

'You're too smart for your own good, sunshine. You know that?' he said, and my heart thumped. 'What is it that you're really doing?'

'Excuse me, Poirot, do you mind? I'm trying to watch this, even if you're not!' Ruby exclaimed. 'Urgh – and I think the dog's doing something in your slipper.'

'What?' said Dad in alarm and looked down under the sofa.

Ruby widened her eyes at me, and I legged it.

I put the postcode into Google Maps and discovered it was only twenty minutes away. It couldn't be her actual address? It took me out past the bunny run and the farm shop entrance then left onto another even smaller lane that led past a couple of houses and wove deeper into the forest. I made the mistake of turning off too soon into a small Forestry Commission clearing. There was nothing else there, only an open track leading right into the woods. I reversed and drove on, almost immediately reaching a cottage set back from the road, behind a five-bar gate.

I parked on the road, and walked down the drive through the garden, in the dark. There were no lights on and the curtains were open. It looked a bit like the family who lived there had gone on holiday. I peered in through the glass and jumped to see Alex just sat on a sofa in the gloom looking back at me. She stood up and walked out of the room as I made my way to the front door. I waited until she silently opened it and stood back to let me in.

Walking into the hallway, which smelt strongly of flowers, I kept my hands in my jeans pockets and turned to face her. 'Do you live here?'

She nodded. 'My husband has taken the children to his parents for the night. I pretended I wasn't feeling well and stayed put.'

I'd not thought about her having children before then. For the first time I wondered exactly how old she was, but then I realised what she'd just said. We had all night.

Maybe that was why she didn't seem in as much of a rush as usual. She slowly walked over to me and I gently lowered my head and kissed her. She pulled back immediately and looked at me, surprised. I reached for her hand and started leading her towards the stairs.

'No,' she said, stopping abruptly. 'We stay down here.'

'OK,' I said, holding up both hands at her sharp tone.

She walked past me into the sitting room, and I followed to find her pulling the curtains. I went to put the light on, but as I reached for the switch, she shook her head.

'Leave it.'

I exhaled, more with nerves than anything – and suddenly remembered Ruby checking that I was going to be somewhere safe. I looked at the closed door on the other side of the room leading to fuck knew where. What if it was all bollocks and her husband was waiting behind that door, and this was just something they did – lure boys like me back to their house before hurting them? I suddenly wanted to be at Olly's very badly, just getting pissed with my mates, getting off with Cherry and posting stupid selfies. I was frightened. I started to edge back away towards the door leading to the hall, but Alex was quickly by my side and took my hand.

'What's wrong?' I could just about make out the concern on her face, and she reached up and stroked my face gently. She'd never done anything like that before. 'You're shaking?'

'I'm…' I couldn't help looking at the closed door again, and she followed my gaze.

'No one's here,' she whispered. 'It's just you and me. I promise. You're safe. I won't let anything happen to you.' She reached up and kissed me very gently, and I realised I wasn't the only one trembling.

*

We did it in the dark on the floor. At first it was good, she kissed me a lot more than normal and put my hands on her body, but then she started making more noise and when she came, she gave this almost desperate moan, like she hadn't wanted to but couldn't help it. I didn't like it; it was the saddest sound I'd ever heard. I didn't want to do it after that, but she started whispering urgently 'just do it, fuck me', and using her hands on me. I did as I was told, and when I came, I felt her go still underneath me, almost lifeless. It freaked me out completely.

'Alex?' I also had no idea why we were still whispering if we were alone. 'Are you all right?'

I reached my hand out to feel for her face in the dark and realised she was crying. I got off and lay down next to her. Her body had started to judder, and she covered her face with her hands while turning to hide in my chest as I put an arm protectively around her. I let her cry for a moment, while I stroked her hair and said: 'it's OK, it's OK.' I didn't know what else to do.

'It's not OK, Jonathan! *This* is not OK. Trust me.'

I hesitated. I didn't know how to handle this new her, and I was feeling increasingly uncomfortable. It was a relief when she pulled back and said: 'I'm so sorry, but I think I need you to go now.'

I didn't need to be told twice. I quickly jumped up and grabbed my clothes. Making my way out into the hall I found a downstairs loo and sorted myself out, glancing in the mirror as I washed my hands. What was I doing here, in her house while she lay crying in the other room? I didn't want any of *this*. I turned off the light and walked back out into the empty hall.

'Alex?'

There was no answer and reluctantly I went back into the sitting room. She was still lying on the floor, only with some sort of blanket round her as she lay on her side and stared into the cold fireplace, still in the dark. I had no idea why: we had to be the only people around for miles.

'I'm going now.'

She didn't turn over to look at me. 'I'm so sorry, Jonathan.'

It wasn't clear for what – and I didn't much care. I just wanted to leave. She was being really weird. 'OK then. Thanks,' I said awkwardly, even giving her a little *wave* as I left. I closed the front door behind me, hurried down the drive and got into the car, driving away quickly and feeling a lot better when I hit the safety of the main road.

I felt better still when I pulled up at Ol's and knocked loudly at the door – trying to be heard over the music coming from within – only to have Ol himself open it and whoop at the sight of me.

'About time, knobhead! Heeeere's, Jonny!' he shouted, grabbing me by the shoulders and steering me inside, to more cheers.

I felt her phone buzz in my pocket as I went into the kitchen to find a drink. When I checked in the downstairs loo, she'd sent an apology.

> I'm so sorry, Jonathan. That all got a bit messed up! :-0 Normal business has been resumed. Sorry again. Just wanted to check you're OK?

For the first time, I ignored her and went off to find my girlfriend. The balance had shifted. I can't describe it any better than that, sorry – but it's honestly true about her not letting me upstairs and refusing to put the lights on. *That's* why I don't know what any of the rooms look like on the second floor. I did NOT go round to her house and look in through the windows while she was at home on her own. I'm no stalker or peeping Tom. I know what the downstairs rooms look like because I was there. She let me in.

But the minute it all got too intense for me, I backed off, and when she realised what was happening she didn't like it and, predictably, did the same as every single girl I've ever known.

She came running… and she became obsessive.

CHAPTER 10

Jonathan Day

Alex messaged every day for the next week – at the same time, every single day. It was pretty freaky – like an automated service. I was on the verge of just throwing the phone away, but realised, if I did that, I'd have no proof whatsoever and some sort of instinct told me evidence might be a useful thing to have, even though all she put was 'Hi! How are you?' Over and over again. I just kept on not replying, hoping she was eventually going to get the message, but on Thursday, 20 July, shit got real.

I'd been at home since lunchtime as school was more or less done for summer and I had free study periods every Thursday afternoon anyway. It was hot, I'd had enough, and the teachers had stopped caring if we were there or not. Angel had started barking, I'd gone to the door and there she was, just standing there on the doorstop.

I hadn't known what to say at first, partly because I was pissed off to be caught looking a sweaty mug, still in my uniform, but also because she looked amazing. I'd forgotten how blatantly sexy she was. She was wearing a bright red dress that made her waist look tiny and sort of stuck out above her knees, and some cream coloured heels, while holding her doctor bag. The hot sun was shining right behind her and I was literally dazzled.

'On your own?' she asked.

'Yeah – but, what if I hadn't been?' I opened the door, and she walked into the cooler hall. I looked at her, exasperated. 'Is this because I haven't texted you back? Is that why you're here?' Then another, much more worrying, thought occurred to me. 'How *did* you know I was here? Have you been following me?'

She looked at me like I was mad and said crushingly: 'Jonathan, I like you, you're very sweet and we've had fun, but things have moved on now. I'm not actually here to see you.' She reached into a pocket in her dress and pulled out a slim, small rectangle and passed it over to me. 'Could you give this to your father for me, when he gets back?'

I took it and stared at her name in shiny black letters. 'What do you want with my dad?'

She looked at me, slightly irritated. 'I heard on the grapevine your parents are looking for a Botox doctor for their new club and spa. I appreciate it's all maybe a bit close to home, but we're both adult enough to put everything behind us, aren't we? Your parents' new facility is going to be a captive audience of some pretty wealthy people and I'm good at my job. There's no reason why this shouldn't be a very successful partnership.'

I looked at her in disbelief but tried to play down my panic. 'I don't think that's a good idea really, do you?'

Alex pretended to look confused. 'I don't see why not?'

I shoved the card in my pocket, closed the door and turned to her.

'Don't do this. This is about us. If you really wanted to work with my parents you'd email like a normal person, you wouldn't come round to their *house*.'

She frowned. 'That's exactly what I did. Sorry, I don't think you understand. Your dad called me back, and I was supposed to meet him here this afternoon for a preliminary chat before I go and pick up my daughters from school. He's obviously got caught up or something, and I don't feel comfortable waiting here with you alone, for obvious reasons, so if you could just give him my card so he knows I *did* come, that would be great.'

'Wait.' I reached out and grabbed her wrist. 'Dad arranged to meet you here? Why not at the new site?'

She shrugged. 'I don't know. Perhaps he just liked the sound of my voice?' She smiled sweetly at me.

I saw exactly what she was up to, instantly. 'You're barking up the wrong tree there,' I said coldly. 'My dad can be a right arsehole, but he loves my mum more than anything in the world.'

'Oh, I'm sure,' she said innocently. Then she stepped closer to me, pressing her body up against me. 'Don't you think you better let me go? He could be back at any moment.' She looked at me and smiled.

I swallowed. I wasn't going to do this. Not again.

She didn't take her eyes from me, just took my free hand with hers and put it up the skirt of her dress. She wasn't wearing anything underneath. I closed my eyes and clenched my jaw but I could already feel her hand moving to the button on my trousers.

'Just quickly,' she whispered.

*

We did it on the stairs. I knew I shouldn't – and I didn't even use anything. She got up carefully afterwards and went straight to the downstairs loo.

'Well, I think I'd better go now anyway,' she said, re-emerging to find me dressed and sitting on the stairs with my head in my hands. 'I'll see myself out.' She paused and sighed. 'Look, just don't give my card to your father if it's a problem, Jonathan. I understand.'

I didn't look up, just waited until the door had closed and I heard her car leave. Then I started to panic. I'd never not used anything before. Ever. She was too old to get pregnant though –

surely? And what was SHE thinking? She was married. My blood ran cold. What if she was actually proper mental and tried to say she'd come round here to see Dad – which he'd back up – and I'd forced myself on her? There'd be stains all over her dress. She was a doctor. No one would believe me and not her. I felt sick and I didn't know what to do.

I waited for Dad to arrive, but he didn't, and it was only after I called him on his mobile – something I never do – and he picked up sounding all concerned, saying 'I'm in a meeting, but are you all right?' that I realised that Alex almost certainly wasn't telling the truth about having contacted him at all.

'Yeah, sorry, Dad. I'm fine. I'll see you later. Don't worry.'

When he did come home, I had to make up something about my car breaking down to explain why I'd called him, which, in true Dad style, he then didn't let go, wanting to get to the bottom of it.

'You're sure you didn't leave your phone charger plugged in again, because that can drain the battery?' He looked up at me over jacket potatoes and ham at dinner, as Mum passed me the salad bowl, and Ruby put some butter on the side of her plate.

'Like I said,' I repeated for the hundredth time, 'one minute there was nothing there, the next it just started again. I thought I was going to have to jump it and if you were at home you could come over with some leads.'

'At home? At two o'clock in the afternoon? I was at the site. But Mum could have come out if you'd needed one of us?'

I looked at him carefully. Was he lying or not? Had he been planning to meet Alex and got delayed? 'Are you looking for any new staff at the moment?' I said. 'Beauty stuff I mean?'

Ruby sniggered. 'Think you should do that instead of vlogging then, J?'

'He knows vlogging isn't a career,' Dad said sharply. 'Don't you, Jonny boy?'

And now was he trying to change the subject and turn the focus on to me instead? I thought about him opening the front door to Alex, her smiling at him and walking into our house, clutching her black bag in her short red dress – and put down my knife and fork.

'Let's not start all that again,' Mum said. 'Jonny knows he needs a backup in case vlogging, or modelling, doesn't take off. He's still doing his exams, and he's still going to apply for university.'

'Which really *is* a waste of time,' Dad said. 'I know that school says you're a bright little bunny, but neither them or you seem to be able to work out that thirty grand of debt for three years getting pissed when you could join the family business and start making money straight away isn't the smartest idea.'

'*That school* gets a lot of kids into the top universities,' Mum said pointedly.

'I should bloody hope so, the amount they charge each term.'

'They've got Oxford in mind for Jonny.'

'You might want to tell Miss Healy that's the plan, then,' I said. 'She asked me where I was thinking of in English and when I said, Oxford, she got all sniffy and "oh no dear, I don't think so". She hates me. They all do.'

'No, they don't. Elsbeth Healy wants to spend a little less time staring at that engagement ring of hers and a little more time actually teaching,' Mum snapped. 'You leave her to me, the stuck up cow. Are you not hungry, love?' She nodded at my untouched food.

I shook my head.

'I really would like you to try and eat.'

I sighed and did as I was told.

Dad pointed his knife at me. 'I want you to do that Personal Trainer module over the summer holidays. I know you're thinking it's all fatties you'd be training, but it's not,' he continued. 'And with your looks you'd get all the mums shoving their kiddies in the crèche. Two birds with one stone.'

I thought of Alex and her stained dress. 'Can I leave the table please, Mum?'

'You have gone a little bit pale all of a sudden.' Mum was frowning. 'I think someone's had a bit too much sun today.'

I stood up suddenly, jolting the table and making all the knives and forks jump. 'Sorry, I need the loo.'

I hastened to the downstairs cloakroom, closed the door and leant my forehead on the cool of the mirror. I didn't know what to think. My proper phone vibrated in my pocket and I pulled it out.

Can I come over and see you in a bit? Thought we could go for a drive and take some nice sunset snaps?

Cherry. She was right, I needed to get updating. I tried to take a few deep, calming breaths. Alex had not been going to meet Dad. Even if she had, she said she'd leave it – about the job – if it was going to upset me. I slid my hand into my other pocket, pulled out her card and ran my finger over the letters.

Dr Alexandra Inglis

Fucking me in the back of her car one minute, crying on the carpet in her dark sitting room the next, and now turning up on the doorstep in no underwear.

If only I'd not gone to football for Dad that night.

I tore the card into tiny pieces and flushed it down the loo. At the very least, if she had been going to meet Dad here, he must have come home, seen my car and driven off again. I'd achieved that if nothing else. I hesitated, went upstairs and fished out the pay-as-you-go mobile.

I think we need to talk about what happened today. Can I see you?

She came straight back to me.

> Going to be difficult. Working and of course children's last full week so – as I expect you are – doing lots of activities/sports days. Then go on holiday for two weeks. Not back until Sat 5 August. Sorry honey! Busy, busy – you know how it is! I'll be in touch on return. Have a good last day of school!

Was she high? What kind of message was that? I stared at it and realised it was deliberately written to give me the information I needed while looking like it was meant for a friend of hers. What was the point in that – unless she was trying to say that her husband had found her pay-as-you-go phone? Warning me that things were becoming too obvious, as well as dismissing me for the next two weeks? Who did she think she was? She was controlling everything, blowing hot and cold. I felt suddenly very angry. I was at her mercy, and I didn't like it.

I was starting to dislike her. And yet I couldn't stop thinking about her. That didn't make me feel so good about myself, either.

*

True to her word, she didn't contact me for the next two weeks. Not even once but, weirdly, it was a relief. I hadn't enjoyed her turning up at the house unannounced. The prospect of being caught on the stairs didn't feel exciting, even in retrospect, it just made me feel a bit sick with stress, but the more time passed, it started to feel like a nightmare that wasn't so bad after all, now the lights were on.

Aside from the rare amazing day here and there, the weather had predictably turned shit as it was the summer holidays, but I didn't even really care. We had a family holiday to Ibiza coming up, so I'd get a tan regardless; I was getting on much better with Cherry – everything felt like it was finally getting back to normal… Alex still lurked in the back of my mind – pretty much always appearing when I was doing it with Cherry, which was both confusing and unsettling – but I felt things were under control again.

So when Mum asked me to drive her to the doctors on Monday, 7 August, I desperately tried to persuade her I couldn't. I didn't want to go anywhere near the surgery – but she ignored me.

'I don't think I'd be safe to drive myself over there, love. I feel hot, knackered – everything aches and I feel sick as a dog.'

'I don't feel well myself, Mum. I think I'm coming down with it too,' I lied. 'Can't you get a taxi?'

Mum gave me a hard stare. 'Well unless you're also menopausal, I'd say you're all right. I'm aware it's the first nice day in forever but I'm not getting a taxi just so you can get Cherry round here while you've got the house to yourself, then hit the sun-loungers. We're leaving in ten minutes.'

I saw Alex's black car the second we arrived in the car park and tried to swing right off to the back, out of the way, but Mum wasn't having any of it.

'What are you doing? There's a space right there, in front of the chemist! There! Get in it quick before someone else does. Why do all men have to drive past spaces that have nothing wrong with them?'

'It's shadier at the back over there under the trees while I wait,' I grumbled and parked up nervously where I was told. 'That's all.'

Mum gave me a look. 'Keep the air con on. I'm sure you'll survive. Or come in with me.'

'No thanks,' I retorted.

Mum sighed and, with an effort, opened the door and winced as she eased herself out, closing the door behind her and walking, hunched over, to the double doors. She obviously was in a bad way. I felt bad for being arsey with her but, the truth was, I was properly stressed out.

After I'd sat there for about twenty minutes, however, I began to relax in the heat and had leant back with my eyes closed, when there was a knock on the glass. I jolted awake, expecting Mum, but it was Alex, standing by the door dressed in a sky-blue sundress, looking very tanned.

Eyes wide, I undid the window all the way down.

'Hello,' she said. 'Someone reported a young boy passed out in his car to the receptionists. I said I'd come out and have a look.'

I had no idea if she was telling the truth or had just seen me and come out using any old excuse.

She lingered for a moment. 'Anyway. I'd better go back in now I know you're OK.' She crossed her arms. 'Um, why are you here, by the way?'

'I've brought my mum down for an appointment.'

'Oh, fine.' She looked relieved and went to step away.

'*I'm* not stalking *you*.' I sat up a little straighter, feeling annoyed. 'You look good though.' I've no idea why I said that. No idea at all. It was asking for trouble. 'Nice holiday then?'

She nodded. 'You off anywhere soon?'

'Ibiza, on the 27th, for two weeks.' I didn't mention it was with my parents and sister, obviously.

She paled. 'Not really? I'm going to be there on the 8th, on a girl's weekend.'

I laughed nervously, waiting for her to tell me she was joking, but she didn't.

'It's almost as if the universe is determined to push us together,' she said. 'Perhaps that's where we were supposed to meet properly for the first time, not here with me cutting your trouser leg off.' She gestured behind her at the surgery. I couldn't believe she was standing in the car park having a friendly chat with me about it all. 'I think I would have preferred that actually – not knowing who you were; a handsome stranger in a hot country and all that. I like *that* fantasy.' She mused over it for a second and smiled, before turning on her heels and walking back to the surgery without another word.

I stared after her, mouth slightly open. As usual with Alex, I had no idea what to think.

It's really hard to explain how she does it. She's like one of those pictures where you can only see a horse head but you're meant to be able to see the duck too, then suddenly you get it and then you can't see the horse head, even though you *know* it's there and you try really, really hard. You only see what Alex wants you to see, her version of reality.

I expected to hear from her later that night after the fate comment, but, disconcertingly, I got nothing. I waited for a summons at the weekend. Silence again. The whole of the next week I kept checking my phone, but she was never there.

I came to the conclusion she'd meant what she'd said at my house. It was over. We'd had fun but moved on. I found myself feeling disappointed and even wondering if maybe I *would* see her in Ibiza, before I realised what she was doing to me again, that this was exactly how she worked: getting in my brain and eating away at it like a worm, destroying my ability to function normally and altering my behaviour.

Even though I KNEW all of that, I still felt rejected that she hadn't called, which was insane. I began to dream about her at night, waking up suddenly, covered in sweat – or worse, my own spunk. I started to wonder why I'd got so worked up about her being weird, when in reality, wasn't it every male wish come true to have a woman who wanted sex and nothing more? What was wrong with *me* that I'd wanted to walk away from that? I was a mess. I didn't know if I was coming or going. I almost needed to be told what to think and do. I couldn't make sense of it for myself any more.

*

So, when she texted me again, on Saturday, 19 August, at ten p.m., asking me to meet her, just like the second time, at the bottom of the hill by the park entrance, I didn't think twice. I just did it. I imagined we'd drive off to the farm shop car park again. I pictured myself putting my hands all over her. I as good as *ran* down the hill from the pub when I saw her car parked up at the bottom. Olly and the others were already busily getting lashed up. Cherry was on holiday at her parents' villa in Spain. I had no one to please except myself.

But when I climbed into the passenger seat, I knew something was wrong. Even in the dark I could tell she'd been crying. She didn't look at me as I clipped my seatbelt in and waited for her to start the car and drive off; she just looked out of the window, one elbow resting on the doorframe, fingernails between her teeth, and tears started to run silently down her face.

'What's wrong?' I said, foolishly, and she didn't answer. Confused, I just sat there for a moment, like a puppy waiting for its owner to tell it what to do next – but she didn't and eventually I asked again. 'Alex, what's the matter? Are you hurt? Has something happened?'

She frowned as if in pain, at that point and, eyes closed, just nodded, apparently trying not to cry some more. I started looking around me for some tissue but stopped suddenly. Oh my fucking God – she was about to tell me she was pregnant. I sat up so fast I banged my head on the glovebox. My whole life literally flashed before my eyes. Dad going ballistic, Cherry screaming at me, Alex's husband coming round to our house and trying to kill me, then a baby being born. An actual baby. I *knew* it. I bloody knew it!

'Can you please just tell me?' I stammered.

'You're going to think I'm mad,' she whispered, looking down, ashamed.

'No, I'm not,' I lied. 'Just say it.'

She turned her head slowly. 'Do you think I'm pretty?' she asked desperately. I could see the tears glinting in her eyes as she waited for my answer.

What? I was momentarily thrown. 'Yes, of course.'

'You don't ever find yourself thinking "urgh, she's really old?"'

'No,' I said. Where the hell was this going?

'So if you saw me in the street and you didn't know me, you wouldn't walk straight past? You'd notice me?'

'Yes. Alex, what's wrong? Could you *please* just tell me?'

Her eyes welled up again. 'I know how this is going to sound – to you, of all people – but my husband told me this morning…' She trailed off.

I waited, now really worried. That he'd found out about us? Was coming looking for me? 'Told you what, Alex?'

She was crying again and shook her head. 'Nothing – forget it. Forget I said anything. It's nothing to do with you, really. I'm sorry.'

So she wasn't pregnant? I began to exhale slowly with relief, like the gasp of air releasing from a pinprick hole in a balloon. Thank you, God. Oh, thank you so much.

'You won't know this yet, Jonathan, but you can be with someone all day every day and be the loneliest you've ever been,' she said suddenly. 'They don't touch you, they don't kiss you – you try so hard and it all just dies anyway.' She closed her eyes again and leant her head back on the headrest tipping her face up to the car roof. 'You wish you could go back in time and make different decisions. Be the person you were then and start all over again.' She breathed in deeply like she was trying to get herself under control.

I remembered her lying on the carpet in her house, sobbing, and not letting me go upstairs. I didn't know what to say. 'I'm really sorry.' It was about the best I could do.

She exclaimed. 'Don't *you* apologise! I shouldn't be telling you this! You've done nothing wrong, not once!' She turned to me suddenly and her voice cracked completely. 'I'm so sorry, Jonathan! I'm sorry for what we've done and why I did it. It was complicated, but I'm sorry that I've even brought you here now. I was trying to prove things to myself that involved me using you to do it. It wasn't that I wasn't genuinely attracted to you. Of course I was! Even though I shouldn't have been. This is all such a mess. Such a sad, stupid and *dangerous* mess.' She let her head hang. 'Just get out of the car, Jonathan. You've got such a good heart and you shouldn't be near me. I'm toxic. I've lied, I've tried to hurt people, to make them see that they're losing me, and none of it has worked. I've just done more and more damage. Please!' She begged. 'Throw away your phone. I won't ever contact you on it again, and I'm so, so sorry for dragging you into this. It's all so wrong! I don't even know who I've become any more.'

After that little speech, I knew I wasn't even slightly equipped to deal with whatever she was talking about. I hesitated after I'd unclipped my seatbelt. 'Are you going to be all right?'

She nodded, silently, but she looked broken.

I slowly reached out my hand to hers, took it and held it tightly for a moment. She gripped it back.

'Thank you,' she whispered, and then let go of me, gently.

I opened the car door to the sounds of happy and drunken shouts from people starting to make their way down the hill running parallel to us, on their way to the local nightclub, and climbed out.

I started to walk back up to rejoin Olly and the others, turning at the sound of her car starting. I watched her pull away and drive off. I tried hard not to mind about her being so blatant about having used me – it wasn't as if I'd got nothing out of the experience after all, she didn't force me to do anything, but I couldn't stop thinking about her saying it was wrong.

I walked back up to the pub feeling suddenly really unhappy in a way that I couldn't put my finger on and went off to find my mates, to get as pissed as I could. Later on that night, I got into my first fight in a club. I threw a punch at someone because I thought they'd shoved into me on purpose and it kicked off. I remember being really angry – a rage I'd never experienced before.

The bouncers chucked me out, and I tried to get back in again. Olly and Rufus managed to stop me, and I flounced off to the park apparently. Ol messaged Ruby, who came to pick me up with her new boyfriend, Matt. He was really good about it and they took me home.

What *is* clear in my mind is that the exact word Alex used was 'wrong' – and she definitely told me to throw away the phone. But I didn't, I kept it. By that point, I was actually a bit worried about her.

I didn't hear from her for another three whole weeks after that. If Ibiza hadn't happened, I like to think that would have been the end of it – but it *did* happen, and she lost control completely.

CHAPTER 11

Jonathan Day

'Come on, we've *got* to go!' Ruby wheedled as she did her make-up. 'It's tradition.'

'Pacha is a giant cliché, Rubes,' I said lying back on the hotel bed. 'I can't be arsed. Plus, I'll just get hit on by a load of old boilers.'

'Oh shut up!' she said, irritated, her reflection glaring at me in the mirror. 'It's Paris by Night – there'll be loads of half-naked dancers in Marie Antoinette wigs.'

I gave her a look. 'How shallow do you think I am?'

'Well, if nothing else, it'd be better Instagramming from there than dinner with Mum and Dad, then your room. Don't be a pain, we booked the table ages ago.'

I sighed, all of that was true, but still… 'You don't need me,' I grumbled. 'You've got India and Bea to keep you company.' I thought crossly about the insanely annoying daughters of Mum and Dad's long-term friends and regular holiday partners, Lindsey and Chris. Both sets of parents had hundreds of photos of me and Bea from age about eighteen months; holding hands, looking confused at the camera, being forced to kiss each other 'cutely'. Fifteen years later Bea had got on board with their plan, but I wasn't quite so enthused. In fact, I'd had it with two weeks' worth of trying to avoid her lingering looks over the loungers and suggestive licking of ice creams, to say nothing of both girls' appalling attempts at banter. They looked all right but their craic stank.

'Bea isn't going unless you go. India won't go unless Bea goes, and I WANT to go – so you're coming,' Ruby said firmly. 'Come on, I do favours for you, now it's my turn. I'm asking you to go to a club, for crying out loud!' She turned round and pointed at the door. 'Go and get ready. Café Del Mar for sunset, then dinner with the olds, maybe the strip for a little bit of kitsch value, then in Pacha for midnight.'

I sighed and did as I was told.

In fact, by quarter past ten, I was only too pleased to have an excuse to get away from the parentals. Dad was loudly pissed after a long, boozy meal. As the four of us stood up to leave, there was lots of 'don't you all look lovely?' and 'stay together and stay safe' from Mum and Lindsey, while Chris and Dad told me to 'look after the girls'. Dad was giving me loads of hugs and roughly ruffling my hair using his knuckles, which hurt, but I refused to say anything.

'Isn't my boy handsome?' he said, loudly, to the other tables and my embarrassment. 'He's going to be a model. He gets it from me, of course.' He and Chris guffawed, and Ruby looked at her watch before saying sharply: 'Put him down, Dad. We need to go.'

'All right, all right. Here.' Dad reached into his wallet and pulled out a wodge of fifty euro notes. 'Have a good time, kids.' He only did it to wind up Chris. He *had* to be the alpha male, but I took them quickly nonetheless.

'Thanks, Dad. See you in the morning.'

'Bright and early for the last breakfast!' He held his arms open wide and smiled at his disciples beatifically. It really was like watching the second coming of Christ. If Jesus wore Paul Smith, had sunburn and was a complete wanker.

As we made our way to the strip, I thought about Alex. She was here somewhere, right now… but I dismissed it just as quickly. It was way too busy to bump into anyone by chance, the odds would have to be really small and, in any case, I wasn't going there any more.

I started posting a few pictures on Instagram with #Pachatradition and got a message immediately from Cherry saying:

This is awesome! More!

Encouraged, I uploaded again outside Pacha's VIP entrance before we went in and then from our table once we'd been escorted to it. I quickly got quite a few likes, which felt really good. We got a bottle of vodka on the go, then I decided to go for a wander as Bea was getting frisky.

I happily went up to the roof terrace for some air and to watch the girl in the glass, but after a quick drink headed off left, to the Funky Room, en route to the Main Room. As I walked down, I had the feeling someone was watching me, but when I turned and looked into the sea of strangers' faces, there was no one I knew.

I couldn't shake it, however, and spun round again, looking through a brief break in the crowd to see Alex standing there, holding a drink and her phone, and staring back at me. Even despite the lights, I could tell she was pretty pissed. She was doing that drunk thing of trying to stand up tall and act normal, but as she flicked her hair, she slopped her drink out of the glass and stumbled. I thought she was going to properly fall over, so hurried across to her and took it from her hand.

'Do I know you?' She giggled and put her arms round my neck.

I pulled back for a moment, but then realised she was acting out her 'fantasy' she'd described in the surgery car park. I looked around but it didn't look like she was with any of the people nearby.

'My name is Alex.' Then she mumbled something unintelligible.

'What did you say?' I couldn't really hear her over the music, so bent down closer.

'My name is Alex,' she said louder, right next to my ear.

'Yes, I know.' I tried to keep my cool. 'How did you find me?'

'I didn't, it's fate!' she said delightedly and let go of me with one hand, swayed dangerously and held up her phone, while putting a finger to her lips. 'You put pictures up!'

Fucking Instagram.

She laughed again as she lost her balance and grabbed onto me for support, hands tightly clasping round my neck as I put my hand on her waist to steady her and tried to hold onto her glass. She quickly leant in and kissed me. I started to try and pull back, but she was leaning into me so much we both staggered a bit. Finally, I managed to get her standing up properly, but her expression had changed.

'I don't feel so good,' she said, and put her hand up to her mouth.

I looked around in alarm. Where the hell were her mates? 'Alex, who are you here with?'

'What?' She was struggling to hear me.

'WHO ARE YOU HERE WITH?'

She closed her eyes briefly, and I saw her stomach heave. Oh shit – she was going to puke.

She put a frightened hand out to me. 'I need some air. I'm too hot. Can you take me outside, please?'

I didn't have any choice. We wove our way through the crowds and eventually pushed out onto the street in a blast, several people staring at us, amused. She staggered, and I thought she was going to throw up on one of the palm trees, but she seemed to steady a bit when she started breathing in the clearer air and visibly sobered up, before beginning to push through the crowds and apparently walk off down the street.

'What are you doing?' I said, following her. 'You can't just go off on your own?'

'I need to go back to my hotel. I don't feel so good. I'm going to get a taxi, that's all.' She held out a hand defensively and carried on. I could see immediately she was one of those really annoying pissed people who looks in control, but isn't, won't listen to a word anyone says, thinks they're sober – then randomly steps out into the road and gets instantly flattened by a car.

I sighed crossly and went after her. 'I'll help you find one, hang on.'

Luckily, it was so early we didn't have any problems, and, even better, her hotel was only ten minutes away. I didn't exactly have her down as a San An girl. She sprawled in all over the back seat when I opened the door though, dress riding right up. I glanced at the taxi driver looking in his mirror at her and I thought about how I'd feel if some strange bloke looked at Mum or Ruby like that. I couldn't leave her in the car on her own.

'Fucking hell, Alex!' I said furiously and got in next to her. She instantly leant on me and closed her eyes, snuggling in. I messaged Ruby en route to tell her I'd bumped into a pissed friend and was taking them to their hotel – and she messaged back to say Bea was in a right state out of nowhere; crying and wanting to go, so they were going to have to take *her* back.

What a mare! Should have listened to you and not bothered with Pacha!! Message me when you're back so I know you're safe.

I slid my phone back into my pocket, wondered what Bea had lost the plot over and hoped it had nothing to do with seeing Alex's attempt to get off with me. That was going to be fun to explain in the morning.

I just about managed to wake Alex up when we arrived back at her hotel. 'Can you please take me up to my room?' she whispered. 'I don't want to fall over and make a scene.' Given how much I'd already done, that didn't seem much more of an imposition, so I led her up a flight of stairs and along a corridor until we arrived outside a door.

'You're sure this is yours?' I said, and she nodded before sliding a card she'd pulled out of the inside of her mobile case into the slot. Thankfully, it turned green and opened.

She sighed and walked in, immediately kicking her shoes off and pretty much flinging herself onto the double bed. 'Praise God for that,' she said. 'And thank you so much for getting me back safely.'

'You're welcome,' I said. 'Drink some water.' And I turned to go.

'No, really. Thank you.' She turned on her side to look at me. 'It's not many men that would walk a woman up to her room and leave without trying it on. You're a gentleman, I can tell.'

'Alex,' I said tightly. 'Please, can we stop the "stranger and damsel in distress" act, please? I know that's what you said you wished that's what had happened, but—'

'What's your name?' she spoke over me. 'Actually, don't tell me. I'd rather not know.'

'Alex,' I said warningly. 'Seriously?'

'I'm leaving tomorrow, and I won't ever see you again.' She got up slowly and started peeling off her dress.

I couldn't not look. The now familiar sick loathing and excitement began. It was like watching porn. I didn't particularly want to, but it was there, and once it had started…

She didn't break eye contact, just reached behind her back and unhooked her bra, bent down and climbed out of her knickers, and waited.

*

Someone knocked on the door just after we'd finished. I sat up in alarm, but Alex put a hand on my chest.

'Ignore it. They'll go away.'

But whoever it was, didn't – and knocked louder. Alex swore, and got to her feet, dragging the top sheet round her and leaving me with nothing on. I couldn't see round the corner, but heard a whispered voice and Alex say: 'I'm fine, honestly. Yeah, in the morning. OK. Night.' Then the door closed, and she returned. 'All sorted. I need a wee.' She yawned, stepped out of the sheet and walked casually into the bathroom.

I took the opportunity to message Ruby that I was safe, and still at my mate's. When Alex came back out, I went in, before coming back into the room and reaching for my clothes. The now typical comedown had already begun, and I was not feeling good about what we'd done.

'You don't have to go.' Alex watched me. 'It's so late. Just stay and sleep for a bit.'

I shook my head.

'We've never done that,' she said, 'just lie next to each other in bed. Please? Just this once?'

'I can't, Alex.' I pulled on my boxers.

'You don't want to?'

I exhaled, feeling stressed and she held up a hand.

'OK, OK – I'm sorry. Could you just do me a favour though? Wait ten minutes until the others have all gone back to their rooms and don't see you coming out of here?'

'You're unbelievable. Were you even that pissed earlier, or was that part of the game too?' I lay back on the bed suddenly, hands on my head. 'Alex, I can't do this any more. It's fucking me up.'

She reached out and started tracing my tattoo sadly with a finger. 'I know,' she whispered. 'I'm sorry.'

'You keep saying that and then you start doing this sort of thing.' I gestured at her stroking me. 'It's gone beyond sex now, I feel like I'm in some sort of weird non-relationship with you.'

'I know,' she said unhappily. 'It really does have to stop. I meant it – this really is it.'

I sighed again, got off the bed and climbed in next to her. The air con was freezing my bollocks off. 'I was so flattered when you turned up at the house that Monday. I couldn't believe my luck. But this isn't good for either of us, any more. Please.' I was basically begging her, for the first time, to leave me alone. It can't have been easy for her to hear. No one wants to be dumped.

She put a brave face on it. 'Of course,' she said. 'Anything else that happened back at home after this would just feel like a cheap version anyway.'

'Yes, it would,' I agreed. 'I'm glad you feel that way.'

She smiled at me and deliberately pulled the sheet down slightly. 'We're still here now though?' She shrugged. 'Go out on a high one last time? Ibiza 2017?'

That really *was* the last time. We haven't had, nor ever will have, sex again.

I passed out afterwards though, exhausted, but also partly because we'd turned the aggressive air con off and the room quickly became sleepy and stuffy. I woke up to see sunlight coming through the curtains as my phone pinged with a text message.

> Where are you??!! And don't give me the "at your mates" shit. Are you still with the girl Bea saw you getting off with last night? Get your arse back here pronto. Dad thinks it's funny. Mum going mental.

Girl? She must have only seen Alex from the back then.

On my way. I texted.

I should have just gone back after the first time. That was always our problem, we never knew when to stop.

Alex groaned, turned over and looked at me blearily. 'Oh God. This wasn't part of the plan.'

'I know. I'm going now.'

There was a knock at the door, and Alex's eyes widened.

'Shit. Stay there.' She got up and grabbed a towel from the bathroom, then quickly kicked our clothes under the bed. Especially, I noticed, mine.

I listened to her open the door, then heard a woman's voice say loudly: 'You got rid of him then?'

I don't know what Alex said or did in response, but the door shut again and she came back in, looking really uncomfortable.

The crazy thing is, it was THAT comment which finally tipped me over the edge. I'd thought what we did was just between me and Alex. That no one else in the world knew. It didn't make it right, but it felt somehow special and secret. We had a connection. I fell for her stupid 'fate is pushing us together' story. But some stranger whose face I didn't even see had summed up the entire thing perfectly. Alex had no respect for me whatsoever. It made me feel dirty.

Used.

And ashamed.

It made me feel like shit.

'I'm so sorry,' Alex said. 'My friend, she…'

I forced myself to smile. I was determined not to let her see how it had hurt me. 'It's OK.'

I dressed quietly and then I left. I didn't touch her. I didn't say goodbye.

I didn't owe her anything.

CHAPTER 12

Jonathan Day

We flew home on Sunday; Dad still teasing me and calling me a chip off the old block, Bea all puffy-eyed, and Lindsey's lips pursed crossly like a cat's bum. Mum didn't hold back and gave me a comprehensive recap of effective alcohol and diabetes management, followed by a lecture on sleeping around, which boiled down to a bunch of *Loose Women* soundbites.

'I did not bring you up to disrespect women, Jonathan. I don't care that men can do that sort of thing without any feelings involved. A woman isn't the same. There's always an emotional cost when she has sex with a man that is not to be abused – and you're not to take advantage of looking the way you do. That's before we think of Cherry, who is a *lovely* girl and doesn't deserve to be treated like this.' She glared at me.

I said nothing as I swallowed that completely unfair assessment of me, and gross generalisation about men AND women. She couldn't have been more wrong if she'd tried, and I felt angry that she'd tarred me with such a shitty brush. Mum, of all people. She knew I wasn't like that. It really hurt. I wanted her to see how wide of the mark she was, but I didn't know where to start and the more she went off on one about women's rights, I began to wonder if perhaps what I'd done with Alex *had* made me into the kind of man she was talking about after all, and it WAS my fault. I could have said no. Yes, Alex and I had done a lot of stuff I now wasn't comfortable with, but I wasn't sure if I could honestly say it had happened every single time because I didn't feel like I had a way out. Part of me had wanted it too, hadn't I?

But mostly, I couldn't stop thinking about what her friend had said.

You got rid of him then?

'Jonathan, are you listening to me?'

I looked up at Mum and nodded. 'It won't happen again.'

*

I went back to school the next day, which felt weird as well. I'd missed the start of term and everyone else had already done the settling back in bit.

'That's probably why it's a good idea not to throw over the first few days because you're on holiday,' my psychology teacher said bitchily, when I complained about only having three days to do an essay when everyone else had already had a week. 'Turning up to lessons *does* benefit students funnily enough, Jonathan. Even you.'

Luckily Cherry took pity on me when – by Thursday – I still hadn't done it. My mind was all over the place, so she offered to help me pull something together using her class notes. We went over to hers – I wrote it quickly – then we drove back over to mine so I could email it from home. It would look too suspicious if the email was sent from my iPhone. I wasn't going to be caught out by poor attention to a detail like that.

Right away as we pulled up on the drive, I saw Alex's car. Fear enveloped me like a plastic bag and shrank to fit my skin; the air simultaneously sucking out of my body.

What The Fuck?

I saw her lying – in every sense of the word – on the hotel bed, smiling at me.

Go out on a high. Ibiza 2017. Last time ever!

How could I have been so stupid as to believe her?

I climbed out unsteadily, staring at the black BMW, as Cherry chattered away alongside me – I didn't hear a word of what she said. All I could concentrate on was Alex's empty car. She was inside the house. She had to be. Had she come to see Dad after all? She'd said she wouldn't. I thought all that was done with.

LAST TIME! We said that. We agreed.

I opened the front door, my hands shaking, as I tried to hold onto my key. I could hear voices in the kitchen. Cherry was in front of me drivelling on about a selfie she'd taken and wanted to show me because it was so bad it was hilarious, apparently. She was laughing and holding up her phone in my face. I just wanted to tell her to shut up and get out of the way. I needed to hear what was being said. Whatever lies Alex was in there telling, I needed to know exactly what was going on. This had changed and become something much darker. It was harassment, it was clear to me now. She was stalking me.

Cherry stopped to try and find the picture, and, in my frustration, I practically shoved her into the room. She slightly stumbled in surprise and I had to yank her back by her bag, slung around her body, to stop her falling over. We burst in through the door and there they were, stood in an odd line: Mum at the back with her arms crossed and looking really angry, Dad next, frowning, and Alex at the front, dressed in her work gear – looking right at me.

I stared back and watched as Alex let go of her bag, which thudded to the floor with an ominous crack. She did it to break the silence. It was a deliberate diversion. Everyone came to life as she bent to pick it up. Dad reached out *and put a hand on her arm*. Why was he touching her? Was that why Mum was looking so angry?

Perhaps he just liked the sound of my voice.

I remembered her taunt when she'd come to meet Dad privately, at his request. Had that gone ahead at a later date after all? Was she having a relationship with him too? I felt sick.

She lifted up the bag.

'Oh for fuck's sake!' Mum lost it. 'Look what she's done!'

I couldn't though. I was transfixed by Alex.

'I'm so sorry!' she said not breaking my gaze. Her eyes were wide, and she looked manic. 'It was an accident. I'll go. I'm sorry.'

She shoved past Cherry as she ran out of the room, violently enough to make Cherry exclaim 'hey!' in surprise as Alex bashed into her.

Mum and Cherry looked at each other in amazement; Mum shouted: 'And what the fuck was that?' before rushing after Alex.

I was torn between following them and needing to find out what had happened.

'What's going on?' I turned to Dad immediately, but he didn't admit to anything.

'Just a minute, all right?' He put his hands up. 'Your mother's having a bit of a set-to. I'll be right back.' And then he belted off down the hall.

Cherry was rubbing her arm and looking confused. 'Who was that bitch?'

I hesitated. 'She's the doctor who looked after my AstroTurf burn.' Even at that point I was still protecting Alex. I have no idea what I was thinking.

Her eyes widened. 'You know her?'

Luckily, Mum and Dad returned to the room and I was able to avoid having to say anything else.

'Those chips in the paintwork are going to need to be buffed out.' Dad looked furious now too. 'Well what do you want me to do, Chris? Phone the bloody surgery and complain about her? I can't exactly do that after what YOU did, can I?'

'The snobby cow.' I'd not seen Mum so angry in a long time. She was shaking. 'I'll chat to anyone, but the second that woman strutted in like she owned the place, I knew we'd made a mistake. And did you see her shove Cherry like that? Cherry, sweetheart, do you know that woman who was just here? She's a local doctor.'

Cherry glanced at me and then shook her head. 'No, I don't.'

'Someone tipped us off that she was very good at Botox, and we thought we'd try and get her to come and work at the new spa.' Mum snorted in disgust. 'But I wouldn't let her so much as clean my shoes now. She just pushed past you for no reason whatsoever then? How dare she?'

'Do you know her, Jonny?' Dad asked suddenly, and my heart thudded.

'Me?' I said and looked up.

'She was looking at you,' Dad said. 'Not like most women, like she'd met you before, I mean.'

Cherry crossed her arms and stared hard at me.

I cleared my throat. 'She's the doctor who patched me up after that Astro-burn. Who did you say tipped you off about her?'

'A friend of mine is a friend of hers, apparently.' Mum almost spat out the last word.

Dad wasn't listening and carried on watching me suspiciously. I felt myself starting to blush guiltily under his gaze.

'Could I have some water please, Gary?' Cherry stepped between us. 'I feel a bit faint all of a sudden.'

''Course you can, sweetheart.' Dad turned abruptly and walked over to the cupboard, getting a glass and shoving it under the filter dispenser in the fridge door. 'Ice?'

Cherry nodded gratefully. 'Thank you. Sorry for asking.'

'Don't be daft.' He handed it over to her with a smile, and she took a delicate kitten sip.

'Thank you so much.'

'You're very welcome. Jonny, get Cherry a brandy if she needs it, too. Christy, can I talk to you a second, please?' Dad beckoned Mum and walked grimly out of the door.

Cherry waited until they were out of earshot, then shoved her glass down on the side. 'OK, I got you out of that one with your dad, but you better tell me the truth. What's really going on?'

I closed my eyes for a moment. For the first time, I wondered if I should just do what she said and come clean. She'd go ballistic, but I was scared. Alex had somehow manipulated her way into my house. She had been stood here with my parents in my house. I'd seen that old movie *Fatal Attraction*. Alex's actions had become more than just reckless, they were chilling. I saw her again in my mind, shouldering Cherry violently as she left. Was that what this was about? Hurting my girlfriend? Or my family? She didn't want to share me with anyone? She wanted in on every part of my life?

'I'm not sure, but it's possible my dad might be having an affair with that woman,' I said, not entirely untruthfully. Nothing would shock me about Dr Alex Inglis any more.

Cherry gasped. 'What?'

'She's been here before. I was at home on my own and she called round saying she'd come to see Dad.'

'Urgh.' Cherry looked disgusted. 'And you ended up having to cover for him? That's so gross! Does your mum know?' Her mouth fell open. 'Do you think she came round tonight to confront your dad or something and now it's all come out?'

'I don't know, but I think maybe you better go.'

She nodded understandingly. 'Yeah, of course I will. I'm so sorry, babe. This is really shit. Call me if you need me, or if you want to come and stay at mine if it all kicks off?'

'Thanks.'

She kissed me and hurried away. I didn't feel bad for lying. Until I'd had a chance to work out exactly what Alex thought she was playing at, I'd say whatever I needed to if it meant protecting everyone from her increasingly malicious games.

*

I went off to find Mum and Dad who were in the cinema room, sat in front of the huge blank screen, talking calmly. Mum wasn't crying, and they both looked up when I walked in.

'Dad, can I ask you something, but promise not to get angry?' I said. 'That woman who was just here came round to the house when I was at home before the holidays. She said you'd told her to meet you here to talk about this Botox job.'

Dad frowned in confusion. 'No, I didn't.'

I took a deep breath. 'You're not having an affair with her, are you?'

I expected him to go nuts, and it was actually Mum who exclaimed: 'Jonathan!'

But Dad just looked at me, like he was considering something. 'No, son, I'm not. I never make mistakes when it comes to your mother.' He reached out and took Mum's hand, and I felt almost sick with relief to realise that he was telling the truth. I wondered why I'd let Alex make me doubt it.

I nodded and turned to walk out.

'Jonny?'

I looked back.

'Are you all right?' Dad said. 'There's nothing you want to tell us?'

I hesitated. 'Like what?'

'I don't know.' Dad looked at me coolly. 'Just something doesn't feel right to me. I can't put my finger on it. I might be way off the mark, it's been a long day.'

'You could tell us though, if something was bothering you.' Mum looked at me, concerned.

'Did she say anything else to you, that doctor, the day you say she came here to ask about a job?' Dad said.

I tried to push the image of us on the stairs from my mind. It made me feel dirty, and not in a good way. I didn't want to discuss that with my parents, of all people, even though events had taken a turn that was downright scaring me. 'No,' I said. 'I'm going to go and email my essay now if that's all right?'

'Oh that's good, love!' Mum brightened. 'Well done for getting that finished.' She smiled encouragingly, and I felt like an A-grade shit. She did not deserve this. Any of it.

Upstairs, I lay on my bed and wondered what the hell I should do. Alex had lost the plot and she needed to understand that this had become completely unacceptable. Coming into my house when I wasn't here, for fuck's sake?

I also knew, however, that that was exactly what she wanted: me to come running to her. She would be waiting for my reaction, craving it. I felt panicked and trapped, it was beyond claustrophobic, but she had also crossed a line by involving by my family and Cherry. I wasn't going to let her contaminate them and invade those parts of my life too.

Enough was enough.

CHAPTER 13

Dr David Harper

Sometimes a patient will come into your room and say something so unutterably ridiculous that it's quite hard not to jump to your feet, point at the door and bark crossly: 'get out of my room *now* and stop wasting my time, you bloody idiot.'

I'm thinking, for example, of the woman who complained to me that she was pregnant, despite using the vaginal ring I'd prescribed her. 'OK, some medicines can interact with it and reduce its effectiveness,' I'd said sympathetically. 'When did you put the last ring in?'

She looked at me blankly. 'What do you mean? Put it in where? I'm wearing it now.'

Then she lifted up her *sleeve.* She was wearing it round her wrist like a bracelet.

I felt much the same sense of incredulity when Day reached the middle part of his allegation. All of a sudden his account turned into sex at Alex's house, sex at his house on the stairs (no one actually has sex on the stairs in real life. I mean, honestly), sex at a hotel in Ibiza, sex with his girlfriend, sex, sex, sex – all with Day in the starring role. I didn't react, just listened gravely to this verbal dribble of a wet dream, taking notes and nodding as if I was taking him seriously.

And right up until the shag on the stairs, I had been. I had been seriously worried at first that Alex had made a heinous error of judgement; I even found myself wondering at one point if she had stolen Day's iPhone from outside the surgery, worried that it might still contain evidence of their first illicit messages, but as the whole tone of his complaint began to change, it simply stopped ringing true. I didn't recognise the Alex I know. He painted her by turns hard and demanding, then in the next breath, vulnerable and obsessive. As I listened carefully to his earnest account of how he'd had to firmly tell her it was over in Ibiza – which she'd accepted, even gamely offering him one last roll in the sack for old time's sake, because he was just *that* damn irresistible – I felt an overwhelming urge to sit back, cross my arms and raise an eyebrow. He was, I realised, projecting his own personality traits on to his imagined Alex, re-writing the story so that he got to reject her, rather than vice-versa – which was all well and good, but the only problem was Alex actually existed in real life, was a thoroughly decent person and didn't deserve to be sacrificed at the altar of Jonathan Day's narcissism.

He also carefully mentioned two more specific dates: 15 July and 7 August, both of which he would have known could be verified, and it occurred to me while he waited for me to write them both down, that if a highly intelligent individual were busily constructing a story such as this he would know how important dates tallying were. He would not – as I had casually assumed earlier – wing it. He would know that such specifics would lend weight to his account. He might possibly ring a surgery to check if said doctor was at work that day. Which he might also do if he were stalking said attractive doctor too, of course. I played with my pen thoughtfully. Not such a silly boy after all.

Ultimately, however, what gave me the gravest cause for concern in his whole account, and really caught my attention, was that Day junior – by his own admission – decided for reasons best known to himself to bring his tale of lovesick woe to our morning surgery. I found it quite hard to remind myself at that point to stay objective and not pass comment. I listened, but I also remembered how severely compromised we were that morning while the systems were down, all doing our level best to provide safe and effective care to patients in need – and doing, if I may say, a damn good job. Day gained access to Alex's room and once he was finally alone with her, he threatened her. She must have been terrified.

GPs act as the gatekeepers to the rest of the services within the NHS and with that comes great privilege, but make no mistake, genuine risk. As a doctor, you simply never know if the next person in through the door will be the person with mental health issues so severe they are about to suddenly attack you for simply saying the wrong thing.

Yes, Alex made a mistake when paralytic in Ibiza, which is regrettable and, in my opinion, totally out of character, but it does not justify Jonathan Day's response. He harassed and intimidated a dedicated doctor, for whom I have great personal respect, at her place of work. I really do find that completely unforgivable, no matter how Day attempts to excuse it.

CHAPTER 14

Jonathan Day

I drove to the surgery straight after class, in my first free period. Luckily Cherry was in History – I didn't need any complications or questions. When I arrived at the doctors, though, it was chaos. There were several people giving the receptionists proper grief. Confused, I went and sat down for a moment while I tried to work out what was happening.

'Excuse me, mate,' I said to the bloke sitting next to me, who was busily texting someone. 'Do you know what's going on?'

'They've got computer problems, everything's running really late and *they* don't know what the hell is going on.' He nodded tersely at the receptionists. 'I've been here nearly three quarters of an hour already, missed two lectures and I've still not been seen.' He went back to his screen.

I fell silent. This didn't look promising.

The bloke jiggled his leg, looked at the clock on the wall and said under his breath: 'In fact, fuck it.' He scrunched up a piece of paper he was holding into a ball, dropped it on the floor and walked out in disgust.

I watched him go, picked it up and unfolded it. It was some sort of form he'd filled out. The woman at the desk was still arguing with another patient, but just as I was deciding how best to play this, some double doors opened and another woman appeared saying loudly: 'Shahid Khan for Dr Inglis, Room 10.'

I waited, but no one got up.

She looked around and repeated: 'Shahid Khan?'

I looked down at the name on the form I was holding and realised she was calling the bloke next to me who'd given up and gone. All I had to do was get in a room with Alex. I didn't need long for what I'd come to do.

I stood up. 'Sorry, that's me. I was miles away.'

She didn't bat an eyelid. 'Room 10,' she repeated, and disappeared.

I made my way up the corridor and knocked on the almost closed door. The déjà vu wasn't even funny. It was exactly like the very first time, three months ago.

'Come in,' Alex said cheerily.

She glanced up as I walked in and, satisfyingly, looked horrified. She jumped to her feet quickly as I closed the door behind me.

'What are you doing here?'

'Not nice when someone turns up unannounced, is it?' I said. 'Although obviously you will have been hoping I'd come running after last night's little stunt, so this can't be *that* much of a surprise?'

She didn't say anything, just glanced at the door, but I was stood between it and her.

'How did you get in here? I've got a patient waiting.'

'Shahid Khan? Yeah, that's me.' I waved my scrunched-up paper.

'You gave a fake identity?' That unnerved her, I could tell. She looked genuinely frightened. 'Jonathan, you shouldn't have come here. If anyone sees you—'

'I had a row with Cherry after you left yesterday.' I spoke over her and watched carefully for a reaction to my lie – but she didn't say anything; she was busily recomposing herself again, becoming blank. 'Even my dad knew something was up.'

I waited, but she was back under control and just looked at me, impassively.

'Is that what you wanted? All of this to come out in the open? What were you playing at, worming your way into my house yesterday?' I took a step closer to her. 'Getting your friends to recommend you to my parents, then upsetting my mother and shoving my girlfriend around? Who do you think you are, Alex?' I hadn't realised quite how angry I was until that moment. 'We agreed we were over. "Have you got rid of him?" were your friend's exact words, I think?'

'Wait, Jonathan.' She held up a defensive hand. 'I had absolutely no idea you lived there. Your mother requested a home visit for medical attention.'

It took a moment for her words to sink in – I hesitated, completely confused. 'What are you talking about? Of course you knew I lived there!'

'Jonathan, I want to make it absolutely clear that my friend recommended me to your parents without my knowledge.' She spoke slowly and deliberately. 'I didn't come to see you yesterday. I'm your doctor at the practice you're registered at. There are very strict rules about that sort of thing.'

'Right, because that's bothered you up until now, the way it bothered you in your hotel room in Ibiza, in fact?' I looked at her incredulously. 'The LAST time we were going to do it, remember? Go out on a high? Ibiza 2017?'

'But I didn't know then. We were just two strangers.'

Then it dropped, and I saw what she was doing. How psycho could one person be? I had to close my eyes for a moment while I made a huge effort not to lose my cool. 'Alex, that's just not true, is it? I know you got off on that whole idea of us being strangers in Ibiza, but this isn't funny any more. You've just called me Jonathan for a start, you know exactly who I am. I've got a phone back at my house full of messages from you. Stop playing games.'

'A phone full of messages?' She looked completely confused. 'I realised that was your name when I saw it on your mother's notes this morning. Jonathan, have I seen you before? Here, I mean, as a patient?'

I stared at her in disbelief and nearly yelled with frustration. 'Alex, you need to stop this. You came to my fucking house! Have you no concept of how messed up that is?'

'Jonathan, when we met at the club, did you think I knew who you were?'

'This is not going to work,' I warned her, somehow keeping calm. 'I see what you're trying to do, but I KNOW I have not imagined this whole thing. You're playing a very sick game. *Of course* you knew who I was.'

'But I didn't. You do understand that, don't you? I *didn't* know who you were. I don't know what you mean, you've got a phone full of messages? I think it would be best if you left now, actually.'

I laughed when she said that. I couldn't help it. '*You* want *me* to leave?'

'Yes, I do. I really am very sorry, Jonathan, that you thought my coming to your house was some sort of signal, but please don't feel embarrassed. I can see it was an honest mistake.'

I stared at her, scrunched my fake form back up and put it in my pocket. 'OK, whatever. If this is how you want to make yourself feel better about the fact that it's over between us, I can live with that. Pretend whatever the hell you want. But you are NOT to come to my house again. You stay away from me, and my family, and my girlfriend, from now on. This is my official last warning to you.' I stepped right up into her face and whispered, 'or I will make you wish you really had never met me.'

My hands started tingling. I was so angry with her, the strength of it surprised me. I realised how easy it would be to just reach out and put my hands round her neck. I wanted to do it so much, I felt frightened and had to quickly spin around and bang out of the room – before I did something I'd regret even more than laying a finger on her in the first place.

*

The rage burst out of me when I got back in the car, however, and I actually did shout. I couldn't believe what she'd just had the nerve to do; stand there and barefaced act like I was having some kind of mental flip out, when *she* had been the one to creep into my house within touching reach of my parents.

I leant my head back on the headrest for a moment, exhausted by the adrenaline surge I'd experienced back in her room. I just wanted it all to go away. If only I'd not put that bloody message on her windscreen.

I drove back to school for lunchtime to find everyone messing around in the Year 12 & 13 common room.

'Hey!' Cherry was delighted to see me. 'Where have you been?' Her face clouded over with concern. 'Everything all right at home?'

I flopped down onto one of the sofas, and she got on alongside me. I didn't know what to say and sat there for a moment trying to formulate the jumble of thoughts in my head, when suddenly a football smacked me on the side of the face out of nowhere. Everyone laughed, and I know it was just the lads pissing about, they didn't mean anything by it, but it tipped me over the edge.

'For fuck's sake!' I roared, jumping up and booting it as hard as I could back at Rik, who was holding his hands up in apology. He ducked but it hit the pillar anyway and crashed down onto one of the tables, knocking over several cans of Coke and decimating two of the girls' lunches. 'Could you just all FUCK OFF!' I shouted.

A silence fell as everyone stopped what they were doing and looked at me. The only sound was the cheap school radio in the corner tinnily playing that sodding James Hype track, 'More Than Friends'.

I closed my eyes, trying to ignore the lyrics and the sudden wave of panic I was experiencing, but when I opened them again, everyone was still looking at me uncertainly, even Cherry – her mouth had fallen open in disbelief. My heart started thumping with embarrassment and anger. I grabbed my bag and banged out of the room, shoving past the Year 8 kids running down the corridor towards me, and out through the main door to the car park.

I heard my iPhone start ringing in my bag the second I'd slung it on the back seat, but I ignored it and drove off so fast I did an accidental wheel spin as I turned to drive down the hill. All of the younger boys playing out the front cheered, but their reaction barely registered with me. On autopilot I drove out of the town and along the back roads to the bunny run, turning right suddenly in front of an oncoming Lexus that blasted the horn angrily. I didn't even care. I drove too fast along the windy road, almost losing it on a bend. I was lucky that nothing was coming in the opposite direction. I pulled off into the closed farm shop car park again. There were actually a couple of cars there, just two people eating lunch in the front seats of a Peugeot and one older bloke letting a dog out of the back of a Volvo. I bounced over the potholes and stopped in front of the five-bar gate – staring at it. In the cold light of day, I couldn't believe it was so exposed. Anyone could have pulled up and seen us. A hot wave of humiliation and shame washed over me and, to my surprise, I realised I had tears in my eyes. She had used me – and she'd known it. She'd told me herself what we'd done was wrong: she was sorry, and I should stay away from her.

I jumped as a man with a dog suddenly appeared alongside the window and walked past the bonnet, glancing at me briefly. I quickly brushed the tears away and started the engine up again, reversing quickly, before turning around and re-joining the main road.

I began the drive back into town and started to think about Dad. I remembered him on the last morning of holiday – less than a week ago – smirking and patting me on the back, happily calling me a dirty little stop out, when I came back from my night at Alex's hotel. He'd been pleased as punch. I took my hand off the steering wheel and felt under my rolled-up shirt sleeve, pulling it up slightly so I could glance at my tattoo, the one Dad had come with me to get when we'd gone to Paris to watch the footie with two of his mates. A boys' weekend.

'He would have got one anyway.' He'd been completely unapologetic when Mum had spied the plaster on my arm and hit the roof. 'Better I was there to make sure it was a safe place and not some dodgy gaff where he'd have come out with a cabbage inked on his arm and Christ knows what else from dirty needles?'

The thing is, I'd not even especially wanted one in the first place. It had been his idea. I let him pressure me into doing something I didn't feel comfortable with because I didn't take control of the situation.

On impulse, I took a left-hand turn and started to drive back towards the surgery. I was going to sort this out properly, once and for all.

I parked up on the street rather than driving back into the doctor's car park, where she might see my car and refuse to come out, holding herself hostage in her consulting room. I walked down the slope and noticed her car parking space was empty. Confused, I looked around but spotted her BMW parked right at the back, out of the way, where she was obviously trying to hide from view. Well, I'd seen her.

I carried my rucksack up to the grassy bank beside it, took my coat off and sat down behind the car, out of sight – and I waited.

*

I don't know exactly how long I sat there – I did a bit of work and went on my phone, ignoring the hundred odd messages from

Cherry – but I was cold by the time Alex appeared, ready to go home. She blipped the car then jumped.

'What the hell are you doing?' she gasped. 'You scared the life out of me! You can't jump out at people like that – Jesus Christ!'

I realised suddenly how much she liked the drama. 'I didn't jump out.' I got up stiffly. 'I just want to talk to you, that's all.' I opened the passenger door and climbed in.

She opened the driver's side, her eyes wide, and said in a terrified voice: 'I need you to get out of my car *now*. Or I'm going to scream.'

My heart sank. She was determined to persist with this stranger crap. I sighed, climbed out again and walked round to her.

She moved back. 'Did you not hear what I said to you earlier? Even if I wanted to, doctors aren't allowed to have relationships with their patients. I would lose my job. I want you to leave, now. Just go home, Jonathan.'

She went to step round me and I reached up and calmly took her wrist.

Her eyes widened with fear. 'Let go of me, *now*.'

'I'm not going to hurt you. Stop being dramatic,' I retorted. 'I don't actually want to touch you ever again. But what you tried to do today when I came to see you was wrong. You know what has happened between us and how many times you initiated it. You were using me. So, I don't understand why, after we agreed to end it, you turned up at my house last night, but it's pushed this over a line for me. I told you earlier to stay away, but that's not enough. I know you'll ignore me just like all of the other times. So, I'm taking control of this now. If you contact me again, or pull any more weird stunts like last night, I will make a formal complaint about you. Everyone will know what a hands-on doctor you are, and how committed to your patients you like to be.'

She sighed wearily. 'You've got absolutely no proof of everything you just said. No one would believe you. Yes, we had sex in Ibiza, but I didn't know who you were. That's not a punishable offence. It was a one-off mistake on my part.'

I glanced up again and noticed a sharply dressed older man across the way, stood between two cars, watching us. There was something odd about the expression on his face and I realised he must know Alex, even though she had her back to him and he couldn't see her face at all. He was clearly very familiar with her.

I had an idea, and without thinking twice, I lowered my head and kissed her softly on the lips. She couldn't help but kiss me back for a moment, but then remembered where she was and pulled away.

'Oh look,' I nodded at the man, just stood there, watching us, 'I think I've just found my first witness.'

She spun round and watched the man climb into his Land Rover and drive off at pace. Her mouth fell open.

'I take it you know him?' I said, pleased.

'He's my colleague.'

I gave a sympathetic shrug. 'Oh well now, *that*'s bad luck.' Irritatingly, although I badly wanted to enjoy the personal satisfaction of a pivotal moment I'd just created out of thin air, I felt nothing at all. Just empty.

She wiped the back of her mouth in disgust, glared at me, got into her car and drove off, leaving me just standing there, alone.

But my mind suddenly felt clearer and lighter than it had for a long time. I knew that I'd begun the end. It was all going to come out, but it felt really good that I'd done something positive to stop her game playing. I walked back to my car and climbed in. I already felt a sense of relief.

I drove home, had a shower and waited for Mum and Dad to get back. I heard them come in together chattering away; Mum was laughing at something. When I went downstairs they were in the kitchen, Mum sat on one of the stools rubbing her heels and Dad pouring her glass of Friday night fizz.

'Hello bubba!' she said, her face lighting up and holding her arms open as I walked in. 'How's your day been?'

I took a deep breath. 'Mum, Dad. I've got something to tell you. That doctor who was here last night? I've been seeing her. I wanted to, at first, I was even the one who came on to her, not the other way round, but now she's gone weird and obsessed. I think she's started stalking me, and I need your help.'

*

Ruby came in later when I was in bed watching YouTube and waited while I took my headphones out.

'Hey,' she said. 'So, Mum and Dad have told me everything, like you asked them to.'

I didn't say anything, just looked down at my duvet.

'I just want to say I think you've been really brave. That woman should never, ever have abused her position of trust like this. You're doing the right thing in speaking out. She shouldn't be a doctor, it's as simple as that.'

I frowned. 'She didn't abuse me, I knew what I was doing – it's just she's gone really weird now and I don't feel safe.'

She took a deep breath. 'The thing is J, and I don't mean this to sound patronising, you can't even see that abusing you is *exactly* what she's done.'

I coloured. 'She didn't force me to do anything.' But as the words were out of my mouth, I started to think about her putting my hand under her skirt and felt uncomfortable. 'I just want her to stop stalking me. It freaked me out that she came here last night.'

'I bet it did, and I'm really sorry that I didn't notice something was going on, and that you didn't feel you could tell me. I'm here now though, J. Whenever you need me. All right?'

'Thanks.' I shifted position awkwardly. 'Are Mum and Dad OK? Mum couldn't stop crying earlier. I felt really bad.'

'She'll be fine,' Ruby said quickly. 'They both will. You don't need to worry about anyone else. We just want to help *you*.'

'I didn't want to hurt anyone.'

'You haven't,' Ruby said firmly. 'You've done nothing wrong at all. Mum said they're going to take you to the surgery on Monday morning to make a proper complaint. If you want me to come too, of course I will. I know what they can both get like when they're angry.'

'Dad's going to go off on one.' I bit my lip nervously. 'He keeps ranting about how she's abused me, but it really wasn't like that – I just want some help in making her stay away from me.'

'Of course you do, and we *will* help you.'

'It all got out of control so quickly.' I felt exhausted and, despite everything, I yawned. 'She's mental.'

'Are your sugars OK? Do you need something to eat?'

'They're fine, but thanks. I'm just tired.'

'Try and get some rest then,' Ruby suggested. 'Come and find us if you need anything and maybe turn your phone off, hey?'

I nodded obediently and did as I was told. She turned the light off too, like I was ten again. It was actually really nice to just lie there quietly listening to her and Mum walking around in their bedrooms while the sound of the TV drifted up from downstairs, where Dad was watching *X-Men*. I fell asleep quickly and for the first time in ages, didn't dream at all.

*

On Monday morning when Mum came into my room to wake me I was already staring up at the ceiling.

'Morning, bubs.' She smiled at me as she sat down on the edge of my bed, but I could see – despite her cleverly applied make-up – her eyes were still puffy from all the crying she'd been careful not to let me catch her doing since Friday night. 'Did you get much sleep?'

I nodded, and she looked relieved. 'Want to get up and come and have something to eat before we get going?'

I sighed, and she looked worried. 'You don't have to do this, sweetheart. Dad and I can go and get things started. You don't need to come if you can't face seeing her?'

I twisted my head on the pillow to look at her. 'I know what she's like, how she'll try and twist things,' I tried to explain. 'She's clever, Mum. Really devious. I don't trust her not to try and pull something I can't defend if I'm not there – she's the kind of person who comes out fighting when she's cornered. This is all my fault.' I closed my eyes. 'I should never, ever have left that note on her windscreen.'

'Hey!' Mum said sharply. '*She* should have thrown that note away and ignored it completely, which is what any normal, sane adult would have done in those circumstances. You are not to blame for her actions.'

'I just want to get on with my life. Is Dad still really angry?' I looked away.

'Not with you, Jonny. Not with you at all.' Mum reached out and picked up my hand. 'But, yes, he's very upset that she took advantage of you the way she did, and he blames himself for you having to go and see her in the first place because of your football injury.'

I exhaled again.

'We'll get through this, all of us together.' Mum reached out and took my hand. 'We're not going to let anything else happen to you, Jonny, I promise.'

*

I felt numb as the three of us climbed out of the car outside the surgery, ready to go in and make my complaint. I walked behind Mum and Dad across the car park to the main door and, for the first time, I thought about Alex's husband and her children, and I hesitated.

'You all right, love?' Mum turned back to look at me.

'I just want her to leave me alone,' I said. 'That's all. I don't want to make trouble.'

Mum stopped and came back to me. 'Jonathan, she's had chance after chance to walk away and she keeps coming back. You don't have to let her carry on hurting you just because she can't or won't see that this is wrong. You've asked her to stop, and she hasn't. That's not OK, and whatever happens now as a result of that decision on her part, is her own fault.'

Dad held out a hand. 'Come on – we've got you, Jonny. I'm going to sort this all out, I promise you.'

I followed him, and felt my stomach tighten into a knot as he pushed the glass door open with the other hand, marched into the surgery and straight up to the desk. 'I want to see the manager out here, straight away.'

The receptionist looked slightly taken aback at his tone. 'She's in meetings this morning, I'm afraid. Can I take—'

'No, you can't,' Dad cut across her. 'I don't care if she's in a conference with the Queen. You get her out here *now*.'

'Will she know what this is regarding?'

'I want to make a complaint about one of your doctors.'

'OK, well it might be our Operations Manager that you need to see, rather than Cleo. If you could just tell me what the—'

'I'm not telling you anything!' Dad started to raise his voice, and I shrank back away from him, aware that everyone in the waiting room was now staring at us. 'Just get the person in charge, down here, *now*, all right, love?'

The receptionist narrowed her eyes. 'We don't tolerate abusive behaviour in this surgery. I'll have to ask you to leave if you continue to speak to me in this aggressive manner.'

'Oh, you don't tolerate abuse? Is that right?' Dad leant forward on the desk with both hands. 'You told your doctors that? Because one of them has been abusing my son here.' He gestured back to me, and I felt my face start to burn with hot shame. I hadn't even told Cherry yet, and he'd just announced it to a whole room of strangers. 'For the last *three months.* So, don't you stand there and tell me what you will and won't condescend to deal with, just *get me your manager*!' He shouted the last bit and for a moment I thought the receptionist was going to cry. Mum was grasping my hand, as I stood there rigidly, while the room full of strangers stared and wondered what I'd been forced to let happen to me.

Before the receptionist could answer, the side doors that led up to the consulting rooms swung open, and Alex herself appeared alongside the man who had watched me kiss her in the car park on Friday night.

Dad turned and saw her too. 'There she is!' he exclaimed and pointed at Alex. 'That's the doctor who's been sexually abusing our son!'

Maybe it was hearing the words said out loud that had such an effect on Mum, or perhaps it was just the sight of Alex in the flesh, but she let go of me and rushed straight up to Alex. I thought she was going to attack her.

'Shame on you!' she hissed. 'And you came to my house? You have the brass neck to get one of your slapper friends to put you forward so you can *come into my house to get at my child*?'

'We need to calm this down.' The car park man stepped in front of Mum, looking down at her. 'This is a very serious allegation you're making here, and this isn't an appropriate—'

'*Appropriate?*' Mum rounded on him. 'Don't you dare talk to me about what's appropriate! You're supposed to be able to trust your doctor with your children. She's been preying on him for months!'

'What? No, I haven't! That's a lie!' Alex finally started to defend herself.

'So you haven't had sex with my son then?' Mum demanded.

Alex hesitated and turned to me desperately. I stared back blankly, offering her nothing, not because I was taking a leaf out of her book, but because I was terrified.

'You see!' Mum exclaimed to the rest of the room. 'She's not denying it! She can't, because it's true. Well we're not going to let you get away with this. I'm going to make sure you never get your dirty hands near another child.' She pointed firmly at Alex, who melodramatically jerked her head back in terror as if Mum was holding a knife to her forehead.

'That's enough,' the car park man said to Mum, and I realised he must be Alex's boss to be assuming charge like this. 'I've just had the police here and I'll call them again if you attempt another assault on my colleague.'

'My wife isn't the one doing the assaulting.' Dad was there like a shot. 'You *best* get us a room where we can make our complaint properly. I assume it's you who runs this place as you're acting the big billy bollocks.'

'Dad,' I said quickly. Defending me was one thing; Dad would lose it completely if anyone insulted Mum and he might well become violent. I didn't want that, for everyone's sake.

'Don't worry, son, I'm dealing with it.' Dad just held a hand up to silence me. 'She's not going to be allowed to hurt you again.'

'Yes, he's the one who runs it,' Mum answered Dad, nodding at car park man. 'He's the doctor I saw last month.'

'This is outrageous.' Alex turned to Dad. 'You're making public allegations that are completely false, and which you can't have any evidence of, because they're not true. That's slander, and I'll sue you if say another word.'

'You're threatening me?' Dad laughed in her face, and I remembered thinking they might be having an affair. Weren't they way too similar to appeal to each other? 'Did you hear that everyone? The kiddy-fiddler doctor says *she's* going to sue *me*!'

'I mean it, I'll call the police if you continue this.' Car park man was starting to get really aggressive with Dad now too. It was like watching two lions starting to prowl round each other. 'We either discuss this privately or not at all.'

'Jonathan – you know this isn't true.' Alex turned to me suddenly. 'Why are you making this up? Is it because I said I'd tell everyone you tried to blackmail me into sleeping with you?'

And there it was. My gut tightened again. I knew she'd try something… some sort of lie to point the accusations at me instead.

'Don't talk to him,' Mum rounded on her furiously; well prepared, after my warning that Alex would attempt to twist everything. 'Don't so much as look at him, love, all right?'

'Please, Alex, don't say anything more.' Even car park man was now trying to shut Alex down. 'Just go into my office and wait there, OK?'

'Jonathan?' She looked at me desperately, but I refused to engage with her, refused to let her play her games. At long last I'd finally managed to prevent her from having any more power over me, ever again.

She had no choice but to turn around to leave the room, everyone watching her. As she opened the door I heard one of the older patients tut and repeat Mum's verdict with a muttered: 'For shame!'

I felt sick with relief. They believed me.

Thank God. Everyone could see I was telling the truth.

*

Why did I choose Shahid Khan as a name? I didn't. I just picked up a form off the floor and pretended to be someone else, so I could have the opportunity to safely ask her to leave me alone. I knew she wouldn't be able to go crazy in a full surgery. That's all.

Yes, I still have the pay-as-you-go phone. I can't prove the messages on it come from her. That was kind of the point in the first place. I doubt very much she has hers any more. She's not that stupid. But my phone definitely exists. The number is 07887— call it right now if you like? It'll ring. It's genuine.

I also want to make the point she was safe from me. I had no intention of going to the surgery to hurt her. I've told the truth. What kind of person would I be to have made everything up?

What kind of person could even suggest that I had?

PART TWO

The Aftermath

CHAPTER 15

Rob

Five days after the General Medical Council began to gather their statements, the first news story appeared. As Al was still suspended and there was no detail on the Medical Practitioners Tribunal Services website about the investigation at all, it was obvious that someone directly involved had leaked the story.

Admittedly, a whole room full of patients had heard that bastard Gary Day publicly accuse my wife of 'sexually assaulting' their son, but none of them would have known anything more than that. The level of detail that appeared in the press, however, was astonishing, and Alex fell apart.

'Oh my god. Oh my god,' was all she could say, over and over again, staring at one of the articles on my laptop screen, as we both sat at the kitchen table after I'd dropped the girls off at school. She'd been sleeping so badly she was pale as anything anyway, but looking at the accompanying photo of herself in a tiny dress outside the club in Ibiza, clutching a drink – helpfully lifted from Stef's Facebook page – she went actually white. It was the first time I understood what seeing the blood drain from someone's face really meant.

'I look like an old slag, someone who does this sort of thing all the time.' She put her head in her hands and stared at herself.

'When in fact I had to buy something new to wear because I don't even own any going out clothes any more.'

'You don't look like a slag at all. You look lovely,' I said truthfully. She didn't hear me and turned instead to the headline:

40-YEAR-OLD FAMILY DOCTOR DISCIPLINED FOR AFFAIRS WITH PATIENTS IS SUSPENDED AFTER ADMITTING TO SEX IN IBIZA WITH 17-YEAR-OLD

She read aloud, then continued in disbelief;

A GP who married one of her patients after having an affair with him, has been suspended pending a full investigation into a second allegation of misconduct. Dr Alexandra Inglis, of Crowborough, East Sussex received a warning when her relationship with a married patient was anonymously reported to the GMC, but now Dr Inglis faces allegations of conducting a sexual relationship over a three-month period with a second patient, aged seventeen years old.

Jonathan Day, now eighteen years of age, has waived his right to anonymity. Day insists that while the relationship was initially consensual, after it ended, Dr Inglis encouraged Day's mother to receive a home visit for a minor medical aliment, enabling Dr Inglis to gain entry to the family home where she is said to have 'shoved' Day's girlfriend 'violently'

Alex looked up at me, horrified. 'Firstly, how about pointing out I met you eight years ago, rather than making out this all happened yesterday, plus – a three-month relationship? That's just a blatant lie, and I didn't encourage his mother to do anything of the sort or shove his stupid little girlfriend.' She scanned the rest of the article, stunned. 'They've referenced the weekend in Ibiza, David witnessing him kissing me at work, that weekend he supposedly came here, they've quoted Gary Day and there's a huge picture of *him* too.'

She pushed the laptop away from her and started to visibly shake.

'Hey!' I said, quickly moving my chair to get up and put my arm round her. 'It's OK.'

'It's not OK.' She went completely rigid at my touch and, thrown, I quickly removed my arm. 'Everyone will see this. Our families, friends, colleagues, people I barely know, complete strangers – but most of all, what about Maisie and Tilly? This is going to be there forever now. What do I say when they're old enough to find this? When their friends look at it and know what I've done?'

'But you didn't do it. Not what he says you did.'

She closed her eyes, barely moving – as if undergoing an invasive medical procedure so painful all she could do was wait for it to be over. 'I had no idea who he was. I swear.'

I didn't know what to say, and as I sat there unable to make it go away for her, or fix it, the now familiar feelings of powerlessness, rage and guilt began to burn within me. This was all my fault – and his.

'Rob.' She opened her eyes suddenly and looked at me, desperately. 'You still believe me, don't you?'

I stared at the mother of my children and the woman I had fallen in love with on sight ten years ago. 'Of course I believe you.'

And I do.

There are some messed up things that can happen in life – I'm not oblivious to the fact that some people find themselves going through truly horrendous experiences when literally the day before their lives were totally normal – but if anyone had told me Alex would one day walk in through our front door and announce that she'd been publicly accused of sexually abusing a vulnerable seventeen-year-old boy, I would have laughed. Not because it's funny, but because it is so offensively ridiculous. When it actually happened and she said the words out loud, waiting, terrified, for my reaction, I didn't even have to think about it. I got to my feet, walked over to her, and I held her while she cried.

My wife is not what you would call a shy, retiring person. She's outspoken, and what she would say is standing up for what's right, other people might describe as being bolshy. I know she can appear unlikeable. Our first landlord ended up serving notice on us after Alex got into a heated argument with him about a faulty fridge he hadn't fixed as fast as Al thought he should have. I've watched her have confrontations with restaurant, shop and hotel managers, listened to numerous draft complaint letters to the council, a window company and our bank, and not said anything when she's threatened legal action over, among other things, a pair of faulty shoes.

But my wife is also genuinely one of the kindest, most generous people I have ever met. Being a doctor, friends of hers often ask her for 'informal' advice. That can range from expecting her to diagnose their kids' rashes over the phone, to wanting her to dispense advice when they're worried their children's behavioural problems are in fact the first signs of autism. She gets texts at all hours, and I've never known her not call anyone back because she was too tired to deal with it after a long day at work. When she asks people how they are, they actually tell her. Warts and all, as well as at great length, but she always listens. If one of her friends called in the middle of the night needing her, she would go. Without question.

There aren't, however, anywhere near as many people she talks to about things that bother *her.* She would say that's because she's a private person, but it's more about her finding it hard to open up, because she doesn't feel comfortable relying on people. Her father ran up thousands of pounds worth of debt behind her mother's back, and it only came to light when he did a bunk, leaving Alex's mum to sort everything out, with Alex's help. They almost lost the house. Alex got used – fast – to having to sort things out for herself and as a result is a very competent person, who is now often mistaken for being strong to the point of invincibility. Her self-reliance can also come across as arrogance when she gets frustrated with people not doing things as fast as she could do them herself – just as her difficulty with trusting people can appear as aloofness to people who don't know her well. But she let me in. In spite of the fact that she knew how much she was risking the second we crossed the line and kissed, she overrode her instincts.

'All of my friends have warned me that if you'll cheat on your wife with me, one day you'll cheat on me too.' She'd looked up worriedly as she lay in my arms in her bed after the first time we slept together. She was understandably afraid of getting hurt as well as the risk to her career and who could blame her? I didn't think about Bella's feelings when I slept with Alex. I knew I was going to devastate Bel and I did it anyway. Bella and I were childhood sweethearts. We'd long outgrown each other and reached the point where we either split up or got married. We went the wrong way and got married. That was our only mistake.

I knew the second I met Alex that *she* was the one. She always has been, and she always will be. I explained all of that to Alex as we lay there in her bed and added: 'I will never cheat on you like this with anyone else, and I will never leave you. I promise.'

And while I know how pathetic it sounds to say I kept my promise – because when I slept with *Hannah* it was just sex and it meant less than nothing – I honestly believe it's true. I had, and still have, no feelings for Hannah whatsoever. I don't even particularly like her as a person. I made a mistake – but it's scarily easy to do.

Sorry, but it is. It's *easy* to find yourself getting pissed much too quickly when you've got kids and you never get to go out. You're overexcited to be out in a real-life pub, you start acting like you're on day release and neck drinks on the company card that you don't have the tolerance for any more. The alcohol kicks in and you start to feel invincible and reckless. You remember how funny you used to be, you're enjoying yourself immensely and everyone is having a great old time. Then someone in particular appears at your elbow, laughing and smiling up at you. She's pretty and acts like you're amazing. She touches your arm, and you jump like it's an electric shock because you don't get touched much these days. Not like that anyway.

Your wife is so tired when she comes to bed that if you turn over to hug her, she wriggles away and says she just needs five minutes peace to herself to read her book, so you wait, but you're knackered too and by the time she turns the lights off you're already pretty much asleep – which you can't help thinking was your wife's aim all along. You might try to talk to her about it for the hundredth time – tell her you want things to be different, you need to make time for each other… and she will respond that she has a really demanding job, two small children and she's 'giving' all the time. What she really wants – rather than being told her marriage is in trouble and only a shag can fix it – is to be kissed and hugged a bit more? Paid attention to? Supported?

Which is confusing and pretty fucking irritating because the last time you did all of that, you were told to get off, because she was reading.

'So maybe don't just hug or kiss me when we're in bed?' she might suggest, an edge creeping into her voice when you bring it up again while she's clearing up after tea and you're about to go and run the kids' bath.

Again, baffling. 'But that's the only time we have together. You're either at work, or we're with the kids, or one of us is at the gym.' Then one of your children will come in and announce they need a wee before your wife has the chance to answer.

So, when you are accidentally touched by this girl in the pub who thinks you're really funny and because pretty much any kind of physical contact turns you on, as she tells you a story, you will lean in a little closer to hear properly. It's much louder in the pub now, more raucous. She touches you again, this time her hand stays resting on your arm. Blood begins to pump. You can feel her warm breath on your skin and smell her perfume. You find yourself wondering what it would be like to kiss her. She says she's going outside for a smoke, and you're pissed enough now to realise you really fancy a fag, even though you gave up years ago.

Once you're standing in the warm, summer night air and dragging on the cigarette, London at night suddenly feels like a place that belongs to Bond – all glamour and shimmering possibility, rather than the late trains and limp lunchtime sandwiches of your usual daytime routine. She's chatting away as someone pushes past her on the street and accidentally knocks her into you. You reach out to catch her, shout abuse at the stranger already out of earshot, look down at her to ask if she's all right as she looks up at you wide-eyed like you actually *are* Bond, then all of a sudden you're kissing, you're in a taxi, you're pushing in through the front door of her flat, you're fumbling with clothes, gasping on the bed… and then it's over and a possibility no more – just a sickening reality. You've fucked everything up forever for one throwaway moment of physical release.

You think about your wife and kids and you shrivel away and die inside. Fully dressed and in the cab on the way home, you numbly stare at the text your wife sent you hours ago saying

Hope you have fun! Don't drink too much! xxx

and you realise you've just traded eight years of fidelity to become a man of the moment – the person you promised you would never be – a serial cheater.

But because you haven't fucked up quite enough, the following morning, you actually tell your wife what you did the night before, because you're a gutless shit who hasn't got the balls to live with the guilt of what he's done and keep his mouth shut. You want your wife to make even *this* OK. So you tell her, and you watch her heart break in front of you and no matter how many times you say you're sorry, you keep coming into a room to find her in tears. She is by turns both devastated – and furious. She goes out and gets drunk herself. In Ibiza, miles away from the hurt you've caused her – looking for some reassurance and revenge all of her own.

Once the initial shock of Alex's confession – and my confusion when she told me who he was – had worn off, I became very realistic about the impact of my behaviour on her actions. I deserved what she did in Ibiza – it was my own fault. But *she* does not deserve people telling lies about her. Especially not people who have already taken advantage of her and tried to manipulate her to their own end.

Alex stood up suddenly, interrupting my ever-deepening, drilling spiral of loathing for the Day family, wrapped her arms around herself and said: 'I think I'm going to go and have a lie down, and you've got to get on with some work anyway, so…' She glanced at the kitchen clock reading 9.05 a.m.

'Do you want me to bring you a cup of tea?'

She hesitated. 'I'll make one before I go up. Do you want one too?'

'Yes, please.' I pulled my laptop round to face me as she reached for the kettle and began to fill it.

I stared at the photo of Jonathan Day, also accompanying the news item, fixating on the now-familiar eyes staring back at mine; the foppish brown hair, faintly amused smile and clean-shaven chin. They'd lifted the shot from his Instagram feed; it was one I'd already seen. I had become obsessed with looking at the boy that had offered the open arms for my wife to fall into, laced with a very real desire to smash his fucking face in. It was a complicated mix of emotions.

I was starting to feel like I almost knew him myself, I'd now read so many social media posts of his and looked at so many photos. It wasn't that I was trying to see what had attracted Alex to him, that was blindingly obvious: youth, muscles, classic good looks – all qualities I was well aware I didn't possess any more. I was searching for answers behind that smug little smile: *why* had he told such blatant lies? What was in it for him? 'Do you think he's fallen in love with you?' I'd asked my wife.

She'd looked confused. 'I can't see that he can have, to be doing this to me?'

'You say that, but it's very successfully keeping him linked to you, isn't it? He's still part of your life – connected to you – albeit in a very messed up way.'

She shook her head. 'He started all of this because he thought I was going to tell everyone he'd tried to blackmail me into having sex with him.'

'Exactly. You'd have to be *desperate* to sleep with someone to do that. He's in love with you. Or whatever his version of that is.'

'No. He attacked to defend. He got in there first with his own far more shocking story, but it snowballed. Now, he – or just as likely his horrible parents – has spotted an even bigger opportunity: fame.'

That startled me. I hadn't considered that. Jonny boy made for an arresting photo, that's for sure, and the more papers that picked up the story, the bigger the accompanying pictures of him became. I obviously wasn't the only one who couldn't stop staring at him, but as I noticed his social media numbers beginning to soar, I realised Alex was absolutely right. Whatever his reason for starting this, Jonathan Day had now found a platform, something that was getting him noticed and making him stand out among a lot of other good-looking eighteen-year-old boys searching for a space in a crowded market. Now he'd created his fifteen minutes, he wasn't going to waste it. It became clear to me that the whole thing had become a massive publicity stunt – with him as the star and Alex collateral damage. In my much darker moments I felt a fool for having wondered if they *had* been sleeping together for three months and if that explained why Alex had stopped being interested in having sex with me? He had made even *me* momentarily wonder if she'd done it, when I KNEW Alex wasn't that person. Bottom line: her version of events made sense and was plausible. His didn't, and wasn't.

But everyone seemed to be too busy looking at him to notice.

*

On Monday, 2 October, I came back from taking Maisie and Tilly to school – Alex had not left the house since the first news item about her appeared – to find her speechlessly sat watching TV. Jonathan Day was beaming out of the screen in front of me, sat on a cosy sofa holding the hand of a simpering blonde, being interviewed by some stand-in male presenter I didn't recognise.

'What the hell is this?' I exclaimed in shock to see Day animated and talking where I was used to a static picture.

'Shhhh,' Alex instructed, and I obediently fell silent, reaching for the TV remote to turn it up.

'More and more people have contacted me telling me similar stories to my own,' he was saying. His voice was accent-less and inoffensive; middle-class quinoa bland. 'And that's why I realised it was important to do the book.'

'He's writing a book?' I said out loud, in disbelief. 'About what?'

'It's really more of a manual with practical advice sections in it,' he answered me himself. 'Things like having a backup plan for when you find yourself in a situation you're not comfortable with, and learning it's OK to say no and how to say it. The pressures we face as young people like, every day, are crazy mad and parents genuinely don't know how to help their kids with current problems.'

'What sort of problems?' interrupted the presenter.

Jonathan shrugged. 'Being stalked on social media and groomed, just for a start – and that's while we're in our own bedrooms. I just hope that because I'm actually the same age as the people the book will be aimed at, and I've had direct experience of these issues, it will make everything more accessible and maybe it will make a difference. I really hope so.'

'"Groomed"?' I repeated. 'You little fucker.'

'Hmm,' said the interviewer. 'You're not cashing in on the publicity surrounding a case that hasn't even been determined yet? You say this story of yours has hit a nerve; that you were effectively stalked by your female GP and harassed, but you've no proof that any of this actually happened, have you?'

I had no idea who this wannabe Piers Morgan was, but I could have kissed him.

'It's very rare for victims of sexual abuse to lie about it.' Day didn't even blink. 'The way you've just spoken to me is pretty much the number one reason most victims don't come forward.'

'But you've never alleged you were abused. In fact, quite the opposite; you've maintained very firmly that everything was consensual. So apart from a very pretty boy having sex with an older woman who just happened to be his GP, what's the story here? Apart from you using "your experiences" to make a lot of money?'

'Have you got a son?' Day asked the presenter directly, who nodded. 'Ok. If he came home and told you he'd had sex several times with an older woman who was in a position of trust and he didn't feel comfortable about what had happened, that he felt a real sense of shame about it, would you tell him to man up, that he should be pleased for seeing some action and stick the stripes on his arm? Or would you listen to what he had to say with as much compassion as you would offer a daughter who came home and said the exact same thing to you?'

Jesus. He was good. I began to feel very afraid for Alex.

'Look – I think if you're going to conduct media interviews where you're being paid money and doing a book for thousands of pounds, before there has been any kind of formal determination about what actually happened – and let's remember it isn't a trial because there's no question anyone has done anything illegal here – people are entitled to ask you difficult questions.' The Piers-bot turned to Jonathan's girlfriend challengingly. 'You've not once been tempted to chuck him seeing as he cheated on you, by his own admission?'

'Of course not.' She smiled at him. 'I'm really proud of Jonny for having the courage to speak out.'

'Right – and you want to be a model yourself, don't you?' He dismissed her and turned back to Jonathan. 'So to clarify, what would you say to anyone who accused you of cashing in on this story?'

'Yes!' I said, focusing intently. 'What would you say, Jonathan?'

'I've never wanted to make trouble,' Jonathan replied earnestly. 'I felt as if I had to speak out, otherwise people will keep abusing their positions of power and nothing will change. You're right, everything that happened was legally consensual, but that doesn't make it right. It was inappropriate. As I've said, I felt pressured on many occasions in a way I wasn't comfortable with. I didn't know how to stop it, and when I tried to walk away, she started appearing in my house out of nowhere. It was chilling, and—'

'Can we turn this off now, please?' Alex asked.

'Hang on a minute.' I held a hand up, trying to catch what had just been said.

She got up and quietly left the room.

'I'm aware some people have judged me unfairly based on the fact I've done some modelling in the past. Should it make a difference what Cherry—' he looked at his girlfriend 'or I do for a living? Isn't that as unacceptable as saying a woman should expect attention if she wears a short skirt?'

I hit live pause, suddenly unable to listen to another word myself, but the more I stared at his perfect, confident teenage face, full of the arrogance of a kid who didn't know his arse from his elbow in terms of real-life problems and stresses and probably couldn't care less about the damage he'd done to my family, the more I hated him.

He had fucked my wife and now he was fucking her over.

*

I went to find Alex. She was lying on our bed, in tears. I gathered her up as she sobbed properly. I felt disgusted with myself for bringing all of this down on my family. 'No one is going to believe me,' she cried into my chest. 'Not with my record, and with him saying all this stuff all over the place.'

'Of course they will.'

'I'm a doctor because I want to help people. That's all, and I'm good at it. I'm a good doctor, I *care*. I get worn down by it all, sometimes, but I'd never abuse my knowledge or position. I'm not the person they're saying I am.'

'Alex, look at me,' I said fiercely. 'You've done nothing wrong and you've nothing to hide.'

But hiding away was increasingly all she wanted to do. She would get the girls ready for school, I'd take them, then she'd go back to bed, emerging once I left to pick them up again in the afternoon. She'd do tea, baths and bed, then return to our bedroom herself. I did all of the shopping, pickups and drop offs, told my boss I might need to work at home for another couple of weeks and took the girls out on my own at the weekends to soft play and birthday parties. It was the least I could do, but by the time we hit two and a half weeks after the Days had confronted her in the surgery – in which she had not left the house once and was only speaking to Rachel and her mother, housebound herself while recovering from a hip operation – I was seriously worried. It wasn't something that could continue on a practical basis for one, I needed to go back into London for meetings, but I was also concerned that Al was becoming full-on agoraphobic.

I didn't know what else to do, and pretty much forced her to come with me on the morning school run the next morning, pointing out the more she withdrew, the guiltier she was making herself appear.

'Everyone's going to stare at me,' she'd said as she pulled on the same jeans and jumper she'd worn the day before and looked at herself in our bedroom mirror, while Maisie and Tilly ran around excitedly upstairs in their uniforms before breakfast.

'They won't. Everyone knows what he said is complete bullshit.'

She didn't say anything to that, just picked up the hairbrush and began to scrape her hair back into a ponytail. She hadn't washed it and it looked a bit grim, but I didn't say anything. I didn't care for me, but I wanted her to feel better about herself and not letting things slip was an important part of that. She didn't put on any make-up either and gripped my hand tightly as we made our way into the playground, Maisie and Tilly running ahead, thrilled to have both of us doing the drop off.

She'd been right, of course, they *had* all stared. I tried to pretend I wasn't noticing them looking, and instead smiled widely and waved hello at the parents in Maisie's year group, like everything was totally normal, as we walked over to the nursery. Most of them were polite enough to smile back, but they all darted curious glances at Al as we passed. She'd very noticeably lost weight and kept her eyes down on the ground, not making eye contact with any one.

'You need to look up,' I said under my breath, 'Hi, Paul!' I called cheerily to another Dad I knew well enough to have gone out for a few pints with on several Dads' nights out. He hesitated, glanced at Al and nodded a silent greeting before scurrying off. 'Seriously, look up,' I ordered my poor wife. 'You're acting like you did it.'

It was, of course, my own guilt that made me so hard on her. I couldn't bear that what I'd done with Hannah could have led to this: my children skipping along unawares that all of their friends' parents were looking at their mother like she was at best a slut and at worst some sort of predator.

We walked into the nursery and the busy hum of chatter noticeably stilled. Several of the teachers glanced over curiously, and poor little Tilly said proudly: 'my mummy and daddy are taking me today!' My heart almost broke.

'Aren't you a lucky girl, Tilly?' said one of them, kindly, but I felt Al's grip on my hand tighten, and she practically dragged me into the cloakroom out of the sight of prying eyes.

'Come on then, Tilly – let's get your coat off,' I said, letting go of Alex and starting to undo the zip.

'I'll put her water bottle in the box,' Maisie said helpfully, and disappeared back into the main room with it.

Alex just stood there watching and then jumped slightly as Melissa appeared in the doorway with Zach. I watched both women eye each other, and Al cleared her throat and said bravely: 'Hey Mel.'

I smiled encouragingly and waited for Melissa to say something back, but she simply stepped past Al like she wasn't there.

'Let's take your coat off, Zack!' she said cheerily.

I saw Alex frown in confusion and then glance at me.

'That's it, hang it on the hook, well done!' Melissa grinned at Zack. 'Come on then! Now, let's go and see who's here!'

She simply walked past us as if we weren't there. I watched my wife's eyes fill with tears and I went to march out after Melissa, but Al caught my sleeve.

'Don't,' she whispered. 'Let's just go.'

We kissed Tilly goodbye and walked Maisie to her classroom. There was a good deal of chatter going on because so many people were there, but somehow that made it easier for Alex to sink into the background and not need to say anything. I knew she'd be devastated by what Melissa had done. Understandably so. I was livid with the short-sighted ignorance of the woman. Whatever the hell happened to innocent until proven guilty?

'Let's go and get a coffee,' I suggested afterwards, like everything was normal, as we got back to the car.

'Don't you need to go home and start work?'

'I've got another half an hour. It's fine. Come on.' I took her hand and led her off before she could protest any more.

I spotted the photographer when we were coming out of the coffee shop. At first, I was stupid enough to think he was capturing the building behind us, and even turned to see what had caught his attention, but then I realised it was us he was focused on.

'Oi!' I shouted, from across the street, but he didn't even bother to put it down, just calmly took another snap of us, then ambled off.

Alex got straight back into bed the second we got home. I texted Rachel to ask her if she could possibly come and see her at lunchtime, but when she arrived, Al refused to see her, saying she felt as if she might be coming down with flu.

'I'm really concerned,' I admitted quietly, on the doorstep. 'She's such a strong person but because of everything that she's been through already over the last few weeks…' I wasn't prepared to gloss over what I'd done or try to discount it, and I knew without doubt Al would have told Rachel everything anyway. 'I'm terrified she's heading for some sort of proper breakdown.'

'How does it work, going to see a GP when you *are* a GP?' Rachel said quietly, glancing up the stairs.

'Doctors don't tend to tell people if they're struggling themselves. Mentally I mean. They just keep their heads down in case they're judged. Plus, technically, if they have mental health issues they're meant to notify the GMC and are investigated under the same procedures as misconduct.'

'God, really?' Rachel looked disgusted. 'No wonder it's a taboo subject. She's not – suicidal or anything?'

'No, no.' I shook my head emphatically. 'But she's very, very low. And not sleeping at all. I think that's part of the problem too; she's somehow managed to reset her natural body clock. She can't sleep at night and catches up by dozing during the day, just so she can basically function, but then isn't tired enough to sleep at bedtime and is too anxious anyway. It's a vicious cycle.'

Rachel sighed. 'It sounds like she needs something to break this new pattern.'

'I thought that as well, so we took the kids to school together this morning and one of the mothers completely blanked her, then on our way back to the car, someone took a photo of her.'

'Oh God!' Rachel exclaimed. 'That's horrible. The poor thing.'

'*He* on the other hand, seems to be enjoying his moment very much.'

Perhaps it was the naked hatred in my voice, but Rachel shifted uncomfortably, and I realised I was in danger of overstepping the mark.

'Yes, I saw him in another online piece,' she said. 'He's got a very good publicist, whoever they are. But what I really meant is it sounds like Al needs something like sleeping pills to help break this new sleep cycle.'

'Oh, I see.' I felt a bit stupid. 'Yeah, I hadn't thought of that. I'll see if I can persuade her.'

'I know her mum isn't able to come down and help, but is there any mileage in your parents coming to stay, to give a bit of a practical hand?'

I shook my head. 'I've asked Al that, but she doesn't want them in the house right now.'

Rachel nodded diplomatically. We both knew Al suffered my parents under duress, finding my mother's insistence on ironing all of my shirts as well as dusting, baking and generally reorganising, stressful at the best of times.

'Maybe just this once it needs someone to take over for a bit though?' Rachel said. 'What about a mother's help or something? There have got to be loads of agencies who supply people at short notice.'

'That's a good idea. I guess it's no different than if she was recovering from an op, or something. Perhaps that's how I should treat it. And I'll definitely see what I can sort about the sleeping pills. Thanks, Rachel. And sorry she didn't actually let you see her.'

'It's fine,' Rachel assured me as I opened the front door again for her. 'Hopefully all of the press stuff will start to settle back down in a couple of days, which will help a lot. Are you all right?' she added, and I paused, surprised. 'Er, yeah? I think so, thanks.'

'You've got someone you can talk to?'

I thought about my university mates for a moment. I'd had a couple of texts offering an ear if I needed it. Workmates were obviously out. Ditto the school dads WhatsApp group – this was all too private for that. Karl, my oldest schoolfriend and best man would fit the bill, but I couldn't actually remember the last time we'd spoken. He also now lived about two hundred miles away, and I hadn't seen him since before Tilly was born… How would I even start that conversation? 'Yes, I have,' I said, because it was easier.

'Good.' She looked relieved. 'And remember; today's news, tomorrow's fish and chip papers.'

*

I wish she'd been right about that, but unfortunately two things happened. Firstly, the picture of Al coming out of the coffee shop appeared. It was an unflattering shot of her, holding her takeout cup and seeming to frown at the photographer in disapproval. In fact, she hadn't been wearing her glasses – she's short-sighted – and was just peering over in confusion. They'd also cropped me out of the photo completely, making it look as if Al was out on her own, having a nice relaxing time of it, while suspended on full pay funded by the taxpayer. What a lovely reward for being brave enough to finally leave the house and face everyone in the playground. Alex looked at it silently – she appeared to have run out of tears – and I was gutted for her.

Then the Harvey Weinstein story broke on 5 October.

Immediately, everyone began talking about how it was a watershed moment, and that this was going to change the way women responded to sexual abuse forever.

The following day Jonathan Day uploaded a new vlog to his new YouTube channel:

> 'None of this is confined to Hollywood, this is in every area of real life too. It's also not just about women being abused by men, it's the continued abuse of power full stop that has to change. If you know what that powerlessness feels like, that shame, that sense that it was probably your fault anyway, you don't have to suffer in silence. There are people who will listen and will help. No one will laugh at you, no one will call you a liar.'

'But you are a liar,' said a voice over my shoulder.

I jumped, not realising Alex was stood behind me as I watched it on my laptop over my lunch. I paused it quickly. 'Hey! You're up! Fancy something to eat? I could make you some pasta? Or maybe a sandwich? Talking of food, shall we get a Friday night curry later, and watch a movie?'

She stared at the screen. 'How does he live with himself, exploiting other people's genuine suffering? Knowing *everything* he says, he's made up? I hate him so much.' She darted down and inspected the screen. 'Twenty thousand views? Are you fucking kidding me?'

'It's all going to die down,' I reassured her. 'The spotlight will move off him now. You've just got to hang on in there.'

'I wish *he'd* die.'

She said it so vehemently I glanced up at her in surprise. There was a moment of silence and then I cleared my throat and said: 'I've arranged for an agency girl to come over to meet Maisie and

Tilly after school, just to have a chat with me about helping us out next week, I hope that's OK?'

But Alex didn't seem to hear what I'd said. She was fixated on Jonathan Day's face, paused, with the play button under him. She reached out and clicked it so he sprang back into life.

> 'If you're not sure you've been the victim of inappropriate behaviour, ask yourself how you'd feel if it had happened to someone you love – your sister or brother maybe – instead of you. If the answer is you'd be unhappy, or angry, it was inappropriate and it shouldn't have happened. It's OK to speak out.'

'Argh!' Alex shrieked. Before I realised what was happening, she reached out and grabbed my mug of tea and hurled it at the screen as hard as she could. It shattered instantly as the whole lid almost rebounded with the impact. The hot tea arced up and splashed over the table into the keyboard and began to drip on the floor as the mug rolled off the edge and fell to the ground, smashing instantly.

'Alex!' I said incredulously. 'Stop!'

But she didn't. She reached out and shoved the laptop sideways off the table, and as the whole thing somehow landed on the floor right side up, she started *kicking* the screen with the side of her bare foot, as she stepped in among the shards of broken china on the other one.

'What are you doing?' I shouted. 'You'll hurt yourself. It's glass, Alex!'

I reached out and tried to pull her off, but she half shook free and, still screaming, tried to bend down, reaching out her fingers, attempting to pick up the screen. Terrified she was going to manage it and then throw it through the kitchen window, or hurl it at the wall, I grabbed her round the waist and with all my strength lifted her completely off the ground, away from it all. I was shocked to realise how comparatively easy it was – how light she'd become, how thin her frame felt beneath her baggy T-shirt, jumper and pyjama bottoms.

She kicked and thrashed about wildly, hammering her fists on my clasped hands, but just as quickly as it had started, she ran out of energy; her screams turned into desperate wracking sobs, and she leant back first against my shoulder, turning her face into my neck, and went completely limp. I half staggered over to the kid's sofa in the playroom part of the room, more or less completely carrying her, and we collapsed down as I held her tightly.

'This is so unfair!' she cried. 'I didn't do it! I got drunk, I had a one-night stand. That's all, and I've lost everything!'

'No, you haven't. It just feels like that.'

'Everyone's acting like I'm a dangerous, obsessive sex-offender.'

'No, no they're not.' I stroked her hair, and rocked her like I would Maisie or Tilly.

'Then where are all of my friends? Who has come to see me, or called me, apart from Rachel and David? They've sent me emojis or texts and that's it. They've ticked the box without actually having to talk to me. Who has offered me actual support? They all looked and whispered at school or ignored me completely. I have told the truth about *everything*. I KNOW the injury he first came to see me with was made slightly more unusual given he's type 1 diabetic and perhaps I should have been able to remember him on first sight in the club, but I just didn't! I was hammered. I wouldn't have noticed him as being good-looking when he came to see me about his leg. He was a schoolboy! Even if George Clooney had walked in for an appointment I wouldn't have taken any notice, because I'm *too fucking tired*! I see someone pretty much every ten minutes of every working day I'm there. Yes, that's a lot of people with a lot of very ordinary problems, but it's also a lot of really weird ones too, kids with bizarre things they've shoved up their noses and in their ears, hideous inflammations or cysts people have been too embarrassed to come and get checked out, lumps they've tried to cut out of themselves. A kid with an AstroTurf burn just isn't that memorable. That probably offends his precious little mummy's boy ego, but it's true. *I didn't notice him.* Maybe that's even part of what's pissed him off so much. He's evil. He doesn't care about ruining us, what this will do to the girls or you, never mind me. You didn't see him in the car park when he threatened me unless I slept with him again – he was totally comfortable saying it, like it was no big deal at all. And now all of this other stuff is in the news and such a hot topic he'll use that and feed off it. In this climate, no one will dare suggest he might be lying, and the GMC will be desperate to show how well *they* handle sex allegations, and they'll make an example of me. I'll get struck off and it's so, so unfair. I've done nothing wrong.'

She began to weep, finally burnt out after her lengthy tirade, and as she fell silent, I carried on stroking her hair and making calm soothing shhhh-ing noises, while trying to hide my fear, because I just hadn't realised the relentless extent to which she was chasing every dark detail round and round in her mind, like tracking a flock of ever-circling birds. It was making her ill – really ill. I could see that now.

'Sweetheart, let's take you up to bed. You're exhausted. Would you mind if I called David to come and have a look at you? I know you won't want to go and see anyone formally, but I'm sure he'd be happy to pop round as a friend. Maybe we could ask him about the sleep issues you've been having?'

'You really wouldn't mind?' she asked, so quickly that I wondered instantly if that's what she'd been hoping I'd say. 'I know you don't like him, but he's offered to help when I need it – and I do.'

'Of course I don't,' I said. The truth was, I wasn't happy about it. While he's never been anything but respectful to me, I'm not stupid and I know how he feels about my wife. You just do when someone fancies your other half, it's instinctive. But, I wanted Alex to get some proper help and feel like there was someone else on her side other than me, far more than I cared about my own feelings. 'You go up and I'll call him now, if you give me your phone?'

'It's OK. Surgery won't be finishing for another five minutes. I'll do it then.' She sighed and leant her forehead on the side of my temple for a moment. 'Thank you.'

'You don't have to thank me for anything,' I said quietly as she got to her feet stiffly and looked at the screen on the floor by the table.

'I'm so sorry I did that.'

'It's fine,' I said quickly, 'I'll sort it. At least it wasn't my work one; I was just messing around on mine over lunch. Go on, you go up and I'll bring you a sandwich in a bit.'

She nodded and left the room. I waited until I heard the creak on the top stair, then the click of our bedroom door and finally the groan of the ceiling as above my head she walked over to the bed and climbed back in. I exhaled heavily, got to my feet and walked the few steps over to the table, staring down at the mess. I have never, in all the time I've known her, seen her lose control like that. Her rage was extraordinary and terrifying. I didn't recognise her as my usually calm and controlled wife.

I looked at the now white screen with what looked like a massive black ink spot pooling beneath a gunshot in the glass. Jonathan Day had been successfully silenced and was gone.

CHAPTER 16

Rob

I saw the outline of David's body through the obscure glass side panels of the front door as I came out of the downstairs loo, and waited for him to ring the bell, but he didn't. What was he doing? I crossed my arms suspiciously. Still nothing. I frowned, walked down the hall and flung it open. He smiled warmly, completely unperturbed by my attempt at the element of surprise.

'Hello, Rob. I expect Alex has mentioned she called and asked me to pop over?'

My confusion that perhaps he *had* rung the bell and I just hadn't heard it was instantly replaced by irritation. Of course she'd mentioned it. I tried to swallow down the implication that he and Alex had decided something without me, and he was kindly letting me in on the grown-ups' plans. This was about Alex, and I had to set aside my personal feelings. Although he was still a smarmy git. I stepped to one side and gestured for him to come in.

'Hi, David, thanks so much for this. We're very grateful.'

'Not at all,' he said in surprise. 'I'm glad to help. Dreadful old day, isn't it? Feels rather like autumn has properly arrived with all this rain and the sudden drop in temperature.' He shivered.

'Can I get you a cup of tea?' I couldn't not offer him one, it would have been downright rude otherwise; although I didn't want to, because it would mean missing out on whatever they were going to start discussing while I was stuck in the kitchen making it. I moved towards the stairs to discourage him from saying yes, but he hesitated and said: 'Do you know, I'd actually love one. Thanks, Rob, that's decent of you. Do you have decaf?'

'We certainly do!'

'Excellent!' he said, equally as heartily. 'As it comes, no sugar. Thank you.' He took off his wet wax jacket, stepped past me and hung it on the end of the bannisters, adjusted the belt on his suit trousers then smiled and pointed to the first floor. 'OK to go on up and find her?'

'Of course.'

He took the stairs two at a time with his lanky legs, holding his doctor's bag, and I listened to him call out: 'Alex? You decent?'

Our bedroom door opened, and I craned to hear the low voices, but couldn't catch what was being said.

I quickly strode into the kitchen. Thankfully, the kettle had recently boiled, so I grabbed a cup, the teabag, and threw it in. I was about to pour the water on when I realised I'd used a caffeinated one. I hesitated but poured the hot water anyway. He'd manage, and I didn't much care if he didn't. When I got as far as the kitchen door I began to feel a bit pathetic for taking such a cheap shot. I stopped, swore under my breath, took it back and made a decaf after all – before hastening upstairs with it and walking in to find David sat on the end of our bed, Alex propped up on several pillows.

'Ah, excellent! Thanks so much, Rob.' He reached out to take it as I looked in surprise at Al. She'd showered, put on clean clothes and was even wearing a bit of make-up in his honour. On the one hand that was obviously encouraging, but as I glanced back at David, I wished fervently I'd kept the caff cup after all. He might actually be allergic to it. Or at the very least get the shits.

'Rob?' He raised his eyebrows. 'Shall I take it?'

I realised I was just standing there blankly like a twat and passed it over. 'Sorry. I'm a bit tired.'

'Of course you are,' he said sympathetically. 'It's a shocking time for you both. Off the record, of course, but I was just saying to Al that we've all been stunned by the media attention that Patient A – as we are required to call him, despite him outing himself publicly – has been receiving. I really no longer know what to make of this world. Anyway, Alex, this sleep situation – or rather lack of it – that we discussed on the phone earlier…' He put his tea down on our chest of drawers, unlocked his bag, reached in and pulled out a tiny envelope that he flicked over to Al, before picking up his mug again. 'Some Zopiclone for you.'

She picked it up, peered in it and said tiredly: 'oh thank you – that's great, but how did you sort this?' Her eyes widened. 'I don't want to get you into trouble? You didn't self-prescribe, did you?'

He looked embarrassed. 'No, I didn't. They're my mother's. She won't notice.'

I suppressed a smirk. Not such the big shot doctor now, handing out his elderly mum's medication.

'It's only enough for four nights and, to be honest, I'd do one tonight, one the night after and see how you feel after that. It might be all you need just to reset the clock.' He moved on quickly. 'Obviously you won't take it at all if you know a good reason that I don't, why you shouldn't, but I trust you.' He smiled at her. 'Can I also make a small suggestion? I don't know how feasible it would be, but if you had any chance of the little ones staying with granny, or a friend, tonight, it might be advisable, because these will help you get to sleep but, as you know, they won't keep you asleep. Really you want as clear a run at an uninterrupted rest as possible. But obviously that's for you to decide.' His smile slowly faded, to be replaced by an expression of doctorly concern as he took a mouthful of tea. 'Anything else been troublesome, or just mostly the sleep?'

I waited for Al to mention her earlier outburst of rage, her reluctance to leave the house, how she was barely eating, but she didn't. In fact, she didn't say anything, just looked worriedly between us.

'Oh, I'm sorry,' I said, the penny finally dropping. 'Did you want me to step out of the room?'

'Would you mind?' she said quietly. I minded very much, but I turned to leave anyway. As I got to the door, though, she suddenly blurted: 'Actually, it's OK, Rob. You don't have to.' She swallowed and admitted: 'I had a major panic attack when I went out the other day. I was in the car, driving, and suddenly I couldn't breathe. It was textbook really: sweating, nausea, my chest was hurting, then I felt like I was choking. I honestly thought I was going to die and I wasn't going to be able to pull over in time. It was horrendous—'

David frowned in sympathy.

'Hang on,' I interrupted, 'you were in the car? Where were you going? And where was I? You've not left the house apart from that one time with me to go to school?'

'Please don't be angry with me,' she pleaded. 'I was driving over to the Days' house.'

My mouth fell open in horror, and I saw David sit up a little straighter.

'I know, I know,' Al said wearily. 'This is exactly why I didn't say anything earlier. And I didn't actually go there. I was just so desperate.' She adjusted the pillow behind her. 'It's become very obvious to me as a result of everything that has happened, that society needs some way of treating people fairly and to find a system that makes sure everyone is protected, but that also doesn't ever put people who have been accused – as I have – in a position where they don't feel they have any chance at all of fighting their cause. I feel like I've been found guilty before I've had any opportunity to defend myself. The media has already made up their mind, along with all the people who have put all of those horrendous "comments" under each and every article I've seen. It's made me feel so powerless. All I wanted to do was to ask Jonathan to reconsider everything he's said. To beg him, basically, to tell the truth. I didn't see any other way of clearing my name.'

'When you say you've felt "desperate",' David said, 'do you mean suicidal?'

I caught my breath. The thought of Alex hurting herself made me feel physically sick.

'I couldn't do that to Maisie and Tilly… and Rob,' she said quickly. 'I suppose I'm only really flagging up this panic attack because, while I don't want to take any anti-anxiety drugs at the moment when I'm just about coping, that might change, and I don't want it to apparently come out nowhere if it turns out I do need to take something at a later stage.'

She blew me away. How on earth did she manage to keep putting one foot in front of the other like this? And stay so dignified with it?

David obviously thought so too, because he looked down at the duvet thoughtfully for a minute and said: 'I think you're very wise.'

'How long does it typically take the GMC to resolve complaints like this, David? Do you know?' I turned to him.

'OK, so answering as a friend hypothetically, rather than on a specific case, which I couldn't comment on,' he said, with a touch of self-importance, 'it depends how far through the process a case progresses. After a complaint is made, is goes to an investigating officer. If they decide it needs to go further, they have to gather statements from everyone, show the doctor concerned the complaint, and give the doctor a chance to respond, then collate all of the information.'

'That's where we are now,' Alex said to me.

'Then, a case goes to two examiners within the GMC, one medical, one not. They might then decide to close the case with no further action, issue a warning to the doctor, impose sanctions such as the doctor has to agree to some sort of retraining, or refer the case to the Medical Practitioners Tribunal Service. At that point they can also request an interim tribunal to suspend the doctor while the investigation continues—'

'That bit won't happen because I'm already suspended on full pay,' Alex interrupted, still explaining to me.

'Then the final stage is the medical practitioners hearing where they decide if the doctor's "fitness to practise" is impaired, and if so, what action to take.'

'Strike them off, you mean?' I said.

'Yes, or suspend the doctor. Or decide they don't need to take any action and dismiss the case.'

He turned back to Alex. 'I meant to say, I really hope you're using the Doctor's Support Service at the moment. Just speaking to another person who is a doctor themselves would be really helpful, I think.'

'You honestly thought Day might just withdraw his complaint completely if you asked him to?' I looked at Alex again, too, who gave a small nod. I thought suddenly about his vlog, how he'd encouraged people to address abuse of positions of power. The hypocrisy was breathtaking. He had all of the power, *all* of the control. And he knew it. I was suddenly so hotly consumed with anger and frustration, I could see exactly why Alex had shoved the computer off the table earlier. Had Day been stood right in front of me, I dread to think what I might have done in the heat of the moment. I understood my wife's feeling completely.

David stood up. 'I better get back.' He put his tea down again. 'Sorry, Rob, I haven't finished it. Occupational hazard I'm afraid.' He patted his jacket. 'Have I got everything? Keys? Where's my phone?' He drew it out of his inside pocket 'Ah! Got it. I'd lose my head if it wasn't screwed on.' He held onto it and picked up his bag too.

'I'm so sorry,' Alex said instantly. 'You must be swamped at the moment with doing everything yourself.'

'I'm not really. Cleo's been magnificent. We'll cope until you're back. Because you will be back. We miss you though.' He smiled, and Alex's eyes filled with tears again.

'Sorry,' she whispered. 'Just ignore me. It's just because you're being nice, that's all. I'll be fine.'

'I know you will,' he said, as, to my surprise, he leant down and kissed her briefly on the cheek. 'Bye, bye, love. Take care and shout if I can do anything else.'

Coming from him, in his well-spoken, authoritative voice, the use of the word 'love' actually sounded elegantly old-fashioned and rather beautiful in its kind sincerity. Fatherly, almost. I let my head drop quietly and felt glad I'd made him the fresh cup of tea after all. Thank goodness she knew someone else was behind her – it wasn't just me.

'Goodbye, Rob. Don't worry about coming down, I can see myself out. I will just pop to your loo on the way out, though, if that's OK?'

'Of course,' I said and, once he'd left, sat down on the end of the bed where he'd been. 'That was good of him. Are they what you need?' I nodded at the pills.

'Yes, they'll be great.' She put her finger to her lips and waited until we heard footsteps downstairs, David call cheerily: 'Bye, both!', then the click of the front door shutting.

Alex sighed deeply, leaning back on her pillows again. 'I'm exhausted. It sounds ridiculous but it's completely taken it out of me having to shower and get dressed to make it look like I'm coping and not falling apart at the seams. Pathetic, isn't it?'

I felt a little better still to hear *that's* why she'd done it, not to look good for him. 'Not at all. You ARE coping. And you'll be even better after a night's sleep.' I pointed at the little envelope lying on the duvet and came over to sit on the bed next to her, on my side. I put my left arm round her and she leant on me. I could tell she'd closed her eyes without even needing to look down at her. I let her just sit peacefully for a moment, then said tentatively 'Al, will you promise me you won't go to the Days' house, or try to contact Jonathan to ask him to change his mind, because he's not going to. You do know that, don't you?'

'Yes,' she said. 'But I felt like I had to try. Exhaust every opportunity. Like I said, I was desperate. Not desperate to see him.' She sat up quickly and urgently looked up at me. 'Oh God, you do realise that, don't you? I wasn't going to try and see him because I AM obsessed with him, like he keeps saying. I really did just want to beg him to walk away from this. But I think he's in too deep now, he's got too much to lose. I don't know what I was thinking really.' She sank back down again.

I hesitated again. 'When did you go?'

'Last week. When you went to the shops before picking up the girls.'

'On Thursday? How did you know he was going to be at home then? Wouldn't he have been at school too?'

There was a moment of silence.

'I didn't know for sure. I just hoped he would be. If he wasn't, I was going to wait until he got back. I just didn't want his parents to be there as well. I realised pretty much straight away how stupid it was though, how he'd twist it to everyone else that I'd gone to the house, and I pulled over when I began to panic about how close I'd come to making such a huge mistake.'

'OK.' I moved us on quickly before she asked me again if I believed her and began to disappear down another rabbit hole of doubt. 'Seeing as you're dressed, why don't you come downstairs? I'll light the fire and put on a movie for you. You still haven't eaten anything and you really do need to.'

She rested her head lightly on me again. 'Thank you.'

I kissed her hair. 'I need to pop out in a minute to the shops before I get the girls. Will you be all right? You won't jump in the car straight away, go off and do something completely mental?'

She snorted sadly. 'No, I won't. I promise.'

*

I climbed in the car and thought hard, for about thirty seconds, made my decision – and set off.

I'd worked out easily – from one of the many, many Instagram shots of his that I'd looked at over the previous two weeks – which school he went to from the tie he was wearing in one of the pictures. It was a pretty smart private one – surprisingly, given how Alex had described his parents to me – but then perhaps they wanted opportunities for their son they hadn't had themselves.

I parked on the road outside and walked in through the wide gates into the car park and up to the 'gatehouse reception'. A friendly looking, middle-aged woman came to the door when I rang the bell and looked at me enquiringly.

'Hello, I'm sorry to disturb you, but I've come to collect Jonathan Day's car for him? He phoned to let us know it had broken down and needed recovery from this address, but I can't reach him on his mobile now? It seems to be turned off.'

'Hmmm,' she said disapprovingly. 'That'll be because he ought to be in class. Hang on a moment, and I'll find out where he is.' She looked me briefly up and down. 'Which garage did you say you were from?'

'Kemptons,' I said, out of absolutely nowhere, then added, 'I'm just doing this to help out his dad, Gary. He's a mate.'

'I see. Would you like to take a seat?'

'Actually, I'll wait outside if that's OK, I've got a few calls to make.' I held up my phone, as if that made me the very epitome of a busy garage manager and not, in fact, a marketing account manager, very probably going to lose his job for pretending to work at home when he blatantly wasn't.

I made my way back out into the overcast afternoon, checking the time on my phone. I genuinely did need to get something for tea before picking up the girls.

I waited for another five minutes, leaning against the gate pillar, and was just starting to panic that, in fact, they'd called the police, who were on their way, and I was about to be arrested, when the main door opened and out he came.

I was momentarily transfixed to see him in real life, striding across the car park towards me, white shirt untucked and billowing, the sleeves rolled-up despite it being chilly, presumably to show off the tattoo on his arm I could just see the bottom of. He was pretty tall but not as good-looking as he looked in the papers, with rather boyish features. He was obviously just extraordinarily photogenic. I straightened up as he approached me, frowning.

'Wotcha mate,' I said smiling. Wotcha? And 'mate'? I wasn't in an episode of *Grange Hill*, for God's sake. I tried to calm down as he stopped about two feet away in front of me, and gave me a bland, but wary social smile.

'Hey. Mrs Hornsby said Dad has sent you to pick up my car?' He scratched his head. 'I've just tried him but, as usual, he isn't picking up. Sorry, but I don't know anything about this. What's wrong with it, and who are you?'

The last question managed to be both slightly dismissive and condescending. It was quite hard to remember he was only eighteen.

I held my hands wide in generous mock surrender. 'You've got me. I haven't come to get your car, and I don't know your dad.'

'I thought as much, seeing as I got a lift in with my girlfriend this morning, and my car's on the drive at home.' He put his hands in his pockets and chewed his lip thoughtfully. 'So, go on then. Who are you really?'

He'd waited to catch me out? The arrogant little toad.

'I'm from the *Daily Mail.* I wondered if you might—'

He laughed, spun round on the spot and started walking back to the school. 'Come on "mate"!' he called over his shoulder. 'You're going to have to do better than that.'

'You don't want to hear about the evidence that's come to light which suggests you've made up your story completely?'

He stopped, turned round again, hands still in pockets and stared at me. 'You're not from the *Mail.* I know that partly because my main contact there is called Sadie, and she's a lot more attractive than you, but mostly because I know exactly who you are. You're Alex's husband, aren't you?'

My muscles tensed with anxiety, fight or flight beginning to kick in, and as I stood there, my hand started to fold into a tight fist.

I saw his gaze flicker to it, and he froze. I actually saw his body go rigid.

'That's how the big boys like you solve things, isn't it?' he said. 'Well, no problem. Go for your life. A black eye will look great with a filter; proper vintage fight club. I might even take my shirt off before I post the pic. Alex will like that.'

I rushed right over to him, I couldn't help it, but although his eyes widened with fright, he just stood there, shaking. He didn't lift a hand to defend himself, and he didn't try and escape either. I got so close up into his face I could feel the heat of his body and smell his florid aftershave; it made me feel nauseous. I have never wanted to hurt anyone so much in my entire life. I wanted to burn the world around him, leave him standing on the last scrap of space and have him beg me for mercy so he knew how desperation felt.

'*Do not* talk to me about my wife.' I was furious.

'Are you going to push me around now?' he blurted. 'Threaten me unless I retract everything? Abuse me just a little bit more? Go on then. Do you know how I recognised you when we've never met? From the photos in your sitting room. Alex and I had sex there when you and your daughters went to stay with your parents that weekend.'

Ironically, it was that mention of Maisie and Tilly that saved me. I stepped back instantly, realising what it would do to them if I was arrested right there and then for GBH. Alex wouldn't cope, she was barely functioning as it was. I couldn't deprive my children of two parents. I had made an epic miscalculation.

'I don't believe you,' I said, my voice shaking. 'Alex was at home on her own that weekend, that's true. But I bet all you did was come round, hide in the dark and peer in through the windows at her without her realising, like the dirty little perv you are. Do you know what I think, Jonathan? I think you were obsessed with my wife from the second you met her when she looked after you – but that's what she's *paid* to do. She doesn't care about you, you're nothing to her. She didn't even remember who you were.' Jonathan flinched, like I actually *had* hit him, and I realised I was bang on the money. He really did have a thing for Alex.

'As for "recognising" me,' I continued 'there are plenty of pictures of me online. I'm on LinkedIn. It would take you five seconds to find out what I look like. I'm flattered that you care enough to have bothered, though.'

Day hesitated, then spat on the ground at my feet. 'Fuck you.' He turned round and began to walk away, only to stop again and call back over his shoulder. 'That's what she's *told* you, and what you want to believe. I don't blame you for that, but it doesn't change the truth. For the record, I only care about what she's done to me. I genuinely couldn't give a shit about your wife.'

'Liar!'

He glanced back at me and shrugged. 'Think what you like. I also knew it was you the second I walked out and saw your car parked on the street, by the way.' He nodded at the bumper of the BMW, just visible. 'I've been in that car a lot. If you're going to do this sort of thing, you need to get a fuckload better at it. Fast. Goodbye.'

He turned and ambled off. My moment of 'victory' had already slipped away. I'd achieved nothing.

'I'll pay you!' I shouted after him desperately. 'I'll pay you to withdraw the complaint and leave her alone. She doesn't deserve this. She's a good person.'

'I don't need it!' He laughed. 'I'm going…' he called out teasingly, and I felt the rage whirling up inside me all over again at that, as he made it all into a *joke* while pausing to briefly punch a code into a security keypad. I almost ran up behind him, saw myself grabbing around his neck and dragging him backwards, wrenching him from left to right, choking the humour out of him. But the heavy door swung open, he disappeared back into the building and it slammed shut again – leaving me breathing heavily and blinded with frustrated rage, just standing alone in the car park, like the fool I was.

*

'Do you know how guilty that makes me sound? You'll *pay* him to withdraw the allegation? What were you *thinking*?' Alex had her hands on the side of her head, fingers threaded through her hair, as she stared at me in disbelief from the bed. 'I can't believe this can be happening. After the way you and David looked at me earlier when I said I'd almost driven over to his house. You made me promise not to go near him again, and then you go out the very same afternoon *to his school* to threaten him?' She picked up a magazine next to her and flung it across the room so suddenly I jumped. 'What if they've got security cameras filming the car park? What if he's audio-recorded you on his phone without you realising? You've just GIVEN him his next burst of publicity! You stupid idiot!'

'All right, calm down.' I put my hands up. 'I just—'

'Calm down?' She raised her voice; her eyes were wild and unblinking as she glared at me. She looked deranged with anger.

'I get that I've fucked up, but please, shhh!' I begged. 'The girls are downstairs watching *Paw Patrol*, I don't want them to hear you like this.'

'Then don't do irredeemably insane things like this that make me want to kill you.' She actually shook both her fists at me. She'd gone white. 'I'm so angry!' she gasped in disbelief.

I was completely taken aback by her reaction. 'I was trying to help. I wanted to go there and ask him to reconsider, instead of you doing it,' I said quietly, 'so that you'd know you HAD tried everything, without actually placing yourself at risk. I just did it without thinking.'

'Isn't that exactly what got us into this mess in the first place?' she shot back immediately. 'You acting without thinking?'

Wow. I just stood there, not sure what to say to that, as she collapsed back onto the pillow again, exhausted.

'I think David might have had a good idea earlier – I'll take the kids to Mum's tonight if that's OK? I've already cancelled the agency girl coming,' I said after a moment's silence. 'You've had a really difficult day, I get that. You're overwhelmed with stress, you've literally not slept in God knows how long, and tonight's the first night you're going to take a sleeping pill. Like he said, let's try and make this a success and clear the decks so you haven't got any little voices calling out in the night and disturbing you.' Plus, I thought privately, your behaviour today has been at best unpredictable, and you're really starting to scare me.

I didn't want Maisie and Tilly around Alex when she was like this. She had done so well at keeping things as normal as possible for them, but it was clear she had reached a tipping point, needed space to rest, and the opportunity to pull herself back from the edge. 'I'll give them tea, pack them a little bag, drive them over and come straight back. Mum would love it – she's already offered a million times. I'll go back and get them tomorrow, after you've rested.'

Alex was staring out of the window. 'It might be best.' Her voice was flat again, as if she'd simply given up. 'At the very least they're sensing our tension, and it's not fair to them. They've done nothing wrong.'

'Agreed. Well, that's settled then. I'll go and call Mum.' I felt relieved and turned to leave the room, as she said suddenly: 'I was serious earlier. I want to kill him, Rob. My daughters are going to think the very worst of me forever. This will change the way they feel about me for the rest of their lives, and *it is not fair*. If I could do it and not get caught, I would.' She looked at me, frightened. 'And I'm a doctor. I'm supposed to protect life.' She held out a hand to me desperately. 'What is happening to me?'

'You are very, very tired. You are suffering from extreme stress.' I repeated it again, went straight over, took her hand and sat down on the bed in front of her. 'These are normal feelings. I wanted to kill him earlier too. He said some stuff about you that…'

She tensed. 'What sort of stuff?'

I hesitated. 'That he was going to post a picture with his shirt off, because he knew you'd like it.'

She looked disgusted and shuddered.

'I honestly think this is all about his feelings for you. He's used to getting what he wants. I could see that.'

'You might be right.' She shifted uncomfortably. 'I'd be lying if I said it hadn't crossed my mind. I'm sorry he said things to deliberately upset you. Sometimes I think it can be harder to watch someone you love suffer than go through it yourself.'

'It's wasn't great, no…' I agreed, thinking for a moment about Jonathan stood in front of me, amused, as he waited for me to hang myself and admit, like a total amateur, I wasn't who I'd pretended to be.

'You do still love me, Rob… don't you?'

'Of course I do. He has no remorse about what he's done at all, you know,' I said suddenly. 'It was… quite an eye-opener for me. He's not going to have any problem lying to a tribunal if there's a hearing.'

'Which there will be,' she said. 'He'll love that. It will offer no end of credibility to his nasty little book. Do you think we could get away with it?' She turned her head back, looked at me and smiled sadly.

'What, killing him?' I shrugged. 'I'd do it and get caught if today's performance is anything to go by. I think my behaviour over the last few weeks has firmly established you're the brains in this relationship, but I'll have a go if you like?'

She snorted. 'Thanks.'

'Or I'll just cover for you. Bonnie and Clyde.'

'They robbed banks; they weren't assassins.'

'You see?' I squeezed her hand, dropped it and stood up. 'Like I said, you're the brains of this outfit.' I looked down at her and felt a sudden rush of love. 'We will get through this, Al. I promise you. We'll do whatever it takes to defend your reputation, and our girls WILL know that they have the most amazing mother in the world.' I meant every single word.

She started to tear up again. 'I'm just so frightened that this has become the perfect storm now, what with all of the other stuff that's appearing in the news. What if no one believes me and this never goes away?'

'It will. I promise.'

She nodded but it was obvious she was just agreeing to stop me talking. She'd had enough. 'I'll come down in a minute and sit with them before you take them to your mum's, once I've sorted myself out a bit.'

'Sure,' I said, reaching the door. 'But only if you feel up to it. They know you're not going anywhere, Al. Don't worry. They're fine. Just fine.'

'DADDY!' yelled Maisie up the stairs. 'That *Paw Patrol* has finished. Can you come and put another one on, or can we have a *PJ Masks*?'

'Coming!' I shouted back. 'See?' I looked at Al in what I hoped was a reassuring way. 'They're happy as anything. Really, they are.'

She nodded, whispered 'thank you' and closed her eyes again, but her brow remained furrowed like she was still in pain.

I watched her for a moment more, quietly left the room and gently closed the door behind me.

*

When I arrived back from Mum and Dad's the house was dark and still.

Maisie and Tilly had understandably been a bit unsettled and overexcited, so I'd stayed to read their stories. I texted Alex to let her know I'd have a cup of tea with my parents and hit the road at eight. I wanted to get straight back to her, but I couldn't leave without a quick catch up at least.

'Alex isn't coping any better then?' Mum asked, sipping at her cup delicately in their immaculate sitting room. Everything was ordered and comfortingly just where it had always been. I could smell they'd had a casserole or something for dinner, although the evidence had been washed-up, dried up and the draining board forensically wiped down, to return the kitchen to the gleaming showroom cleanliness it had proudly shone with when we'd arrived. I wanted to lie on the sofa myself, watch some mindless telly, then stagger up to my old room and go to sleep. I knew Mum would be only too delighted if I asked. I imagined her getting some of Dad's clean, ironed and folded pyjamas out of the airing cupboard for me to borrow and sighed wistfully.

'She's not doing great, to be honest, Mum.' I took a mouthful of my tea. 'Actually, that's not true. Given the circumstances she's coping brilliantly. She's been publicly accused of something heinous, she's suspended from the work she loves and has no idea yet when all of this is going to be over. I'd be in pieces if I were her, and that's before you consider she's doing all of this on top of chronic insomnia. She's still getting up every morning to see the girls off, and getting up every evening when they get home, so it all feels normal for them, but I really, really hope she'll get some rest tonight.' I didn't mention the pills. I knew Alex wouldn't want me to. She'd see it as an invasion of privacy and God knows she'd had enough of that already.

'Fingers crossed,' Mum agreed. 'I'll say a prayer for her.'

'Righto,' I said doubtfully, and Mum frowned.

'Robert!'

'I'm not criticising.' I held a hand up. 'I'll take whatever positivity we can get right now. Seriously though, thanks so much for having Maisie and Tilly. This way Al gets the best crack at a whole, undisturbed night, and that might be all she needs to break this messed-up sleep pattern she's got herself into.'

'We can keep the girls as long as you like tomorrow?' Mum offered. 'Another night even, if you want? They're such good, dear little things.'

'They are. Thank you for making a fuss of them. That's just what they need.'

'We're going to make an apple pie tomorrow!' Mum revealed. 'We'll save you some.'

'Sounds lovely.' I drained my tea and, catching sight of the carriage clock, got up. 'Ten past already – I better go, sorry.'

Dad looked at his watch. 'Well, you've missed the worst of the Friday night rush now in any case. It should only take you forty minutes, you'll be back by nine. Although there are works at the crossroads. I'd go via the Tesco's roundabout instead if I were you. I can shave as much as five minutes off, usually, by doing that.' He stood up stiffly, and I hugged him, almost overcome with sudden affection for them both. It had been an emotional day. 'Thanks, Dad. I'll try that.' I planted a kiss on his cheek.

'Well done, son,' he said, hugging me back and giving me a kiss. 'Very well done. This too shall pass, just remember that.'

I whispered it to myself in the car over and over again as I drove back home.

This too shall pass.

This will all become a distant memory. We will reach a point where we no longer think about this even most of the time, never mind all of the time. It felt impossible to believe, somehow.

*

I felt a little strange as I let myself back into the house, switched the hall light on and quietly shut the front door behind me. It occurred to me that I hadn't eaten a thing since lunchtime, and that was probably why. I wondered if it was too late to get a takeaway after all?

I crept over to the stairs and padded softly up to check if Al was awake and wanted one too – but when I reached our bedroom the door was closed, with a note sellotaped to it:

> Taken pill. Hopefully will sleep till morning. OK for you to sleep in spare room? Love you x

That answered that about the curry then. I tiptoed back downstairs, wandered into the sitting room and sat down on the sofa in the dark for a moment.

'*Do you know how I recognise you when we've never met? From the photos in your sitting room, which Alex and I had sex in when you went to stay with your parents that weekend…*' I heard his mocking tone from earlier, closed my eyes and forced him away. Jonathan Day was not going to bother me any more tonight. I wanted him silent.

Impulsively, I got up and went to get a curry after all. It wasn't until I arrived back at home clutching the plastic bag containing the two foil containers, a paper bag with the rest of the poppadums I'd managed not to eat on the way back, and a larger bag containing a garlic naan, that I noticed the BMW was missing. For a moment I panicked. Where had Alex gone? She'd said she'd taken a pill! I was about to rush into the house, go upstairs and open the door, when I remembered just in time that I had actually put the BMW in the garage myself earlier, intending to give it a hoover in the morning because it was filthy inside. I felt ill at how close I'd come to barging in on her and ruining it all. I had to sit back in the car for a moment and try to gather myself. Funny the things your mind decides are important when you are completely overwhelmed with stress. I simply couldn't believe I had forgotten I'd done it. Even then, I had to check I was right, I doubted my own sanity that much. To my relief, it was there, where it was supposed to be.

I went to retrieve my food, found a beer and plonked in front of a Gerard Butler movie, watching him liberate the entire White House single-handedly from a terrorist attack. I dozed on the sofa then crawled off to bed in the spare room at about half eleven, falling instantly and deeply asleep.

*

When I woke up, I was slightly confused to find it light and that it was already quarter past seven. The luxury of a lie-in. No small voices shouting 'my clock is yellow!' No trying to grab another five minutes while they watched the iPad at full volume sandwiched between Alex and me in our bed. I turned over with a happy sigh to go back to sleep, but then wondered if perhaps I ought to go and check on Alex, see if she'd woken up yet.

But when I reached the door, it was still closed with the note on it. I decided I'd take her some breakfast at eight and glanced back at the spare room, considering getting some more rest myself, only I couldn't somehow bring myself to do it now that I was up. I decided to go for a run instead – and, brightening at the thought of some fresh air and five minutes to myself, I went off happily to find my running gear, leaving Alex to sleep a little longer.

CHAPTER 17

Cherry

When Jonny came back into class just before the last bell, something was badly wrong. I tried to get his attention, mouthing 'what was that about?', but he totally ignored me, keeping his eyes straight to the front.

When we were finally dismissed, I was all 'Hey! Hello?' as everyone started packing up, and he was forced to look at me, but he didn't say anything.

'Where did you go, halfway through?' I got to my feet and walked over to his table.

He was shoving his stuff into his rucksack. 'Some bloke turned up pretending that he'd come to collect my car, that Dad had asked him to.'

'But I picked you up this morning? Your car isn't here.'

'Yes, I *know* that,' Jonny snapped.

'All right.' I frowned. 'So who was he really then, this man?'

'A journalist.'

'Oooh.' I brightened. 'From where?'

'I don't want to talk about it. I'm going to message Mum to come and get me. See you later.'

He put his bag on his back and I think he was just going to walk away. It was super awkward for a moment, but I cooled it down.

'Jonny, you don't need to do that. I said I'd take you back.'

He sighed, closed his eyes for a moment, then suddenly opened them again. 'Fine, but I want to leave now.' He started walking out of the room before I had time to answer. I grabbed my own stuff and went after him. He didn't say a word as we walked down to the car, even though some of the others said: 'Bye, JDay' and 'See you later?' He just nodded, not smiling, and they gave me a wtf? look. I just had to shrug, and mouth 'Sorry', practically having to frickin' *trot* behind him to try and keep up as he marched off, getting ever further in front of me with his crazy spider legs.

'Jonny, can you slow down?' I called behind him. 'My skirt is actually too tight to walk this fast?'

He stopped, and waited pointedly for me to catch up, but then instantly strode off again the second I was alongside him. I watched him bomb towards the car and began to feel pissed off. I flicked a V sign at his back and paused to decide how I was going to play this.

He was waiting on Bertie's passenger side when I arrived, having deliberately slowed down to take my time. I was prepared to help and listen. What I was *not* going to do was be a mug. He could NOT walk all over me. I blipped Bertie open and watched Jonny sling his bag on the back seat, and fold himself in. He wasn't designed for small three-door cars. I got in myself and started Bertie up, checking my phone last of all. Alice had sent me a GIF. It was hilarious, and I tried to send one back, but my stupid phone kept crashing.

'This heap of shit!' I pressed the screen repeatedly. 'Time for an UPGRADE!' I sang, finally getting it to work, as Jonny exploded next to me.

'Will you just drive the car, please?'

I turned to him in astonishment, my phone still in hand. 'Literally, what is wrong with you? Are you getting hypo? Do you need a snack?'

'No, I am not "getting hypo". What's wrong with *you*? You've started the car. So why are you sat here on your PHONE sending some pointless message to Alice?'

'OK, Dad,' I said – and at that, he suddenly flung the door open and started climbing out.

'Where are you going now?' I sighed. He could be such a little bitch.

'I'm going to walk home. I need some peace.'

I wrinkled my nose. 'Walk? Are you crazy? It'll take ages and—' I checked my phone again, 'it's like four already? We're meant to be at Alice's around eight?'

'Yeah, and I'm going to flake tonight, so it doesn't matter.' He tried to yank his bag back through the small gap between the side of the passenger seat headrest and the door, but it got stuck. 'Fuck – this – shit!' he exclaimed as he tussled with it, then really pulled when it still wouldn't give.

'Hey! Be careful!' I exclaimed. 'You'll hurt Bertie!'

He turned to me and gave me one of his ice stares. 'It's a *car*.'

'No, she's not. Alberta is my baby.' I stroked the steering wheel.

He let the bag go, and it thudded back onto the seat as he put his hands on his head and looked at me wide-eyed. 'I just can't do this any more.'

'OK – unnecessary drama.' I raised an eyebrow. 'I'll just flip the seat forward if you get out of the way?'

'No – I mean I can't do *this* any more. I want us to split up. I'm sorry, Cherry.'

I froze. 'You're finishing with me? For real?'

'Yeah. I am. I should have done this ages ago.'

Tears sprung to my eyes. 'Because of me, or because of *her*?'

'Because of everything!' he shouted, making me jump. 'Everyone wants a piece of me, everyone is looking, everyone has something to say. Everywhere I go this whole thing is following me. I can't escape!'

'Don't shout at me!' I yelled back. 'And I thought that's what you wanted anyway, to get attention to all of this, and you.'

He sighed and then collapsed back down on the seat awkwardly, facing backwards this time with his legs stretching out of the open door beside him. 'I'm not dealing with things well. You know that. Everyone knows it. I just need some space at the moment. I'm feeling very overwhelmed.'

I started to shiver; the door was open but I felt cold from *inside* as I tried to process what he'd just said. He was ending it. This was actually happening, and it was tragic. 'But I want to help you and support you through this. I love you.' Just like always, he didn't say it back. He'd only ever said it to me once, when he'd not had anything to eat, got completely off his face at Ol's and I was truly out of my mind with terror that he was *actually going to die* because none of us could find his pen.

'I know you love me,' he said, suddenly miserable, 'but you shouldn't. I'm not worth it.'

'That's not true. What she did to you…' I trailed off for a moment as I tried to find the right words. It was really hard knowing what to say. Instead I reached out very slowly, took his hand and just held it. But that was kind of stressy too, not knowing if he wanted to be touched, or if I would make him feel all invaded – but like, if I didn't touch him, would he think I didn't want to because he was in some way dirty? Which wasn't true at all. It was really confusing. He looked so sad though. I wished I'd let him call his mum.

I'd known for a while, obviously, that he had *something* to tell me. At Ol's party, when he turned up really late – his sister was having some kind of crisis and he'd needed to be there for her – he was actually totally wired. He wouldn't tell me what was wrong with Ruby, only that it was personal to her. I didn't say anything to him, but I saw Ruby in town the next morning coming out of Costa as I was going into Fenwick, and she didn't exactly look like she'd been having a meltdown the night before. In fact, she was with a new bloke; holding his hand and laughing. Where ever he *had* been, it wasn't with his sister. Dr Bitch said she was in her house alone all night and that Jonny drove to her house to watch her from outside like some sad perv. While that might have explained why he was 'excited', that's not exactly Jonny's style. Just look at him. He doesn't exactly need to window lick. That's pretty obvious.

Anyway, after I got back from holiday we had a really great three weeks; some beautiful moments. We drove Bertie to Brighton, we talked about when we were going to launch our YouTube channel – Jonny said he was investigating ways to give our profiles a real upswing, fast. Everything was really, really good. It was so hot one day, we just lay on my bed in each other's arms next to the open window and listened to the birds singing, and when he kissed me, I was completely happy. I took a selfie – no filters – just lying there together, holding each other. It's my favourite picture of us.

But then he came back from Ibiza. I had planned everything for when he walked into my room. I was wearing this really cute little dungaree playsuit I'd found in this vintage store – it was so retro but really hot, not actual denim, but dyed really deep blue, and just straps going up over my tits. Once Mum and Dad were out at the pub, I took my top off underneath it and wore it like that. It just about covered my nipples. I heard him let himself in and when he appeared holding some Marc Jacobs he'd bought me, I knew instantly he'd slept with someone else. I don't know how, I just did. I'm very gifted with awareness. He was smiling, and his body language was all the same as usual, but there was nothing in his eyes. I went up to him straight away and kissed him, put his arms around my waist, and he *hesitated*.

'It's good to see you!' I'd smiled. 'I missed you!'

'I missed you too.'

'Still love me?' I teased.

'What can I say?' he said, playing our usual game and, inside, I screamed, for the millionth time.

'You can say "I love you",' I replied.

'You know I do.'

But that's not actually saying it. School was DOA after that. He was just vacant. Everyone noticed and was asking me what was wrong with him – it was quite a lot of pressure actually, because I had no idea what to say. I didn't know anything more than they did, which hurt. It actually makes me sick now to think that the Thursday when we went to his house and SHE was there having some kind of scene with his parents it was *Jonny* that she was sleeping with, and not his dad, like Jonny tried to make out. When she pushed past me, I was just surprised. Now I wish I'd shoved the slag back.

I think his crisis moment came when he got smacked in the face with a football, at lunchtime, the next day, in front of everyone. He went batshit. It was beyond embarrassing. He was so mad. I'd never seen him like that before. He gets moody, of course, and sometimes when his sugars are low you could kill him, he's that much of an asshole, but this was a whole new level of crazy. It was obvious by then that something was really, seriously wrong. *Now* I know that he'd been over to see her at the surgery, to beg her to leave him alone, and that's why he was so stressed, but as it was, I just let him slam out of school. I'm not going to lie, I was starting to re-consider our narrative, but then he called me and asked me to come over. His dad let me in when I arrived – he was really subdued too, not himself at all. He's usually over the top and just that little bit too hugsy for your boyfriend's father, but he just said Jonny was up in his room, and when I got to the top of the stairs he called out: 'Cherry?'

I looked back down, almost frightened by what he was going to say.

'Try and understand, OK?'

I nodded, although I had no idea what he was talking about unless Jonny had actually told his *dad* he was going to finish with me, which was going to be really fucking shit if it was true.

Jonny was sat on his bed when I went in and he asked me to come and sit next to him. He told me the doctor who had shoved me in his kitchen hadn't been there to confront his dad, *he* had slept with her – in Ibiza.

'Her?' I just stared at him. 'But she's so *old*.'

It got worse, a hundred times worse. He told me everything. All the stuff that everyone knows now that was in the papers. I cried. I didn't know what to do with what I felt about her. I still don't.

*

I squeezed his hand again. He was just staring into space, and we were both getting colder and colder sitting there in the car with the door half open.

'Come on,' I said. 'Let me just drive you home and you can dump me after that.' I tried to make a joke of it, but he didn't laugh, just sighed again, pulled back his hand, turned round to face the right way and swung his legs back in.

'Thanks.'

As we drove back, the new Sam Smith song came on, 'Too Good at Goodbyes'. I tensed and tried so hard to keep it together, but as I listened to the words, I wasn't imagining that I was saying them to Jonny, I heard him in my head saying them to her. Was he even mine any more? Had she damaged him so much it had broken us?

I swallowed but I couldn't help the tears streaming down my face.

He looked back across at me, tutted impatiently, and muttered 'for fuck's sake, Cherry', then leant forward and changed the station, flipping around until he found Taylor Swift's 'Look What You Made Me Do'.

'There you go. Perfect. You can #squad power-emote to this instead,' he said and returned to staring back out of the window.

It was legitimately the rudest thing he'd maybe ever said to me. We pulled up at some lights and I turned and stared at him in disbelief. *Power-emote*? 'Just who do you think you are?'

'Cha-ching!' He sighed, like I was that predictable.

'I'm serious, Jonny. I've done nothing but try to help you and support you for the last two and a half weeks.'

'You must be exhausted,' he said, looking out of the window. 'It's so tough to be you.'

'Hey!' I said. 'You say you feel it's following you, but you're *letting* yourself become more and more obsessed by it all – you keep vlogging and posting about it. It's like it's eating you up from the inside out. You can't give her this much power. And I HAVE been there for you, for the record.'

He turned very slowly and looked at me. 'Yeah, it must have been a real pain in the arse to have to come on national TV and watch your own social media numbers soar.'

'That was NOT why I was doing it. I did it to support you.'

The car behind us honked. The lights had changed, and as I pulled away I sniffed.

'Oh God, stop *crying* about it.' Jonny glanced across and rolled his eyes. 'You don't even understand any of this, Cherry. It's not your fault. But you really don't. Trust me. I'm sorry for what I just said about why you were with me when I did that TV thing, I know that's not true. All I want is to try and get something good to come of this; use it to help other people, because what's happened has been so wrong. So messed up.'

'I know it has,' I said.

He shook his head, exhaustedly. 'No, you don't. That's exactly what I mean. You don't know what I'm talking about at all.'

We drove out towards his house, but as we were about to turn left, he suddenly said, 'can you go down towards Sainsbury's before we go back?'

I did as I was told. Anything to delay the *actual moment* of leaving him for the last time at his house. We reached the roundabout.

'You know what?' he said. 'I've changed my mind. Can we go out to the forest and just drive a bit? I want to clear my head. Take the second exit… that means you need to be in the other lane. Cherry! Watch out! There's a woman about to step out!' he raised his voice in alarm.

'Don't shout at me!' I shrieked as I swerved round this stupid bitch in the middle of the road – frozen and staring at me, all wide-eyed. 'She shouldn't be looking down at her phone while she's crossing the road!'

'No, it's this dumb electric car, you can't hear it coming. It's fucking dangerous,' retorted Jonny. 'Especially with you driving it.'

'Can I actually do anything right any more?' I demanded but carried on out towards Eridge.

'OK, OK – I'm sorry. Calm down. It *is* dangerous though.'

'I had the noise sensor on, OK? You have to switch it off if you want it to be totally silent, and I didn't. It was her fault for being a dick and wandering out into the road without looking.' We reached the bunny run and I indicated to go left, but he shook his head.

'No – turn right here.'

I had to break at the last minute and some asshole in a lorry behind us leant on his horn, properly freaking me out as he, like, *thundered* past us. I'd almost totally had enough. I was a shaky mess and breathing fast as we drove into the forest, but Jonny didn't say a thing, just stared out of the window. I glanced at him. He honestly just wanted a pretty drive? Seriously?

'Slow down a bit,' he said after a moment of my grumpily wondering if I was allowed to speak while he 'cleared his head'.

We approached a bend – but as we went round it wasn't even tight. I opened my mouth to say I really wasn't that bad a driver, but he was concentrating on a house to our left.

'Slower – please,' he added as an afterthought.

I was almost crawling past. It was just an ordinary house. A car outside, gate shut. Then I saw a figure moving around upstairs at the window. A woman.

It was *her*.

My mouth dropped open. This was where she lived? She wasn't looking at us, and disappeared out of sight, walking into another room.

Jonny sat back heavily in the seat as I drove off in shock, staring out of his window. I was trying to think of what to say, when he blurted: 'I hate her for making me feel this way.'

'I know you do, baby. I hate her too.' I suddenly felt bad for not being more supportive. 'But why are we even here? We—'

'Her husband came to the school this afternoon,' Jonny interrupted. 'It wasn't a journalist. It was him. He threatened me. I was going to tell her, but I've changed my mind.'

My eyes widened. 'He threatened you? Then we definitely shouldn't be here! You do need to tell someone, but—'

Jonny half smiled. 'Someone? I'm going to tell *everyone* what he did.' He looked back over his shoulder. The house had gone. 'Just not quite yet. I want to go home now, please.' We didn't say another word the rest of the way back. No wonder he'd been so whacked out all afternoon. I couldn't believe her husband had come to school. What had this doctor done to all these men? When we finally pulled up at his, only his silver Golf was sat on the drive.

I turned to him. 'Well I'll see you then.' This was it, we were over. The next time I saw him he wouldn't be my boyfriend any more. I wouldn't be allowed to just walk up to him and kiss or hug him. I imagined us at opposite ends of the room, everyone whispering, wanting to know what was going on. I felt totally overwhelmed.

He was staring at his house. 'Just come in.'

'What?' My eyes had filled with tears and I wiped them away quickly. 'You are literally insane. I thought when we left you said—'

'I know, I know. I don't want to be on my own at the moment. My head starts going crazy.' He leant forward and tapped the side of it. 'I don't want to think any more. I just want to go in and watch some crap telly for a bit. Please come in?'

'OK,' I said quickly, before he changed his mind.

I made us both a hot chocolate, and we padded upstairs to his room. I love his house, it's exactly the kind of place I'd like to own one day. My mother would say it's tacky, and it is a bit, because it's all white, really deep soft carpets, candles and twinkly lights, but I also think it's amazing. Angel trotted in after us and we lay on his bed watching *The Inbetweeners*.

His parents got back at about half five. 'Hello my darlings!' I heard his mum call up the stairs. 'We're back! Want a drink or anything?'

'No thanks,' Jonny shouted back, as I adjusted position next to him, and he moved his arm round me to get more comfortable. I snuggled down into his chest, Angel nestled between us.

Moments later Christy appeared in the doorway and smiled at us fondly. 'Ah! Hello you lot.' Angel sat up and wagged her tail. 'Had a good day?'

I didn't know what to say to that, so I looked up at Jonny and he shrugged. 'It's been OK. Glad it's the end of the week.'

'Me too! You stopping for tea, Cherry?' Christy smiled at me.

Again I looked up at Jonny.

''Course,' he shrugged. 'If you want to.'

'Then yes, please, Christy.' I smiled back at her.

'Lovely. I'll go and start putting it on. You out tonight, Jonny?'

'Not sure yet,' Jonny replied. 'See how I feel in a bit. I'm a bit tired.'

Christy frowned. 'Your sugars all right?'

He rolled his eyes. 'See you in a bit, Mum.'

She stuck out her tongue. 'Come on, Angel, I'm not wanted. You come and keep me company in the kitchen.' Angel dutifully trotted off with her and they went downstairs.

It was so nice, just lying there in his arms watching TV and hearing the pots and pans as his mum started to cook below us. I felt totally comforted, and I hope he did too.

*

Christy and Gary had finished their glass of 'Friday fizz' when they called us down to dinner at quarter past six; although Gary wasn't looking like he'd had the best of days either when we walked into the room, still dressed in a shirt, tie and smart trousers.

'Hello, sweetheart.' He looked up at me as he sifted through some post and forced a brisk smile, which vanished almost immediately. 'All right, Jonny?' he added. He was on edge, I could tell.

'Yes, thanks.' Jonny was just as short back.

We sat down at the table in our usual places and Jonny got his pen out. I looked away as he lifted his shirt to inject his short-acting shot. I have no clue how he does it so many times a day. I couldn't. I'd have to be one of those people with a paid nurse who follow them around all the time, or something. Christy was fiddling around with some plates and getting some bits out of the fridge. The boys were on one side, Gary opposite me, with a place set at the end for Ruby.

'Where IS Rubes?' Gary said sharply, nodding at it.

'Running late. Bit of work to finish off.' Christy came over and put a plate of prosciutto, chorizo, hummus and pitta strips in front of me, and then Jonny.

Gary nodded approvingly. 'Good girl, staying until the job's done even though it's Friday night. That's the kind of work ethic that gets people noticed.'

I saw Jonny glance at him sideways and my heart sank. It was going to be one of *those* sorts of meals. Christy obviously thought so too, because she put a plate down in front of Gary and said brightly: 'We're going fancy tonight. I've done a starter! Tapas-styley!'

Jonny didn't say anything, just picked up his fork and began to eat silently.

'Good day then, kids?' said Gary to me and Jonny.

I looked at Jonny, who didn't answer.

Gary looked annoyed, glanced at Christy and cleared his throat. 'I said, good day?' He twisted to Jonny.

'Not really, no. Alex Inglis's husband came to school this afternoon. He nearly hit me, then offered to pay me to change my story.'

'*What?*' Gary exploded furiously as, simultaneously, Christy dropped her fork, which clattered to her plate, making me jump. 'Why didn't you tell us?'

Jonny frowned. 'I'm telling you now.'

'I mean earlier!' Christy exclaimed. 'We've been home for nearly an hour!'

Jonny shrugged. 'I handled it. It was no big deal.'

Gary stared at him in disbelief. 'You *handled it*? He came to your school and threatened you, but you *handled it*?'

'Can you stop saying it like that?' Jonny looked at him.

'Should we call the police?' Christy looked at Gary worriedly.

'Hello?' Jonny waved at her. 'I'm right here. I'm eighteen now, Mum. If I want to call the police, I will. I'm thinking about it, but can we drop it for a minute, please?'

'Did he so much as lay a finger on you?' Gary's voice was ominously low.

Jonny closed his eyes briefly. 'No, Dad, he didn't.'

'Well, that's something at least. Fine. We'll talk about this more after dinner then.' Gary began to eat, but we'd only managed another couple of mouthfuls when he started up again.

'It must have been one of them days all round. I was just telling Mum before you came in,' he pulled his chair in a little tighter, 'we've had a couple of our receptionists come forward and make complaints about two of the gym staff today. Seems everyone's ready to speak out now!'

I watched Christy pause, mid mouthful. 'I thought we weren't going to mention this?' She looked at Gary carefully.

'Nah, I'm getting sick of things I'm not allowed to talk about. It's good to talk. Good that other people have been given the courage to step forward, isn't it?' He turned slightly in his chair again, addressing Jonny directly. He tried to make it sound light, but he was getting ready for a takedown. Fact.

Jonny just swallowed his mouthful, and Gary was forced to turn back to his setting.

'Well, I think it is anyway. You do have to ask yourself where it's going to stop though. Is every single bloke going to be too scared to make a move on a girl at the office Christmas party this year in case he gets the sack for 'inappropriate behaviour?'

Jonny started pushing some chorizo around his plate thoughtfully with his fork. He was biting the bait, I could tell.

'But it *is* a good thing, of course it is,' Gary repeated. 'I've seen so much stuff coming out about how things that were acceptable ten or twenty years ago just aren't now, and that's right.'

Jonny put the fork down, turned his chair to face Gary full on, widening his legs, leaning forward and resting his elbows on his knees and clasping his hands together. It was weirdly aggressive somehow, even though it was supposed to be relaxed. 'It's never been acceptable, Dad. That's the point. There was no "culture" that was different then. If anyone – like your gym staff – still doesn't know the difference between flirting and sexual harassment, then that's really scary and they need to ask themselves some serious questions.'

'Thanks for that,' Gary said. 'Now turn back to the table and sit up properly.'

'Both of you, stop it now,' Christy said warningly.

'I had some woman come up to me today too, giving me grief about something you've put online – it being about men too, not just women,' Gary continued as Jonny turned back to the table and picked up a bit of pitta, dipping it in some hummus. 'She was going on about how men even want to be the best at this. "You can't even let us have abuse," she said.' Gary made his voice all pretend-high, squeaky and outraged.

'Well men *do* get abused too,' Jonny said.

'Not often by women though. You've got to admit that.'

Jonny tossed the pitta back down on his plate. 'What are you actually trying to say, Dad? You're embarrassed and ashamed of me? Well, we all know that already. Perhaps you've had a doughnut and not done your hundred press-ups today; maybe that's why you're so pissy? Or is what's really frying your arse that *I'm* the one getting the – unwanted – attention now, rather than my old man?'

Gary moved so fast I didn't see it coming. He shot sideways, grabbing Jonny by the front of his shirt, but high up round the neck, pulling him out of his chair to his feet, before shoving him up against the kitchen cupboards.

'What did you just say to me?' He roared into his face, his fist still full of shirt 'What did you just say, you little *runt*?'

Jonny looked down at him, terrified, right on tiptoes and his fingertips - trying to steady his balance by bracing them on the work surface, where Gary was pushing him so hard. Angel was barking like crazy, and Christy had already rushed over to them by the time I was on my feet too.

'Put him down, Gary!' she gasped, trying to reach over the top of them and break Gary's clasp, but he kept staring up at Jonny, his eyes had gone small and black. He looked like a pig.

'You don't get to speak to me like that, *ever*, d'you hear?' Bits of white spit had gathered in the corners of his mouth. He gave Jonny one last shove then released him.

Jonny bolted from the room, and I went after him, running up the stairs as fast as I could to his bedroom.

I didn't know how to process what I'd just seen. I was so shocked. Is it possible to humiliate your son more than doing that in front of his girlfriend? I don't think so. It was brutal.

I pushed open the door to Jonny's room and went in. Jonny was pacing up and down, his eyes were full of tears.

'I should have hit him,' he said. 'I should have hit the bastard.'

'I'm so sorry I didn't say anything.' I was stunned. I knew Gary had always been tough on Jonny, that they rubbed each other up the wrong way, but I'd never seen him force Jonny down like that before.

'I hate him. My whole life, he couldn't have made me more aware of how disappointed he is – but at the same time, he's jealous of me. I can't help being *younger* than him. I can't help being ill. I hate him so much. He's nothing but a bully – that's how he's got to where he is today. He stamps on people like they're insects and smiles at everyone else while he does it.' He reached into his back pocket and pulled out his iPhone, tapping in his passcode and holding it up to his ear.

'Who are you phoning?'

'Ol. To see if I can go and stay at his for a bit.'

'Don't be daft,' said a voice behind me. 'You're not going anywhere.'

I jumped and turned to see Christy standing there holding a plate of mains, looking shocked. I moved out of the way awkwardly and sat down on the bed, but she didn't even look at me.

'Put your phone down. You need to eat something. You only had a few bites of starter.'

'I don't bloody want it, Mum!' Jonny exclaimed. 'Stop trying to control me. I'll eat when I want to eat!'

She stood her ground. 'Hang up, please. We need to talk, Jonathan.' She took a step back, holding the door open with her free hand.

'I've got nothing to say to him.'

'Your dad's downstairs. *I* want to talk to you. Now.'

'For fuck's sake!' Jonny exclaimed, throwing the phone on the bed and pushing past her into the hall.

She let the door drop closed, and from the mumbling I could hear, they were obviously having 'words'.

I glanced across at his iPhone and picked it up. It was still unlocked, and I nosily clicked on photos looking to see what ones he had of me. There weren't that many full stop, seeing as he'd not had his new phone for long. I quickly scrolled through the thumbnail shots and, in among the selfies, I found several identical pictures of me asleep in bed, my hair spread out over a pillow, face to one side. Smiling, I clicked on one of them to get a better look – but as it upsized, I realised it wasn't me. It was her. Again. Her at the window, now on his phone… I felt the sick actually come up into my mouth.

I stared at the image hard: she had some white sheet tucked round her, but her shoulders were bare and all tanned. I peered closer – it was natural. You can't fake colour like that. She was abroad, in a hotel room, and I was looking at a post-sex picture. No question. I swallowed. He'd only kept it to prove they *had* slept together, hadn't he?

The voices were starting to rise on the other side of the door; I hesitated, but looked some more. As I studied it, I realised she was out of it. Like, practically comatose, and the harder I focused, the more… I don't know – creepy? – it became. The only time I've ever taken pictures of people sleeping is when they've got their mouth wide open and they're dribbling, or something funny. There was nothing LOL about this picture. She looked almost dead. I threw the phone back down on the bed feeling dizzy with shock and jealousy.

Seconds later, the door flung open and Jonny burst back in. 'How many times? *I don't want the food!*'

Christy was still standing there behind him, holding it.

'Please, Mum,' he begged. 'Just take it away.'

Christy didn't say anything, just finally turned and did as he asked.

I stood up, moving over to him so I could take his hand, but he shook me off.

'Can you just go, please?' I realised he was *crying*. 'I'm OK, but I want you to leave. I don't want you to be here while this is all happening, and I don't want you to see me like this.'

I didn't want to force him to let me stay. I moved to the door. 'Come and sleep at mine tonight, if you want?' I said suddenly. 'For as long as you want – you could move in with us if you like? Mum wouldn't mind.'

'Thanks,' he said, not able to meet my eye, as he furiously wiped his own. 'I'll message you later.'

'Your dad shouldn't have done that, Jonny. He should be supporting you.'

Jonny snorted bitterly. 'You'd think, wouldn't you?'

'You're not a bad person.'

He lifted his head up quickly but, as he stared right at me, his eyes went all wide. 'Shit,' he whispered. 'You're right. I'm just like him. I didn't stop myself either.'

I was confused. *Stop himself doing what?*

He'd started staring into space. 'Please, Cherry, just go.'

But I kept seeing the photo in my head, so I carried on. 'People do dumb things, but that doesn't make you a bad person. Whatever it is, you can tell me, Jonny.'

He focused right back on me again. It was like he was looking into my *soul* or something. 'You'd hate me if you knew what I've let happen.'

I swallowed. I wouldn't, would I? I shook my head. 'Promise.'

But he must have seen I was scared, because I watched him shut back down again. I had messed it up.

'There's nothing to tell.' He shrugged blankly. 'Forget I said anything. I'm a state tonight. It's better if you all just leave me the fuck alone, to be honest.'

I gave up and reached for the door. 'I love you.'

'What can I say?' He looked at me desperately and our ritual didn't seem so cute any more.

'Say you love me,' I whispered.

'You know I do.' His voice was toneless.

I can't lie, I kind of wanted to go – the atmosphere was beyond toxic, and I needed to start getting ready for Alice's, but I should have stayed. I think for the rest of my life, I will see him pushed up against that wall and know that's what it looks like when you break someone who ought to be able to trust you – and you damage their sense of self so badly they won't ever be able to recover.

I ran downstairs and was putting my shoes on in the hall when I looked up to see Gary through the gap of the door, sitting in his study. I straightened up quickly to leave, but the movement caught his eye. He got to his feet, came to the doorway and leant on the frame as I picked up my bag. I tensed and waited as he looked at me.

'I'm sorry about what happened at dinner, sweetheart.' He tried a smile, but I could tell he was still angry. 'I was upset. Christy always says I handle things badly.'

I looked around for Jonny's mum, but she was nowhere to be seen. It was just the two of us.

'I'm just trying to look out for Jonny,' Gary continued. 'Whatever he thinks. I don't always show it right, but what that woman has done to my son really offends me.'

That, I understood. 'I know where she lives,' I blurted, and Gary's smile faded as he straightened up. 'That doctor, I mean. And her husband. Obviously.'

Gary's gaze darted up the empty hall, then back to me. 'Go on, babe. I'm listening,' he said softly.

*

Once I was back at home getting ready, I wished I hadn't told Gary anything, although a part of me liked the idea of him storming round there and giving them what for. *She* definitely deserved it – but then a text from Jonny pinged through which made me feel instantly better. Until I read it.

> Still at home. Don't worry about me. Probably come over later to Alice's but I'll call first. Cheers.

Cheers? I sat down on my bed and tried not to cry again. We were so over. I'd lost him. I wasn't sorry at all then that I'd told Gary how to find her.

I called Jonny again later to see what he'd decided about coming out, but he didn't pick up, so at about quarter to eight I drove back over to his house on my way to the party. I couldn't help myself. I needed to see him again and was prepared to use any excuse. I was only a couple of minutes away when another text pinged in from him. I pulled over quickly. It said he'd decided to stay at home and would catch up with me in the morning.

He wanted to *stay at home* after what had happened when he'd been so desperate to leave he'd been phoning Ol? What?

I paused and sent him the kissing, heart and boy and girl holding hands emoji. Then I waited in the dark, just sat in the driver's seat going nowhere, for him to send something back. He always texted back.

But nothing happened.

He'd gone.

CHAPTER 18

Rob

I began to pick up speed as I neared the house again, going for the sprint finish. My lungs were about to explode, I could feel every muscle, sinew and tendon straining to the max as the lactic acid build up began to take over… and I couldn't do it. Hitting the wall, I gave up and stopped, panting heavily, hands resting on the front of my burning thighs and clouds of breath surrounding me. Bloody kids. I couldn't sleep past seven a.m. any more but was too out of shape to maximise the gold-dust opportunity of a Saturday morning run. The paradox of parenthood had struck again.

I started to walk the last bit, chest still heaving as I breathed the mushroomy dampness in the air and glanced at raindrops clinging to browning leaves. I wiped the sweat from my face and enjoyed the stillness of the quiet woods – but then the birds began to scatter in the trees above, flying away, chattering anxiously as I heard the distant wail of sirens approaching from behind me. I glanced over my shoulder and stepped on to the verge as not one, but *three* police cars and an ambulance, lights flashing, shot past so fast I was covered in a fine mist of wet spray from the road and bits of grit and twig. I blinked and wiped my eyes in confusion, as it dawned on me that they were, of course, heading in the direction of our house.

Alex.

My panic was as physical as the sensation of falling just before sleep, and my body jolted into action. I started to run, fire tearing through my muscles instantly, but this time I didn't stop. I should have checked her before I left. Why didn't I do that? She'd told me she was desperate, and I left her to take sleeping pills, alone. Was I mad? Was I fucking MAD?

'No!' I gasped desperately, rounding the corner expecting to see the cars surrounding the cottage, the police breaking in – but there it was, just as I'd left it forty minutes earlier. No sign of any activity at all. I hurtled to the gate and shoved it open, before fumbling with my keys in the door and crashing up the stairs. I flung open the door to our bedroom, to see her lying on her side, still under the duvet, looking at her phone.

'You're all right!' I exclaimed as the door smacked into the wardrobe. 'Oh, thank God.'

She lifted her head up. 'What on earth's the matter? You look like you're about to have a heart attack.' She looked at my feet. 'You're also treading mud everywhere.'

I glanced down in confusion. She was right.

'Sorry,' I said automatically. 'I thought you were—' I was forced to stop and bend over to rest my hands on my thighs. I literally couldn't catch my breath and thought I was about to be sick, or collapse. Maybe she was right and I *was* having a heart attack.

'You thought I was what?'

'I don't even know really.' I straightened up as I tried to calm down. 'I was just – I saw three police cars and an ambulance go past in this direction, lights blaring. I was coming back from a run. I just – panicked.'

'You thought I'd done something silly?'

'Yes – no… I don't know!'

'I would never do that to you and the girls. Ever.' She sat up properly, put her phone down on the mattress, and for the first time since it had all happened, she smiled properly at me. 'I actually feel great. I slept and it was amazing. I took the pill, closed my eyes and thought "Well this is rubbish, nothing's happening" opened them again and it was *ten hours later*!'

'Wow!' I said weakly, starting to take off my trainers. She was right – I'd made a right mess everywhere. 'That's impressive.'

'Yes – and also very scary,' she said. 'You can see how people get addicted.' She rolled over, sat up, and the open envelope tumbled out of a duvet crease. It was empty.

'Alex, how many of those did you take last night?' I stared at it.

'Just one, honestly – stop worrying. I've left another for tonight, but I flushed the other two down the loo when I woke up. It was amazing to just pass out like that, but genuinely very unnerving, plus I've got this horrible metallic taste in my mouth that feels like I'm chewing on filings every time I so much as take a sip of water. I don't want to take them again after this evening, and I definitely don't want the girls finding them by mistake and popping one, given they're just loose. Last night and tonight will be enough to reset me, I'm sure. I feel much better already, actually.'

She did look considerably more relaxed, but otherwise still pretty ropey. I took a deep breath again and smiled at her, determined to hold on to the positives. She'd slept all the night through.

'That's great. I'll go and have a quick shower, then do you want something to eat?'

She threw back the cover. 'It's OK, I'll make something for you. And then I thought maybe I could come with you to get the girls if that's all right?'

I stared at her. She appeared to have more energy than she'd had for days. 'Of course. Mum and Dad would love to see you.'

She smiled. 'Let's go after breakfast then. We better check the roads, I guess, if there's been a big accident. We might have to go the back way. They really need to do something about how fast people come up that hill when traffic is trying to turn onto it from Bunny Lane.'

'They do,' I agreed. 'You really do seem much brighter today, Al. That's great.'

She hesitated. 'I feel calmer really, not so overwhelmed and desperate. Nothing's changed, obviously – but it's so much harder to cope with things rationally when you're severely sleep deprived too. And I've been thinking... the most important thing to me is making sure that Maisie and Tilly aren't affected by any of this. They need to see me coping normally and, from now on, that's what they're going to get.'

I scratched my head. 'But you were doing that anyway.'

'I mean taking them to school, going out at weekends as a family. Not allowing myself to be distracted by his social media stuff. I refuse to let him ruin every single part of my life until this is resolved and everyone realises he has, in fact, been lying from the word go.'

She sounded determined – and I felt encouraged. Optimistic, even.

'Sounds great to me.'

'Good.' She hesitated. 'Listen, on the subject of *him*, something happened last night while you were at your mum's. Gary Day came over.'

I froze. 'What? Here?'

'Yes. Just after seven. David was just leaving and—'

'Sorry, wait—' I couldn't keep up. 'What was *David* doing here again?'

'He'd called in to pick up his mobile phone; he left it in the downstairs loo by mistake when he came at lunchtime,' she explained patiently. 'Thank God he did, otherwise I'd have been here on my own when Day rocked up.'

'So what happened?'

'I'd lost the bloody pills upstairs, David came up to help me look – worried that I was making it up and going to ask him for more, I expect – we found them, came back downstairs and the door went. I opened it and Gary was just standing there.'

'You were upstairs with David?' I tried to keep my voice calm and even.

She gave me a look. 'Don't. That's exactly what Gary Day said. I opened the door, David was stood next to me – and he said: "well this is cosy. Hubby not in then, I take it?"'

I clenched my jaw but said nothing.

'He's so disgusting,' Alex said vehemently. 'I replied no, you weren't in and would he mind explaining what he thought he was doing, coming to our house? He told me it was very simple. If either you or me go near his son again, he won't be reporting us to anyone else, he'll be sorting us out himself. He was calm – not ranty and out of control like he was in the surgery that morning – which was actually more unnerving, somehow.' She shuddered. 'Anyway, then David said: "just so we're clear, you're happy that I've just witnessed you say that?" To which Day replied – and I quote – "I couldn't give a flying fuck". He wished us a "happy night in" and left. David stayed for another half an hour after that. He offered to stay longer but I said you'd be back for nine. I took the sleeping pill, he left and I went to bed.'

'You took a sleeping pill, in the house, on your own, when Gary Day had turned up out of the blue and had a go at you?' I was incredulous.

She frowned, confused. 'It wasn't pleasant, but [illegible] I wasn't afraid. You *had* been to his son's school, it wasn't completely unjustified.' She shrugged helplessly.

'I said sorry for that.'

'Yes, I know. What I mean is, I can see it from his point of view, that's all. I'd have reported you to the police, to be honest, so…' She shrugged, looking tired again. 'Anyway, I just thought you ought to know.'

'Well of course I should *know*—' I began, but she was already looking at the clock.

'We should get a move on. You put the kettle on, I'll be right down.'

Dismissed, I turned to leave the room.

'Rob?'

I looked back over my shoulder.

'I wasn't having a go, then. I really was just telling you what happened. I actually want to say thank you for your support – practical and emotional. I wouldn't be doing this without you.' She realised what she'd said and coloured instantly, 'I mean—'

'I know what you mean, it's OK,' I said quickly. 'And you're welcome.'

Gary Day had been to our house and spoken to my wife. I was furious with myself for putting her at risk and actually I *was* glad that David had been here too. The thought of her being alone in the house and answering the door to that opportunistic, nasty piece of work made me feel as frightened as he'd intended.

*

'Don't slip on those leaves,' I nodded, walking back from opening the gate, as she picked her way over to the Qashqai an hour later. 'I need to sweep them all up later when it's dried out a bit.'

She breathed the air deeply. 'I love the way it smells in the forest when it's been raining like this; pine cones and bracken, all cleansed. It reminds me of walks with Mum and Dad when I was little. They'd make up stories about fairies living in the tree trunks, then we'd go home to tea in front of the fire and watch *The Muppets*. Maybe that's why this place appealed to me so much.' She nodded at the cottage. 'I've never thought about that before.'

We got into the car and I started the engine. 'I think people are subconsciously drawn to architectural styles of houses that they were happiest in as a child,' I said, pulling away. 'Which is what sold it for me here – rather than just the setting.'

'Hmmm,' she pondered. 'Maybe. I *have* always had a weird thing about townhouses – people being either side of you. You might be right. Anyway, do you want me to close the gate?'

'Leave it,' I said. 'Saves a job on the way back. I checked and there's no report of traffic problems, so we'll just go the usual way, I think.'

We carried on up the road, falling into a companionable silence, then turned the bend. Immediately on my right I saw the police cars from earlier, parked up in the Forestry Commission clearing. The place was swarming with uniformed officers and people in high visibility jackets, while a silver Golf was being placed onto some sort of recovery truck.

'Shit!' I exclaimed, and as we passed I saw an officer look up from talking to a man with a dog on a lead before noting something down. I slowed instinctively and glanced back briefly to see, within the trees, the flash of a large white tent.

'Oh my god!' Alex said next to me.

'I know,' I said carrying on. 'It looks like they've found a body. That's why they put up tents like that, isn't it?'

We turned the corner again and the circus disappeared from sight.

'Do you think we ought to go back?' I said. 'They'll only come knocking on the door later, won't they? Ask if we saw anything?'

'No!' Alex said so quickly that I glanced at her. She had gone utterly rigid in her seat and was staring dead ahead.

'Are you all right?' I glanced at her again. 'Do you need me to stop the car?'

'Please, just keep going!' she begged. Then she began to whisper: 'No, no, no…' under her breath.

Worried, I opened my mouth to ask her what on earth was—

'That was his car!' she blurted. 'That silver Golf.'

A cold, greasy fear engulfed me. 'Jonathan's, you mean?'

She nodded, terrified. 'I recognise it. I almost drove into it the day I was trying to get away from their house, when his mother offered me that job and I argued with them.'

'You're sure?' I said.

'Yes. I am. He's got a wanky personalised plate. J05THN.' She was starting to breath faster as we pulled up at the busy crossroads, traffic thundering past us, left and right. 'What's happened? What's he done now? He was blogging, or vlogging, whatever you call it, left, right and centre. He was *enjoying* this too much to have done something stupid.'

I put my hand out on her lap. 'Try to calm down.' I looked up and noticed in the rear-view mirror that one of the police cars was there. 'Look, I've got to concentrate for a minute: they're behind us. Let me get across the road, I'll pull over, and we'll talk.'

'What do you mean, "they're behind us"? A police car?' She whipped round in panic. 'Do you think they're following us?'

'Of course not! Please, just be quiet a minute so I can do this?' I looked both ways and pulled out over both lines of traffic to turn right.

'Are they still there?' Alex asked as we continued up the road.

I looked. 'No, they've gone.'

She exhaled so deeply it was as if she'd just finished a race and placed a hand on her stomach.

'Are you having another panic attack?' I looked at her. 'What do I do? Do you need me to stop? Shall we pull over and get you some water at the garage?'

'Yes,' she said faintly. 'Yes, please.'

I put my foot down and pulled in sharply onto the busy forecourt, dumping the car by one of the pumps. I climbed out and ran into the shop, grabbing a bottle of still water. By the time I'd almost reached the front of the queue, the jobsworth fifty-something assistant was already on the tannoy.

'Lady in the Qashqai, can you please stop using your mobile phone and wait until you're off the forecourt, as per the warning on the pump right next to you? Thank you.' She clicked it off and said pissily to the bloke she was serving. 'They always think the rules don't apply to them – and it's always a "really important call".'

'That's my wife, thanks!' I called out furiously. 'And phones don't actually spark fires on forecourts. Only a moron would still think that.'

Everyone turned to look at me for a moment, and the assistant shouted back warningly: 'I don't make the rules, Sir, but it's my job to enforce them. We also don't tolerate abusive or threatening behaviour against staff? So I'll thank you to lower your tone and not insult me?'

I stared at her in disbelief as she gave me a smug, fat smile and everyone went back to waiting. When it was my turn, I fixed her with a fierce glare the whole way through, arms crossed, but said nothing. I knew she'd be desperate to have any excuse to refuse to serve me from behind her crappy plastic screen. She stared at me when she handed back my card, and I almost said something, but changed my mind, hurrying back out to Alex instead. There were more important things at hand.

I passed her the bottle, put my seatbelt on and pulled away. 'Who were you phoning?'

'David, to see if he knows anything – if the police have contacted him yet. They haven't.'

'Why would they contact him?'

'To get Jonathan's medical records.'

'If it's even him?' I looked at her sideways again. 'I really think you need to try and relax. We don't know anything for sure, Alex. There are a lot of silver Golfs.'

'Not with that number plate. It's him. I know it is. And like you said, they only put up tents like that when they're protecting forensic evidence. Don't you see what this means? They're going to think I had something to do with this.'

I swerved slightly. 'Why on earth would they think that?'

'Because it's happened on our doorstep! Because he publicly accused me of harassing him. Because everyone knows we had a relationship and now he's dead!'

'You don't know that!' I raised my voice.

'I was at home alone last night. I took a sleeping pill and went to bed – no one is going to believe that if something really bad has happened to him. I've just asked David to say he stayed with me until just before 9 p.m. because I was in a bit of a state after Gary Day's unpleasant visit, which isn't a total lie. In fact, it's good that he saw David. It proves David was there.'

'But why are you going to say he was there longer than he actually was?'

'Because I need an alibi.'

My mouth fell open. 'You're not serious? An alibi for what?'

'Whatever Jonathan's done in the woods. Don't worry, I've been very careful about it. David doesn't live anywhere with CCTV on the roads, his mother was out until half nine and you were home by, what, 9 p.m?'

'I went straight back out for a takeaway though.' I struggled to think. 'I was back home by half nine too? Maybe a tiny bit later. I'm not exactly sure. I'd be on the takeaway security camera though; but Alex, this is crazy. What do you think you need to?—'

'OK, so I was "alone" for, at most, ten minutes in between David leaving and you coming home,' she interrupted impatiently, 'and then for another separate half an hour while you were getting your food. That's not enough time to do anything.'

'Do what?' I was genuinely confused.

'Kill him.'

I swung round in shock.

'Keep your eyes on the road,' she said.

I did as I was told and blinked several times while I tried to think what to say next. 'You're worried the police are going to think you've killed Jonathan?' I managed eventually.

'People don't just die in the woods,' she said quietly. 'Whatever he's done, they are going to consider foul play and I have to be prepared. Rob, I know I talked about killing him yesterday. I even said: "if I could do it and not get caught, I would". But please know that I have got nothing to do with this. I *would* be caught, that's the whole point. They would lock me away from Maisie and Tilly forever. I would never risk that. Although the real point here is, of course, I couldn't kill anyone.'

'I've never said you could.'

'I know, but you didn't actually see me when you got back, did you? You just saw a note on the door that said I'd taken a pill and could you sleep in the spare room?'

God – she was right. I realised I had caught my breath.

'Obviously I *was* there,' she said carefully, watching me, 'but that second of doubt you just had? Everyone is going to have that multiplied by a million, because they're not my husband who loves me and knows I would never do that – and *that's* why I need an alibi.'

I pulled over suddenly, making the car behind us break heavily and lean on the horn as they passed.

'Do you know what has happened?' I asked. 'Are you just pretending to guess like this?'

'No. I'm not. But I'm telling you that's his car – and they only put up tents like that if they are shielding a body.'

'Swear on our daughters' lives – you know nothing about this at all?'

'NO!' she shouted, putting both of her hands on the side of her head. 'How can you even ask me that? This is insane, absolutely insane! I took a sleeping pill and I went to bed!' She started shaking, but I couldn't tell if it was with anger, or fear.

'You're not hiding anything from me?'

She hesitated and, horrified, I shrank back away from her.

'I told a lie in my statement to the GMC,' she confessed. 'When I woke up next to Jonathan in the hotel room, I realised then who he was and I did remember treating him in June. Partly because of the note he left me on the car. No, Rob, Wait!' She raised her voice as I exclaimed aloud in disbelief. 'At Pacha, I was blind drunk. I wouldn't have known my own name. I didn't sleep with Jonathan because I knew him,' she changed position again to look at me, 'I did it because I was pissed. I swear to you, I DID NOT KNOW who he was when I went to bed with him.' She paused and took a breath, before continuing. 'But how could I tell the truth about realising who he was when I woke up? It would have muddied the waters. The second I admitted to it, they'd have concluded that everything Jonathan said in his version of events is the truth, and it isn't. I *did not* message him on his phone – no doctor would ever be that stupid. I categorically did not have a three-month relationship with him. I didn't plan to be in Ibiza at the same time as him – it was just coincidence – and that whole sexual fantasy thing he said I constructed about us being "strangers" was utter fabrication. I need everything to stay completely black and white. You can see that, surely?'

I exhaled and leant my head back on the rest behind me. So she *hadn't* been entirely truthful with me.

'Everything else I have told you and the GMC is one hundred per cent true. It was a *tiny* lie, Rob. It doesn't change the fundamental elements of what actually happened, but it does illustrate why I also need David to cover for me now, and why I need you to say that you said hi to me when you got back from your parents and that I was reading in bed when you came home with the food. As far as anyone else is concerned, there has to be no mention of sleeping pills. I've just agreed that with David too.' She paused. 'You have to decide what you're going to say when the police come to the door – if you're going to support me like David is – because, while I know you think this is crazy, they *are* going to come. I can promise you that.'

*

I lay in bed that night in the spare room, the door open, listening to the sound of my daughters breathing in their bedrooms. Alex had taken the last sleeping pill. I was the only one awake.

We had ended up staying at Mum and Dad's for the day. Neither of us wanted to come home, plus Mum had taken one look at Alex and insisted on settling her on the sofa with a blanket and a cup of tea. All of Al's earlier resolutions seemed to have crumbled already and she meekly did as she was told. The girls ran around happily gathering fallen leaves from the garden to make an autumn picture, and I constructed a smouldery bonfire that Dad just about managed to get going. We sat down to bangers and mash, followed by the promised apple pie, then drove the long way home to avoid the girls seeing anything disturbing in the woods and asking questions.

I waited all evening for the knock that Alex said we should expect, but it never came. In the end it was less stressful just to go to bed. I stared up at the ceiling and wondered if they were all still up the road, scurrying around under floodlights, gathering information. Perhaps this really was nothing to do with Jonathan after all. Alex had become pretty obsessive. Wouldn't this just transpire to be nothing to do with us at all, bar being distressingly close to our house?

But she had seemed so sure that she recognised the car.

If only I had gone and checked on Alex, like I was going to when I came back with the curry and panicked that the BMW was missing

Suppose she was right, and questions were going to be asked, what *was* I going to say? Was I going to lie for my wife? Obviously, I couldn't believe for a second that she would hurt someone. Not Alex. She is committed to preserving life, not taking it. You know a person when you've been married as long as we have. You understand what they could and couldn't do; what the bare bones of that other person are when the daily stresses and strains have been stripped away. Yes, Day was single-handedly destroying her life with his lies, and campaigns like that can change people, and yes, she'd said she could kill him, but saying it is not the same as doing it. Not for a moment.

Feeling panicked, I got out my phone and scanned the news headlines, but there was nothing. I wanted very badly to do a search through Jonathan's social media: check the last time he had posted, but I was too scared, in case I might be asked to explain why I'd looked through the accounts the night after he died, in addition to why I had visited his school earlier that same day. If Alex was right and it *was* Jonathan lying in that tent, I was going to have questions of my own to answer. Instead, I did a search on Alex's name, and a new Saturday paper 'comment' piece popped up.

> You must make sure that your conduct justifies your patient's trust in you and the public's trust in the profession. This is one of the fundamental tenets of medical practice. Yes of course there are rare cases where a doctor falls in love with a patient; it's mutual, consensual – they marry, have a family and contribute to society. Dr Alex Inglis herself demonstrated this is possible when she married Robert Inglis eight years ago – still her husband and the first patient she admitted to having a relationship with. But the fresh allegations Dr Inglis now faces are very different. Dr Inglis maintains she was unaware that a man with whom she had sexual relations in Ibiza on a 'girls' weekend' was in fact seventeen and a current patient of hers. The teenager in question, however, paints a rather different picture, alleging that they had an affair conducted over a three-month period beginning after Dr Inglis treated him for an injury to his leg. He admits he initiated their relationship and that it was consensual. He's young, but above the age of consent, nothing illegal has happened – in spite of the Weinstein allegations stunning both

sides of the Atlantic, sexual harassment remains legal, if not acceptable – so why has this small-town case attracted quite so much attention given the size of the Hollywood fish currently on the slab?

It's rare for a female doctor to face allegations of this nature, that's true – but this isn't just because Dr Inglis is a woman and a mother. We've moved beyond that argument – a male doctor would be quite rightly facing the same backlash for having a relationship with a female seventeen-year-old patient. It is because the doctor and patient relationship can only be based on trust. By definition, one party is vulnerable and requiring care. No doubt Dr Inglis does not regard herself as exploitative, but the fact remains that power in the doctor-patient relationship is always inherently unequal and abuse of this position of trust is always unethical. It's well known that doctors are more likely to cross boundaries while facing problems in their personal life, and Dr Inglis has admitted to experiencing marital difficulties immediately prior to when the alleged affair began. Yes, doctors are human – but it's simply unacceptable to use your patient roster as some kind of dating service, as demonstrated by the warning she received after her relationship with her now husband came to light.

And while the judgement of some doctors may well become impaired under such circumstances, there is of course also another type of doctor altogether who commits sexual abuse of patients simply because they are rapacious.

My god.

I realised immediately she was right. If Jonathan was dead, Alex was unquestionably going to need an alibi from David, and from me, when they came looking for her.

*

It happened on Monday. The police car pulled up outside the gate just after Alex had got back from dropping the girls at school, which seemed a particularly cruel payback for her first solo act of bravery.

'They're here!' she gasped, appearing in the kitchen, looking at me wide-eyed with panic as I got to my feet.

We were at least slightly prepared.

The day before, the first local news reports had emerged:

BODY OF EIGHTEEN-YEAR-OLD MAN FOUND

The discovery was made at Broadwater Woods in the early hours of Saturday morning by a member of the public. The police were called to the incident at 07.50 BST and an investigation is now under way with Kent Police treating the death as unexplained. A police cordon is in place at the location. Police are appealing for any witnesses or anyone who may have any information to assist the investigation to come forward.

'You see?' said Alex, shakily. 'An eighteen-year-old man. It's him. I told you.'

'Should we "come forward" then?' I said, looking up from the laptop screen as Maisie and Tilly played happily with their toy kitchen.

'I'm making a salad for you, Mummy!' called Tilly. 'Get ready!'

'Thank you, darling! I'm very hungry!' She turned back to me. 'But *come forward* with what? We don't actually know anything. Wouldn't that be even weirder? I think we just have to wait.'

'Are you all right?' I asked, reaching out and taking her hand.

'Yes,' she said. 'Because I know I haven't done anything wrong. I don't want to have to tell them David was here longer than he was, but there's no other way. I can't have an hour and a half unaccounted for.'

'You're absolutely certain David won't change his mind and say you asked him to cover? I wish you'd just tell them the truth.'

'He won't do that, and I can't. I can't risk them thinking I was involved in whatever has happened. I'm telling a lie to protect the truth.'

'Here you are, Mummy!' Tilly appeared proudly and placed a plastic plate laden with green felt leaves and a carrot on the table between us. 'It's your breakfast!'

'Thank you, Tilly. You're such a kind girl.' Alex kissed her.

'And I made a chocolate cake.' Maisie appeared behind Tilly, carrying a more elaborately laid tray, complete with napkin.

'Well aren't I a lucky Mummy!' said Alex. 'How delicious. Thank you, sweetheart.'

I watched as my wife hugged my daughters to her and they both relaxed into the embrace of the mother they adored more than anything in the world – their sun, moon and stars – and I thought, fuck it. She's right. This is about protecting *them*. Whatever it takes. We'll do it.

'Deep breath,' I said, taking her hand and remembering my determination to keep my family together. 'They're not here to arrest you, they're just asking questions. That's all. Remember everything we've both agreed to say and don't say any more than that. You've done nothing wrong. Stay calm. I love you.'

TRANSCRIPT

DC Teresa Hart: So Mr Inglis, outside his school you asked Jonathan Day to retract his allegations in return for payment?

Robert Inglis: 'Yes. I was desperate. He seemed to be very motivated by money, what with the book deals and the paid public appearances he was undertaking, so I thought I would try and appeal to that side of his nature.'

TH: But he declined your offer?

RI: 'Yes. He was quite agitated and verbally abusive – as you saw in the footage you've just watched, he spat at me as I was walking off. I called out 'I'll pay you' and he replied: 'I don't need it where I'm going.'

TH: And after you left your parents' house on the evening of 6 October, you drove straight home, arriving at nine p.m?

RI: 'Yes. I came in, went upstairs to check on Alex. She told me Gary Day had been to the house. We talked about that and I said I wouldn't go out again to get some food if she'd rather I didn't. She said she was OK but not hungry, so I went back out, got a takeaway for myself, checked on Alex, who was reading in bed when I got back, ate my food, watched a movie and went to bed myself.'

Little white lies. One alibi – all for the greater good – because Alex was *not* involved in whatever happened at the woods that night.

*

A couple of days after our voluntarily helping the police with their questioning, a story appeared on the BBC news website.

No Others Involved in Death of Jonathan Day

Kent Police are treating the death of eighteen-year-old Jonathan Day as 'unexplained' pending toxicology results from the post-mortem examination carried out after the teenager's body was found on Saturday in woodland near his home.

Det Supt Greg King said: 'The post-mortem examination has not identified any injuries to suggest any other person was involved in his death, but our investigation is ongoing at this time.'

Mr Day, a type 1 diabetic, was found by a member of the public in the early hours of Saturday morning. 'The area where the body was located will remain cordoned off until forensic examinations have been concluded,' confirmed Det Supt King.

Mr Day's family has asked for privacy at this time. Mr Day's sister Ruby posted on Facebook, 'I cannot explain our loss. The 'little' brother who I always looked up to and loved with my whole heart has left us. We will miss you forever.'

Dr Alexandra Inglis (40) and her husband Robert Inglis (41) who were known to Mr Day were questioned by detectives and released under investigation.

We knew we had done nothing wrong, and eventually it seemed the police started to see that too – and the flipside of the situation. Whatever had happened to Jonathan that night – whether a tragic accident where he'd collapsed because of his diabetes or that he had taken his own life – he had still been in the woods alone, less than a mile away from my wife who was at the time lying asleep in her bed completely unprotected… I found that so scary a prospect I'd had to push it away from my mind the second I thought it.

We co-operated fully with the investigations and were not arrested, although we were told the police 'had grounds for arresting us on suspicion of Jonathan Day's murder'. I still don't know what that means. We let them into the cottage all white-suited up and with dogs. It was several days before we were allowed back home, but we didn't complain once, made no comment publicly about the stress it had caused us and our children. We didn't want to give anyone any reason to feel aggrieved whatsoever.

Jonathan Day Suffered Health Concerns Prior To Death, Parents Confirm

The parents of Jonathan Day, whose body was found in woodland in Kent on Saturday, have said that their son had long standing issues with his diabetes before his death. After paying tribute to his 'bright and beautiful boy' Gary Day said, 'Jonny didn't always find it easy to manage his illness and could really struggle with it at times'.

The police are treating the teenager's death as 'unexplained' but have confirmed Robert Inglis (41) and his wife Dr Alexandra Inglis (40), who were questioned, have been released from the investigation without any further action. 'Mr and Dr Inglis have remained appreciative that in any investigation like this the police are obliged to investigate every line of enquiry, and we thank them for their co-operation and understanding in a matter that must have caused them stress,' said Det Supt Greg King of Kent Police. 'We can confirm they will face no further action.'

SIX MONTHS LATER

(present day)

CHAPTER 19

Cherry

My Mum and Dad didn't want me to come to this inquest today, but anyone can and I'm eighteen now. It's totally weirding me out, though, that there are people sat in this room who never knew him at all. Even journalists. How messed up is that? One of them is staring at me. I look away. I know authentic voices are really hot right now – and I'm not telling him shit. Not after what happened when someone turned up on our doorstep and, still really upset, I somehow said enough to make it look like I'd given them a whole interview slagging off Jonny's dad. I'm too scared to say anything at all now.

I've been working with a really nice therapist who reminds me all the time that you can't be responsible for other people's actions and that I can't feel guilt for what I think I did or didn't do. But I can't help it.

Jonny is literally the only thing I can think about *all* the time. I keep seeing him walking in the forest. I have nightmares about it.

I feel like I'm going to cry again, so I try and blink the tears back and blow my nose. When I look up, the journalist across the way is *still* staring right at me – and also writing something.

I tense and instead look across at Christy and Ruby, tightly holding hands. They've moved to London now, away from Gary.

We texted for a bit – me and Ruby – but then it got too painful, and we stopped.

I honestly don't know what I would have done without Alice and the girls right now. They have been so amazingly supportive and understanding. They've kept my life feeling normal and grounded. They said today would be good closure, but it won't be. No one understands. I can't forget him. Everyone keeps telling me I'll fall in love again and be happy one day, but there will always be a part of my heart that is just his, even though he lied to me.

I should have done more. If I could go back in time and do it differently, I would. I could have saved him from himself, because that's what I know we're all about to hear – that Jonny killed himself – and I feel so, so sad.

And so guilty.

CHAPTER 20

Rob

'I would like to remind everyone of what I said at the start – this is an inquest, not a trial. Its purpose is not to attribute blame, but rather use the evidence we have heard to confirm the identity of the deceased, where and when they died, and the cause of death.'

I watch the journalist preparing to take notes at the back of the room as the coroner starts her summary. He looks positively excited and I get why, the chance to rehash it all again; two very physically attractive people (nice big front-page sorted), an older woman – a family GP no less. A young, vulnerable, rising social media star, and a passionate night in Ibiza. Allegations of unethical conduct, marital strife, harassment, illicit sex trysts, messages, a pretty, wronged girlfriend, parents publicly gunning for the woman they'd apparently tried to employ… but this juicy bone has culminated in the tragic death of a young man, and those parents are sitting in this very room. This journalist isn't even trying to hide that he's licking his lips.

In return, I don't make any effort to conceal my look of contempt. He doesn't care about the people involved here, just the happy thought that Jonathan Day died less than a mile from his ex-lover's home. Lovely detail. I hope he's really disappointed that we've wound up here, and not in court, the parasitic worm.

After all, God knows Kent Police performed a very thorough investigation. As one of them said to me, they don't actually get bodies in the woods that often. They're excited when something like that happens, and they were all over it, given Day's profile. But they found nothing; there was no criminal case to answer and everything was turned over to the coroner.

'As we have heard,' she continues, 'at approximately seven thirty p.m. on 6 October 2017, Jonathan told his mother that he was going out to meet his girlfriend, Cherry, and would stay at her house – he'd let them know if his plans changed but otherwise he'd be back in the morning. He drove instead to Broadwater Woods – a twenty-minute journey – parking his car in a clearing.'

I watch Christy Day reach out, grip her daughter's hand and close her eyes. The poor woman's face is etched with agony and guilt. I glance over at Gary Day, sat on the opposite side of the room to his estranged wife. He stares at the floor, eyes wide, hands clasped tightly, and I shift uncomfortably. I am sorry for his loss, as any parent would be, but the man frightens me.

We all listen silently as the coroner determines that at approximately 8 p.m. Jonathan walked about a hundred metres into the forest and injected his whole insulin pen into his stomach before collapsing on the ground never to wake up. He had earlier taken his pre-meal insulin shot at the dinner table without then eating enough to balance its effects. He would have already been hypoglycaemic on arriving at the woods. It would have been enough for him to simply lie down and wait to fall unconscious – in the absence of immediate medical attention he would have died anyway. He wasn't taking any chances, however, hence the sleeping tablets that were discovered in his system at the post-mortem – the same brand his mother takes – and the injecting of his whole pen. The forensic post-mortem also revealed extraordinarily high levels of insulin in his system. He meant business.

He was found, dead and soaked to the skin by the night's heavy rain, by a man walking his dog early on Saturday morning. His wallet, keys and his switched-off phone were laid out neatly beside him. There was one typed note on the phone, which said:

Sorry for everything and what this will do.

'Sorry' to whom is not clear. Sorry to his poor parents and sister or sorry to my wife – obviously not present right now and not just because she's back at work – for the damning lies he told about her? What comfort could any of them take from that apology in any case? A young man is still needlessly dead.

When we were first told how he'd died, I was appalled. He'd seemed so in control that afternoon when I'd confronted him, apart from when I'd nearly hit him. I remembered the fear on his face and felt ashamed of myself. What if telling him I had evidence that he was lying had pushed him over the edge? Had he believed me and panicked, having dug himself into his lies so deeply he was unable to climb out? But as Alex says, you cannot take responsibility for anyone else's choices, only your own. It seems that in any case, the row he'd had with his father distressed him more than anything I might have said. God knows what was going on in his head to make him do what he did.

Not, of course, that his death has negated everything he did to Alex. It hasn't. After his death, although the GMC continued their investigation into his complaint, they had no witness testimony other than his supplied statement, which made it difficult for them to take any action against Alex. They could find no evidence whatsoever that Alex had known who Day was when she met him in Ibiza. When we attended the MPTS hearing last month in Manchester, they mentioned that the speed and frequency with which Day had spoken to the media was of 'concern' to them, as was his girlfriend's supplied statement in which she noted Day's determination to become a social media star and provide the two of them with a 'platform'. David also supplied evidence that he witnessed Day force his way into Alex's car outside the surgery, before she pointed at him to get out, at which Day tried to kiss her. Everything Day said was at worst a deliberate lie, and at best a fantasy that existed only in his head. I can hear his voice calling out to me again: "I genuinely couldn't give a shit about your wife." Bollocks, given he chose to end his life so close to our house. I still think he was in love – if you can call it that – with Al. Obsessed would be a better word.

'I don't think anyone around Jonathan could have predicted what he did.' The coroner's clear and calm voice draws me back to the room. 'It was not a preventable death. Jonathan had long-term experience of managing his diabetes and was well aware of the risks of his condition and medication. The pathologist has given his cause of death as drug misuse. I am satisfied beyond reasonable doubt that Jonathan took steps to ensure he would not be disturbed and deliberately took his own life.'

I can't look at his poor mother, I only hear her gasp with pain, and resolve to hug Maisie and Tilly more tightly tonight when I get home. His girlfriend stands up and walks out unsteadily, tears streaming down her face.

As the coroner records her conclusion of suicide, I swallow and stare down at the floor. I am so sorry for them but, thank God, it's over. Thank God.

When I look up, I glance again at the journalist. He should thank his lucky stars that after he's written this up, he gets to go home and forget about it tonight.

I walk back out into the bright spring sunshine and text the news to Alex. When it was first made public that it was a probable suicide, I was terrified that there would be a backlash against Alex, that people would think Jonathan must have been so ashamed by what had 'happened' that he'd killed himself, and because he'd chosen to do it near our house, it would only cement her culpability in people's minds.

In fact, the reverse happened. A well-known tabloid ran an interview with his girlfriend that painted a picture of a vulnerable schoolboy who had never felt good enough for his domineering father, someone who might have easily developed an obsession with a strong adult figure who had shown him attention. I still struggle to align that profile with the boy I spoke to, who showed not a shred of remorse for the lies he had told and was obviously deftly manipulating the publicity and attention it was bringing him. But presumably if the thoughts of someone about to commit suicide were rational, they would be able to prevent themselves from doing it in the first place.

For Alex's part, what scares me most is that her only mistake in all of this was to have a drunken one-night stand. There's a lesson for us all there. I'm never going to cheat ever, ever again – because, while I don't think for one second think my wife has lied to me about what really happened, I still can't help but think she's got away with this by the skin of her teeth.

There but for the grace of God.

*

'I haven't been able to stop thinking about him all day,' Alex blurts, once Maisie and Tilly are in bed, having finally settled. Since we moved back into the town centre, it has taken them some time to get used to hearing the sounds of the family on our right through the walls. 'I wish I could have prevented it somehow.'

'You've said that so often, but he was ruining your life! And what could *you* have done anyway?'

She looks away. 'I don't know. Everybody makes mistakes and nobody deserves a death like that. No matter how badly he lied, I would have forgiven him, rather than this.'

'Really?' I am genuinely surprised.

'Of course!' she exclaims. 'I was never interested in punishing him, or revenge. I just wanted people to know the truth.'

I get up, walk over to the cupboard and take out a wine glass. 'That he was obsessed with you? That he'd never met anyone like you before?'

She sits up uncomfortably, as if someone has placed a hand on her shoulder when she wasn't expecting it. 'You keep saying that.'

'It was obvious when I spoke to him outside his school and he got off on winding me up about you.' I open the drawer and pull out the corkscrew. 'I can count the people I dislike on one hand, but I really hated him.'

'I was reading online earlier about narcissism and the dark triad,' Alex says suddenly, watching me reach for the bottle and start to open it.

'The what?' I frown. I have no idea what she's talking about.

'The dark triad comprises three personality traits: narcissism, Machiavellianism and psychopathy. They all have a malevolent connection: if you have traits of one, you're likely to share traits with the others. Narcissists have no empathy whatsoever in addition to thinking they are more special than everyone else. Machiavellianism is all about manipulation and the exploitation of others, displaying a total lack of morality as the individual focuses on their own self-interest, and psychopaths are completely remorseless as they pursue their antisocial behaviour.'

'Sounds about right,' I say, starting to pour. 'He was an evil little shit, which is why I don't understand you saying you wish you could have prevented what happened to him.' I pass her the glass and cross to the fridge to get myself a Guinness.

'He was only seventeen when it happened, Rob.'

I open the can and get my pint glass. 'Young, yes – but seventeen is plenty old enough to know right from wrong. Even Tilly knows you don't tell fibs.'

'But does someone with those types of characteristics really commit suicide?'

I pause for a moment, then sit back down at the table. 'Well, I still think it's fucking weird that his deranged father came here at seven o'clock, out of the blue, and less than an hour later, his son is here too, apparently topping himself in the woods.'

'It *wasn't* you – was it?'

At first, I think I've misheard her, but as it registers, I blink in astonishment and sit right back in my chair with a slight thud.

She looks at me worriedly. 'I won't ever ask you this again, but did you do it? I promise I'll never tell anyone – whatever happens. I just need to know. We talked about doing it – and I know we were only half joking.'

We're right under Tilly's bedroom, so I've already turned off the kitchen radio in case we wake her and, as we both stare at each other, the only sound is the churning of the water in the dishwasher.

'You're serious?'

She nods.

'No, Alex, I had nothing to do with his death. I've made some huge mistakes, but honestly, even I'm not that stupid.'

'I've never said you're stupid. Far from it. You're not complicated. There's a difference. With you, what you see is what you get. At least that's what I always thought.'

'Until Hannah you mean?'

She nods.

'I told you the next day what I'd done. You think I'd be able to hide something like *killing* someone from you? You think I'm even capable of that? Genuinely?'

'I think you want to protect us and try to fix things. I think if you'd driven past Jonathan skulking around in the woods by our house on your way home from your Mum and Dad's, you might have snapped. I'd kill to protect Maisie and Tilly.' She lifts her gaze and looks unflinchingly right at me. 'Without hesitation.'

'OK, but you don't think the police might have considered that scenario too? We're all well aware I had a motive. They didn't charge me, and they would have if they'd had the evidence.' I pause briefly. 'I can't believe we're having this conversation. Did *you* do it?' I sound more defensive than I intend to. 'Same thing, then; whatever happens I won't ever tell anyone.'

'Because I asked you and David to lie for me?' she says quietly.

'That, and the two sleeping pills you said you flushed down the loo. The same type that showed up on Day's post-mortem.'

'They're a very common brand and I really did flush them away. We've been over why I asked you to lie already.'

'I'm not asking you to go through it all again. I'm just asking if you did it?'

This time the pause is longer. 'You're right,' she says eventually, 'this is a horrible, stupid conversation.'

'You started it.' I can hear the hurt in my voice.

'I know, I'm sorry. And the answer is no, Rob, I didn't do it.'

'Well, OK then.' I lift my pint glass. I know what she means. It's quite something to be forced into a situation where you have to consider if your partner might be capable of doing something like that, and that they must also think the same of you.

'I feel like what we're really voicing is that the way the coroner laid everything out earlier doesn't feel like the whole picture – to either of us,' I say. 'Gary Day must have had a solid-gold alibi, that's for sure. But you know what?' I look my wife in the eye, 'at the end of the day, I'm just glad it's all over. I love you.'

'I love you too,' she says, and takes a sip of her wine.

PART THREE

The Attack

CHAPTER 21

I didn't have much time to get there. I stayed on the road, listening for cars as I walked, ready to jump into hiding, but no one appeared. Once I was in position, crouched behind the tree, waiting, I wasn't thinking anything other than: would he really come?

It's me, I'd texted. Did he have the phone? Was it near him?

I held my breath and felt an almost visceral thrill of satisfaction as it delivered.

Me who?

You know who. I have to see you. Come to the woods. Clearing on left before house. Will signal when you arrive.

I wasn't afraid, waiting for him in the silence. I was focused and determined. It was quite calming standing there in the dark listening to the sound of my own steady breathing. Gradually my senses became heightened. I heard an owl, felt the wind pick up, heard the snap and rustle of an animal of some description moving about in the leaves – and eventually an approaching car engine.

The headlight beam bounced as the driver steered it into the clearing, coming to a stop, facing me. I stayed hidden away. The engine cut, the lights went off and I heard a car door opening, then slamming shut.

I took my pencil torch from my pocket, switched it on then held the light up in front of me, before covering it with my hand, showing it again – and repeating the signal once more. Would he risk it? Would he follow it into the woods to find me?

I held my breath and listened to the sounds of footsteps crashing through leaves, thudding into the ground. Yes, he would. His obsession had won. He couldn't bear *not* to come running. I killed the light and there was a pause as he stopped, disorientated.

'Alex?' I heard him whisper. 'Where are you?'

I flashed the light once more, and he set off again. I reached into my pocket, curled my fingers around the handle of the knife, swallowed, and once he was practically upon me, I stepped out from behind the tree.

He yelped then froze rigid, his eyes widening as I held up the torch to illuminate the blade.

'Do not move,' I said. 'You really believed, in spite of everything you've done, that you'd been summoned here for sex tonight? You're *that* narcissistic?' I put the torch in my pocket, then reached into my coat and brought out the plastic plunger I'd carefully removed from the Calpol packet in the bathroom. Every parent has one these days. I stepped over to him and placed the knife tip at the base of his Adam's apple – but not close enough to actually touch him – in one precise movement. Perhaps I should have been a surgeon, except I prefer to make the difference at grass-roots level.

'Open, please,' I instructed, and with my left hand, I squeezed the 5 ml water solution into his mouth. 'Swallow and then open your mouth again.'

Terrified, he held it – I could see his cheeks bulging. I sighed, put the plunger back in my pocket, reached out and pinched his nose tightly. The fingers of the disposable latex gloves felt almost slippery as I squeezed.

'If you spit it out, I'll shove this knife right into you here and now,' I said pleasantly. 'I don't even care any more.'

He closed his eyes and swallowed.

'Good boy,' I said. 'Open wide, please?'

He did as he was told, and I reached back into my pocket for the torch and shone it in his mouth. All gone.

'What the fuck have you just given me?' He tried to sound angry, but his bottom lip trembled. He was frightened it was going to hurt.

'It'll be painless,' I said truthfully. 'You can relax. I'm going to move the knife a little bit further away from you so that you can sit down. I want to talk to you.'

He watched me warily, but stayed standing, although he visibly wobbled, almost swaying on the spot.

I frowned. The pills wouldn't have an effect that fast. 'When did you last eat something?'

'What do you care?'

His words were slightly slurred and I realised he was sweating. Ah, now this was interesting. I relaxed immediately. This was going to be *much* easier than I had anticipated. 'Jonathan?'

'I had a bit of tea about an hour and a half ago.'

'And your last shot?'

'Same time.'

'So you're already hypo? That's poor management, Jonathan. Really. Reach into your pockets and drop your phones – both of them – your keys, pen, any snacks you have, and your wallet on the ground. What's your iPhone code?'

He didn't take his eyes from me but did as he was told. 'What did you just give me?'

'Your code please?' I held the knife steady.

'2256. *What did you just give me*?'

'Don't shout. Two sleeping tablets – the same ones your mother takes – dissolved in water.'

'Why?' He couldn't hide the tremor in his voice. 'What is it you want from me?'

I raised my eyebrows, amused. 'You think you have any bargaining power now? Really?'

'I'll say it if you want. I'll say sorry.'

I shook my head. 'You don't have to say a thing. Not if you don't want to. I already *know* you lied. For the record, pretending your iPhone was stolen outside the surgery, to cover up the fact there was never any initial message 'stored' on it in the first place, was weak. The texts on that,' I pointed at the android phone, 'were better. Obviously, they could have come from anyone, of course, although I get that was somewhat the point. Quite a nice touch though. Very dramatic. What did you do, buy another handset and message yourself?'

He cleared his throat and eyed the knife. 'I'm sorry I did it.' He looked me in the eye. 'I'll say sorry publicly too.'

I looked at him with interest. 'Will you now? Why *did* you make it all up, Jonathan?'

He didn't answer, just glanced wildly to his right and suddenly bolted off into the dark. I could hear him crashing off through the trees, panting with exertion as he hurtled towards the road. I sighed and got the torch out again, shining it up just in time to see him collapse and crumple to the ground. I bent and picked up his belongings, then walked over to him. It only took me about thirty seconds; he'd hardly managed to get any distance at all.

I stood over him. He was lying face down on the leaves, almost motionless. Perhaps he sensed me there, because he suddenly exclaimed: 'Fuck off, you fucking cunt! You're full of shit with your hands waving near!'

'That's it. You just keep lying down – and thank you.' I said soothingly.

Such insults have not the slightest effect on me. He's not the first and he won't be the last, and actually, as he was making no sense whatsoever, I suspect he already didn't have a clue what he was saying. It was no more than a physiological response; too much insulin in his system and horribly low blood sugar. As if to confirm my assessment, he fell silent and went still. I felt almost cheated. I'd wanted to tell him what was going to happen, how I was going to pour oil on the waters he'd so maliciously whipped up. I could have just left him – he was already as good as dead – but it wasn't enough to make it appear an accident. Questions would be asked: *why* had he come to the woods in the first place? Everyone needed to see that he'd had intent. That there had been a plan.

I crouched down next to him. 'I wonder how it will feel for your parents when they have to listen to an account of how you committed suicide here?' I whispered. 'Because, you know, lies hurt, Jonathan.'

He still didn't reply, which was, frankly, very disappointing. 'Let's pretend you haven't let yourself become hypoglycaemic already,' I said conversationally. 'Although – thank you. It's been a great help. So – *this* is what everyone is going to think: you came to the woods, took two sleeping pills – because no diabetic intending to take their own life would want to wake up here hypo, hungry, confused and alone – and then you emptied your entire pen into yourself.' Moving swiftly, I reached for his pen, gently parted his coat and lifted his top to expose his tummy. I discharged the contents into him and threw the pen on the leaves as if he'd dropped it. He would quite simply never wake up. I can think of worse ways to go – I have seen many of them.

I waited for a moment or two, lifted his heavy hand and selected his index finger, pressing the home button then '2256' on his iPhone. I checked his messages. He'd sent one to 'Cherry' telling her he was still at home – he might see her later– so I sent another saying he'd decided to stay put after all. It was laborious having to use his single finger, but necessary. Once I'd selected the notes, typing 'sorry for everything, and what this will do' – because that was the least apology he owed – I put the phone down beside him. Finally, I picked up his pay-as-you-go phone and put it in my pocket, before beginning the walk back to the cottage. It was useful to have a moment to clear my head. When I arrived there was no car on the drive: Rob wouldn't be back for at least another twenty minutes, and I knew Jonathan would already be dead. I peeled the plastic bags from my feet before I walked up the drive and left them carefully by the front door, reaching into my back pocket, removing the keys and letting myself back into the house. I quietly padded upstairs, but Alex's door was shut; she'd even put a note on it helpfully telling her husband she'd taken the pill.

I thoroughly rinsed the Calpol plunger and put it back in the box, then tiptoed to the downstairs loo, retrieved my 'forgotten' phone from the side by the loo roll and carefully sent Mother a text telling her I was sorry if she was already home from bridge and I wasn't, but that I'd be back soon. Once I re-emerged I placed Alex's keys on the sideboard again and let myself back out, closing the door behind me.

I picked up the plastic bags, blipped my car and began the drive home. The whole thing had taken less than an hour.

As I drove, I felt only the calming of the storm. It had been difficult to watch that filth about Alex circulate in the press. I had started to become distracted myself at work – which unsettled me, as that should *never* happen. Poor Alex herself was evidentially clinging on by her fingernails – so unhappy and exhausted. Her hapless husband didn't have a clue what to do, of course. She needed to be back at work, doing what she did best. I meant what I'd said – I missed having her there, we all did. It wasn't the same without her. We support each other at work; we're a good team.

I *did* wonder once if I might be in love with Alex, around the time she first arrived at the surgery, but before I'd had a chance to explore it any further, Rob Inglis arrived on the scene. I could have overreacted, I suppose, but I managed to calm my own feelings and instead reported her – anonymously, naturally. I was concerned that she might leave the practice in an attempt to 'remedy' the situation; start afresh elsewhere – and I didn't want to lose her in a professional sense. The restrictions she received severely hampered her future employment prospects elsewhere and, as I suspected, she stayed put. So, in reward – I nurtured her, helped her develop her career, made her my partner.

The strategy has paid off very well, we've achieved a great deal together. She's not suffered from not moving on – quite the contrary, she's blossomed. Everything has worked nicely for all of us. I value her input and support; she values mine. We have a lot of respect for each other. Almost better than being married in some ways.

Then Day came along.

I glanced at the bags, tucked into the inside pocket of the car door and peeled off my gloves. I'd get rid of them on my late shift at the drop-in centre where I would be in exactly twenty-four hours' time. The bags were destined for the recycle bin at the supermarket first thing in the morning, and Day's phone would be finding its way into Bewl reservoir when I walked the dogs there after the shopping, along with one of my own pay-as-you-go phones. I've had several at home for years now. We get rotten coverage and I like to be prepared for all eventualities. When you have to make many difficult decisions a day about the one thing we all take for granted and yet could not do without – health – there is no margin for error. You get used to thinking around a problem and you certainly cannot afford to make mistakes.

I thought about Day, again, sitting in my room with his parents, casually feeding me his lies as if I was some kind of idiot. It was insulting that he thought I might fall for his routine. Charming, intelligent and ruthless types like him usually do well in life because they have learnt how to manipulate people and situations to their own end, leaving a trail of devastation in their wake without so much as a backward glance. I boarded with plenty of boys like Day. One of them is now the cabinet minister responsible for the stealth privatisation of the health service – whom I have also had the misfortune to erstwhile see wank into a sock. But here's the thing about these people; they become so enchanted by themselves, so obsessed with power, they begin to believe they are unstoppable and then they overstep the mark. They make a mistake, they interfere and poke around in places they ought not to – upsetting the balance – as Day did when he parked his travelling circus in my waiting room that Friday morning and let his protein overloaded, 'roid-raged father start to yell about sexual abuse at the top of his voice.

What had Alex been thinking, sleeping with him in the first place? I knew she would, of course, need an alibi. Had she not called me first, I'd have contacted her to let her know that the police had been in touch for Jonathan's medical records and did she need my help? I was naturally only too happy to oblige when she did ask.

I suppose had things come too close for comfort I *might* have been forced to retract my story and lay the blame at her feet – 'confess' that I had given her some pills of Mother's that I shouldn't have done, but I knew that wasn't going to be necessary. The devil is in the detail. You just make sure you think of everything. Timings, especially, are what can trip people up, after the event. I really don't like having to clean up like this and, thankfully, I've only had to do it a handful of times for one reason and another – one fellow medical student, but patients mostly. If you're going to do it, however, do it properly and most vitally, *for the greater good.* Do it to affect the world around you for the better. Dispatch for a *positive* reason. Once her reputation has been fully restored, Alex will go on to treat countless patients successfully and she will make an enormous contribution to society. This is a demonstratively *good* thing. We need more people like her in our dark little world right now – shining a light – not less.

Jonathan was dangerous. It was like looking at my teenage reflection – I could see the damage he would do to every single life that became intimately entwined with his, how monstrous he would become, unchecked. Dispatching my younger self in the woods was not cathartic, but it was necessary. There is such a thin line between chaos and order, but Jonathan Day is now no longer a threat to anyone.

I do not mind that this will go unnoticed – no doctor ever seeks thanks for what they have done; I am no hero. I was just doing my job.

The truth does not always out, and for that we must all be thankful.

EPILOGUE

Alex

I knew there was something going on from the second David turned up at the house again with some excuse about having forgotten his mobile phone – he'd left it in our downstairs loo apparently. David is *never* without his phone, least of all for a whole afternoon. He remarked that the house was quiet and I explained that Rob had taken the girls to my in-laws – as he'd suggested. He looked quietly pleased and said he was sure it would help.

Only, I explained, I'd gone and lost the sleeping pills… He'd seemed worried about that and insisted on coming upstairs to help me look for them, which was weird too.

We were momentarily distracted by Gary Day showing up and saying his piece. I was actually quite glad when David insisted on staying for a bit once he'd gone. We found the pills, of course, and when I came back from the loo having brushed my teeth, David was sitting on the edge of the bed putting his phone away in his pocket and glancing at his watch. I got the distinct impression he had plans, yet he seemed to be waiting for something. I wrote a note for Rob and stuck it on the bedroom door, told David he didn't need to worry about staying any longer and pretended to knock the pill back with water, actually palming it instead. I smiled gratefully at him as I climbed into bed. 'Thank you so much for everything, David. Would you mind showing yourself out?' I yawned. 'I'm sure I'm going to get some sleep tonight, thank God.'

He got up. 'Glad to have been of service. Toodle-pip, and sweet dreams.'

I snuggled down obediently, even switching off my light as he left. I heard him creak along the landing, then a moment or two later his light footstep on the stairs. The front door closed and I relaxed slightly, but oddly, there was nothing after that. No car starting up. I turned my head on the pillow and listened carefully. I got out of bed and went to the curtains, peeping through the gap – to see him sitting in the front of his car, on his phone. I climbed back into bed but after five minutes, still no engine turning on. I went back to the window. The car hadn't moved – but David was walking up the road towards the woods.

Astonished, I tried to think quickly, and on a hunch spun round and opened the wardrobe door, reaching inside one of my knee-high boots to retrieve the phone from the toe. I switched it on and almost immediately, a text came through from Jonathan:

Are you there? Just had a message from someone saying 'I have to see you.' Was a different number tho? Told me to come to the woods. They were making out like they were you?

I hesitated. Bloody hell, David. Really? Why was he posing as me? I chewed my lip thoughtfully.

Definitely me. Wasn't sure if you'd barred this phone, so used alternative option. Your father came to my house tonight... He just left.

WHAT? Why?

I could sense Jonathan's alarm.

He had something to say. I'll tell you when I see you.

You're lying. Don't do this to me again. Please.

Cross my heart. Come. It's really important. I owe you the truth. Your mother deserves the truth. He's not a nice man.

A small smile played around my mouth as I turned the phone off. That ought to do it.

Well! David – my knight in shining armour. Who knew he had it in him? I got back into bed, absurdly flattered at the thought of him coming to my rescue in such dramatic fashion, believing he was defending my honour. Dear David, always there for me, year in, year out – after every mistake. The thought of him telling Jonathan to back off, scaring him into silence far more effectively than Rob had managed, was beyond a relief. I shivered with anticipation and unable to settle climbed *back* out of bed to watch from the window, excited to see what was going to happen next.

I felt an actual thrill when I saw a figure come around the corner. It was David. I peered through the gap in the curtain as the clouds blew away from the moon – illuminating something strange on his feet. My smile faded. What *was* he wearing?

Then I realised. They were bags.

He had fucking plastic bags on his feet. I gasped and darted away from the window, scrambling back into bed. My heart was thumping so hard I felt sick. What had he done? *David?*

I listened for the car starting but instead heard a soft click of the front door opening downstairs and froze.

He was back in the house again? How? Why? What was he doing? He'd let himself out! I looked around frantically for my phone, realising as I did that even if I called the police immediately, I'd be dead long before they arrived.

The stairs creaked.

He was coming to find me.

I squeezed my eyes shut tightly and thought of my girls and of Rob. How could everything have come to this? I made desperate and silent deals with God that if he spared me, I would never, ever do anything like this ever again. I would be a better person. A good wife, a decent mother.

He walked past the bedroom, he was going to the bathroom? I heard the tap start running and the squeak of our bathroom cabinet opening… then tensed with fear as his footsteps approached the bedroom door once more. *Oh God, please no…*

But they passed, and he went downstairs again.

Still I held my breath as there was the quiet jangle of keys being placed back carefully down on the side, then the click of the door again, before the best sound I have ever heard in my life – after my daughters' first cries – his car starting and pulling away.

Everything fell silent and after what felt like an age, I was brave enough to get up and go to the window. He'd gone.

I walked shakily over to the phone Jonathan had bought me all those weeks ago and checked it was switched off. I put his iPhone in a tin can at the bottom of the rubbish bag after I removed it from his car, and off it went with the bin men the following day. I knew I also had to get rid of the burner immediately – should I risk it when Rob was due back any moment or wait until the morning? I was pulling some socks on when the familiar noise of our car pulling onto the drive made the decision for me. Rob was home. I grabbed the phone and jumped into bed, under the covers. He must have seen the note on the door, as he didn't come in.

I stayed there all night, wide-awake with shock, clutching Jonathan's mobile.

By the morning I'd managed to convince myself I was being stupidly melodramatic. David wasn't capable of killing someone! There would prove to be a logical explanation – but when I heard the police sirens, I knew what they'd found. I put a smile on my face, but when Rob drove us past the woods and I saw Jonathan's car being recovered, I couldn't hide it – my reaction was physical. I had a panic attack. Jonathan's mobile was in my bag. I lost control when Rob said the police were following us. I thought they were going to stop and search and that would be that.

But they didn't. I tried to think quickly and realised David had been thorough. I was the immediate suspect – and I needed a much better alibi than taking a sleeping pill and going to bed. I had no choice but to ring David, play dumb and ask him to lie for me, which I knew he'd be only too happy to do. His methodical planning was terrifying. He didn't know I'd seen him of course, but what did it matter? I couldn't *tell* anyone. It would be my word against his – what chance would I have? We were better stuck together, just as I know he's always wanted. I never, for one minute believed he would do something like this, however. It makes me physically sick to watch him calling patients into his room with that kindly smile every morning – and yet he saved me. I was able to walk away, my reputation salvaged.

I slipped the mobile into the pond at my in-laws' house. It's given me nightmares. I dream that Jonathan is in there, looking back up at me from beneath the murky water.

I am not a bad person.

I really do love my husband and my daughters. Jonathan was just so beautiful.

What more can I say?

And who would believe me anyway?

A LETTER FROM LUCY

Thank you so much for reading *White Lies*. I hope you enjoyed it as much as I liked writing it. If you'd like to keep up-to-date with all of my latest releases, you can sign up at the following link. Your email address will never be shared, and you can unsubscribe at any time.

www.bookouture.com/lucy-dawson

I came up with the idea for this book on a long car journey. I was listening to the radio and a song came on about a lover realising his ex only wanted his attention, not his heart. When I was a teenager, I wanted to be a songwriter and to this day still listen far too intently to lyrics. This particular track struck a chord with me (sorry) and before I knew it, I had Alex and Jonathan stuck in my head…

If you have time, I'd love it if you were able to let me know what you thought of the book and write a review of *White Lies*. Feedback is really useful and also makes a huge difference in helping new readers discover one of my books for the first time.

I also have a reader's club, which you can join via the following link:

www.lucydawsonbooks.com/join-my-book-club

Alternatively, if you'd like to contact me personally, you can reach me via my Website, Facebook page, Twitter or Instagram. I love hearing from readers, and always reply.

Again, thank you so much for deciding to spend some time reading *White Lies*. I'm looking forward to sharing my next book with you very soon.

With all best wishes,
Lucy x

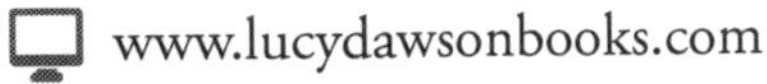
www.lucydawsonbooks.com

lucydawsonbooks

@lucydawsonbooks

ACKNOWLEDGEMENTS

My very grateful thanks to Amit Dhand, Emily Eracleous, Nicky Walt, Paul Dodson, Ellie Nelson, Andrew Cox and Nathan Johnson. All errors are very definitely my own.

Thank you to Paddy Magrane and Jenny Blackhurst for their encouragement when I decided to stop work on a half-finished book with a deadline looming, to write this one instead. Thank you also to Sarah Ballard and Kathryn Taussig for not batting an eyelid when I broke the news to them. It did however mean I pretty much didn't see my husband, family or any of my friends for three months, and when I did, boringly talked about nothing but my word count. Thanks to all of you for being so nice about it and still being there when I'd finished. Wanda Whiteley was as ever invaluable, and I'm very grateful to everyone else who supports me too; Eli Keren and all at United Agents, Kim Nash and the tireless Bookouture team. The bloggers and other authors who very generously give their time to help and cheerlead do not go unnoticed either. Finally, thank you to the CBs. I would get far more done without you, but it wouldn't be anywhere near as much fun.

39258731R00164

Made in the USA
San Bernardino, CA
18 June 2019